J.D. Barrett is an Australian television writer and script editor. She has worked on the writing teams for *Love My Way*, *East of Everything*, *Bed of Roses*, *Wonderland*, *Love Child* and *The Secret Daughter*. *The Secret Recipe for Second Chances* was her bestselling debut novel. *The Song of Us* was her second book and *The Upside of Over* is her third work of fiction. J.D. lives between Sydney, Byron Bay and Los Angeles.

the upside of over

J.D.BARRETT

hachette AUSTRALIA

hachette
AUSTRALIA

Published in Australia and New Zealand in 2018
by Hachette Australia
(an imprint of Hachette Australia Pty Limited)
Level 17, 207 Kent Street, Sydney NSW 2000
www.hachette.com.au

10 9 8 7 6 5 4 3 2 1

 A catalogue record for this
book is available from the
National Library of Australia

NATIONAL
LIBRARY
OF AUSTRALIA

ISBN: 978 0 7336 3797 1 (paperback)

Cover design by Christabella Designs
Cover photograph courtesy of Getty Images
Author photograph courtesy Craig Peihopa
Text design by Bookhouse, Sydney
Typset in 11.5/18.9 pt Sabon LT Pro
Printed and bound in Great Britain by Clays Ltd, Elcograf S.p.A.

MIX
Paper from
responsible sources
FSC
www.fsc.org   FSC® C001695

The paper this book is printed on is certified against the
Forest Stewardship Council® Standards. McPherson's Printing
Group holds FSC® chain of custody certification SA-COC-005379.
FSC® promotes environmentally responsible, socially beneficial
and economically viable management of the world's forests.

To my dear friend Jaki Arthur,

thank you for championing me and insisting I write books.

1

INITIAL DISPATCH FROM THE INTERIOR

11.34 pm, Wednesday, 15 August

'DO YOU REMEMBER THAT TIME NOT LONG AFTER WE WERE MARRIED, at the work Christmas party, when you came on set so I could show you around? It was just the two of us and you'd been eyeing me all night in *that* way while I was showing off my ring and post honeymoon tan.

'You closed the huge sliding doors that led into the studio and I turned on the lights. You looked around the set where I work every day. Got me to show you how the auto-cue worked and this wicked grin crossed your perfect lips.

'You asked me to sit in my chair, which I did, you kissed me lightly and nibbled my earlobe in that way that sets me right off and then you came around the other side of my desk, kneeled in front of me underneath it and lifted my dress up. First, you reached up and pulled my lace knickers down. Then you asked me to start reading the news. And as I did, you gently, but persistently stroked from my ankles up to my upper thighs with the lightest touch until I started to wriggle and writhe. You asked me to continue reading as you kissed all the way up my legs and around my groin, hovering there until I was crying out for you. Then, you went down on me. Right there . . . You told me to read out the headlines as I came. And I did . . . and you just kept kissing and licking and sucking and I just kept cumming . . . till I was pretty much screaming out the auto-cue. And then you pushed back my chair and moved around the other side, lifted me onto the desk, and started to fuck me. Really fuck me. Slamming into me so hard, watching me as I came again and again. And then you came all over the desk. God I loved that. Remember?

'I do.

'I think about it a lot. In fact, there have been times when I read the news that it is all I can think about. I'm reading out a headline about a blocked bill in the Senate, or a cat up a tree on a slow news morning, and all I am thinking about is you doing that to me again. There have been times when I'm so turned on that I can barely keep my hands above the news desk.

Once . . . maybe twice . . . perhaps even more, I've even started to touch myself while I imagine it. Right there at my news desk. No one else knows. Well, maybe Greg on sound had his doubts, but I keep my poker face, telling Australians what's going on in Canberra or wherever while I'm flicking my clit, thinking of you.

I'm sure that's why we won the Logie for best news show these past years – I'm so relaxed in that chair.

'David, I want you to come back . . . and that's how I want you to fuck me again.'

11.45 pm, Wednesday, 15 August

Olivia Law, Australia's most beloved newsreader, puts down her empty stemless Riedel wine glass, attaches her video love letter to her husband to an email and presses send.

12.03 am, Thursday, 16 August

While scrolling through Netflix, Olivia Law passes out on her designer lounge.

2

I HAD THE PERFECT LIFE. PERFECT BLOW-DRIES, WELL-CONDITIONED hair, wrinkle-free face, gorgeous, devoted husband, designer everything. But the truth is, nothing is ever as it seems. At least not with me, and especially not in my marriage. I knew Dave and I weren't working at optimal capacity. There were signs. We didn't have sex the prerequisite number of times a week to make ours a healthy marriage – or at least we didn't according to every lifestyle column I've read. Though, let's face it, the statistics always differ and, having worked for women's magazines as a journalist earlier in my career, I'm aware of the necessity to inflate and scandalise in order to create magazine-selling drama.

How many times a week, a month or a year is it normal for a married couple to have sex? It depends on whether you're asking your best friend, your nemesis or your mum. Not that I'd ever ask my blessed mother, Gillian, anything so obscene.

Dave was as good a husband as you can get. That's what I believed. How did I know he was done, as in packing his stuff and leaving me, as opposed to we had a fight and he was letting off some steam? Because we never fought and because there was no steam, no heat. We weren't cold, we were bath water that had been left to cool for half an hour too long. We were tea that you'd take a sip of and forget. Quality tea of course.

Dave is one for shared calendars. But on scanning I discovered he'd withdrawn his. He was no longer on my 'where to find' app. An app, I might add, that he insisted on us using. He'd been working on a deal and I could pretend he'd had to rush overseas on a trip and had forgotten to tell me. But the pit of my stomach and my reaching for our best wine in the cellar and drinking it alone, out of spite, indicated that wasn't the case.

Booze was still pumping through my veins, sugar jumping my heartbeat, and I had a vague memory of turning the red record button off before I managed two hours of drunken sleep or, more accurately, stupor. I woke before my driver arrived at 4 am and by 4.30 am Shelley in makeup was attempting to cover the humungous bags under my eyes. She is a sweetheart and a miracle worker and, ignoring the fact I reeked of wine, she worked silently until any trace of the night before was eradicated. My hair was shiny, eyedrops whisked the red away and haemorrhoid cream works wonders to tighten the skin around the eyes. As long as I didn't breathe on anyone my secret was safe.

5

Devouring two of the best bottles in our cellar is an impressive solo effort . . . not to mention the love letter, in the name of what? I check my phone again, no response from David.

In the cold, harsh fluoro lights of the studio, I knew getting drunk and pining to Dave on video was a highly unlikely technique to win him back, if he had indeed gone. But there was a feeling I couldn't shake. He was gone and my world was slipping away. I ignored the sadness (and nausea) I was feeling and concentrated on the auto-cue. No matter what else, I know how to do my job.

That's why it was such a shock when I was suddenly hauled off air. I admit I was still slightly pissed, but I definitely wasn't slurring. I was concentrating hard to make sure I compensated for the alcohol content in my bloodstream. If anything, my elocution was more precise than usual. I was watching as Janie, the new weather girl, shone brightly on the screen. The Twitter feeds appearing on the screen underneath her seemed random and completely unrelated to the headlines I'd been reading, but I wasn't going to be distracted and miss a segue. 'Forecast is mild with a chance of showers,' Janie was saying.

The voice in my earpiece told me to throw to a commercial break and step away from the news desk. Like any good presenter, I always do what that voice tells me. But why couldn't I finish my news read? Had something bad happened to Dave? Is that why he hadn't been home last night? Was Finn okay? Before I knew it, I was being led to the elevator. I was right to feel deeply worried.

The lift doors open and I am ushered through to the conference room. There are four lawyers present as well as Len Prior, the head of the network, the PR doyenne Harriet Mercer and my direct boss, Fergus Henessey. This is serious.

Fergus, the head of news, current affairs and light entertainment (doesn't that say something about the state of modern news programming), is on the phone and on a roll, his rapid-fire approach informs me there is definitely a tempest at hand.

'My daughter posted a picture of a fucking pancake this morning – a pancake – what's in that? Is there a show in it? Can someone get onto that?'

He holds out a seat while simultaneously hanging up his phone – even in prime demolition mode there's still something bizarrely chivalrous about him. He squeezes my shoulder, which is intended to be reassuring but isn't. Oh Fergus, what's going on?

Fergus gave me my break all those years ago. I'd been working at a magazine for teenage girls, first for work experience, then answering the phone and smiling while women with recession-era power suits ignored me. Then I got to be Dr Darlene and make up solutions to young women's woeful romances. When there weren't enough letters, or they were too dull, I'd make up the complaint: *Dear Dr Darlene, my boyfriend's stubble is giving me eczema, but I feel we're at a crucial stage of our relationship and he has trust issues due to his parents' divorce. I don't want to turn him off, please help!* My response – *Dear Sorely Scrubbed, you owe it to your beloved and your skin to come clean. But angle it positively, tell him how much you love watching him shave, how the feel of his freshly razored face sends you wild, especially the thought of it gently caressing your inner thighs as he kisses you . . .*

Fergus read the column over his sister's shoulder; he was a fledgling current affairs producer with the network, in need of fresh talent and ideas. He called me the next day and hired me that same afternoon to be an on-air reporter. That was twenty-three years ago. We've always worked together and our success seemed sweeter because we both rose up the ladder at the same time. He's always had my back, and me his, and as a result I'm now the face of the network's morning news.

Fergus continues his ADHD fuelled rant, he's in hyperdrive. He's nervous.

'Right, we'd better get onto it. Liv, you've stuffed up.'

'Okay . . .' I venture. It has to be the hangover.

'What happened?'

Tears well in my eyes. Fergus is someone I can't lie to, even when I'm fibbing to myself. The lawyers look at me blankly.

'David left.' My voice wavers. 'I got home yesterday and his stuff was gone, he's left and I don't know where he's gone, or what happens now.' God, isn't that the truth. Dave and I have been together twelve years, married for eight. Now there's a huge void where his clothes used to hang. There was no note, no voicemail. I'm guessing it's the no sex thing but, really, I don't know.

'Yeah, we know that, toots, but it didn't warrant your reaction.'

'I don't usually drink . . . I was upset.'

'You were more than that,' Len quips, peering over his glasses in a way that makes me feel completely naked. He's always leering, and occasionally groping.

I'm at a loss but before I have time to query what he means, Harriet calls 'Lights!'

The room goes to black. All heads face the screen at the end of the conference table. The network's newsfeed is interrupted by a YouTube clip.

A backlit figure appears. A dishevelled, naked, drunk blonde ... it's ... oh god, oh no, oh please god no ... it can't be. But it is. It's me, it's my love letter to Dave. My entire drunken rant is on YouTube.

'Half a million views and counting,' Harriet announces with a certain level of respect.

The four lawyers note that.

I hear my own drunken, desperate voice in the background. 'Do you remember that time not long after we were married, after the work Christmas party, when you came on set ...'

'Holy fuck.' I quake.

The lawyers note that too.

'I don't understand.'

'You went viral,' Fergus states. He turns to Harriet, 'Switch it off.'

The screen goes mute though my image remains.

'But how?'

'Who the fuck knows? Have you heard from David?'

My mind jumps. 'You think Dave uploaded it?'

'The problem is, your image has been irretrievably damaged,' a lawyer with bad teeth and a posh watch offers these words carefully. I've seen him in the lift from time to time, now he addresses me as though I'm a five year old who hasn't been invited to a birthday party.

'You've brought your private life into the workplace, you're in breach of contract,' Winsome, the network's head lawyer, points out. She always turns up for cake at crew birthdays, but I've never said more than two words to her, though I think I remember her telling me she enjoyed origami once, or was it sailing? Shit, I really am still drunk. This is one of those surreal drunken dreams you awake from drenched in sweat and promise yourself lifelong sobriety as payment for the relief of it not being real. Except it is. I stare around the room. The lawyers, Len, Fergus and Harriet stare at me. I look back up to my muted image.

'But it was private. I recorded myself and sent it to my husband. It was in my own time, at my own house, it doesn't concern anyone else.'

'Except your public image *is* our concern, pet. And you clearly reference a liaison that occurred in the workplace.' Len is enjoying this way too much. He adjusts his position on the chair, pulling it back from the table in a way that suggests his massive hard-on over it needs room to move.

'After a Christmas party, eight years ago!' I appeal. This is insane. I look to Fergus for some back-up. His eyes are on my image on the screen, his head tilted.

'Fergus!'

'If you were twenty-five it could have made your career – even at thirty-five we could have spun it and given you a current affairs show, but at forty-five . . . at forty-five you're just fucking the nation.'

'My intention was to fuck my husband.'

'You're fired. Sorry, Liv.' Fergus doesn't sound sorry enough.

'Huh?' The ground falls out from under my feet. Like a mini-earthquake.

'There's an avalanche of complaints,' Len says. 'People watch you because they feel safe with you. Now they don't know if you are masturbating while they watch. You've effectively desecrated the image of the morning news show and the network. It's going to cost us millions to get the show back on track.'

'I'm fired? Can't I just be suspended? I mean, surely this is just a storm in a teacup?'

'We can't sue you for damages if you're still an employee,' lawyer number three, a recent recruit who has obviously watched a lot of episodes of *Suits*, delivers his killer line.

'You need to get a lawyer,' Fergus says.

'Over six hundred thousand views,' Harriet chimes in. 'Growing by the minute. And here's a copy of the Twitter feed being sent into the network. That was just in your first fifteen minutes on air, before we pulled you off.'

She passes a printout across the table. Most are short. Most say slut. Some say whore.

In my job you get used to criticism. You can't have an on-air career and not expect it. And, yes, it's still worse for women than men. I'm critiqued daily on my hair, makeup, outfit, weight, tone of voice, the lines on my neck, the lack of lines on my face, any whiff of partiality, for being too expressive or not being expressive enough, for having too much fun or looking too miserable. In many ways I gave up thinking my appearance and presentation were up to me years ago. I'm used to it being claimed and judged. It belongs to the network and the viewers more than me. Is that why I stopped sleeping with Dave? Because I wanted something for myself?

The comments are certainly more passionate and colourful than usual. Some involve hating me, shaming me, and there are a few who offer me a 'jolly good rogering'.

'But people can see that it was a mistake,' I appeal.

'You're a morning news presenter, you can't make mistakes,' Winsome offers her statement with a perfunctory air of satisfaction.

'If it wasn't so . . . evocative, we could've played it as a meltdown, a break-up or a cry for help,' Fergus says.

'But?'

'You've violated three separate clauses in your contract, you're not getting the ratings you were three years ago. There's no way around it.' Fergus doesn't look at me as he says this.

'You're over,' Len says, rising from the table as he stares me in the eye.

Desperation kicks in. 'But I've given you my life? I've been here for the past twenty-three years.'

'And that will be taken into account with the lawsuit.' Len attempts magnanimity. I hate him.

'I'll fight you all the way,' I say.

'Good luck with that.' Again, the young buck lawyer offers up his best television delivery.

Winsome begins the dressing-down. 'You are no longer an employee of this network, all privileges and possessions provided by the network are to be immediately retracted and returned.'

'You are not permitted to speak about the network or the case in a defamatory matter, as per your contract, unless you wish to hurtle yourself into another violation, in which case you may end up incarcerated,' bad teeth lawyer says sweetly.

My head is whirling, I try to stand up but I'm shaking so much I collapse back into the chair.

'All bonuses, your car and wages are immediately cancelled. Your super is frozen until such time the network is confident of a settlement and reclaimed damages from loss of reputation and income,' Winsome continues. They're performing a sort of devastation volley between them.

And then I lose it. 'Loss of income? Don't tell me my head on a platter hasn't spiked your ratings this morning? Fergus?'

'I'm not at liberty to disclose the ratings with you, Liv.' Fergus looks sad.

'Oh come the fuck on, Fergus, we're a team.' I stammer.

'You went rogue, Liv. It won't wash. I can't protect you or save you. Sorry.' Fergus stands and pulls back my chair.

'Let me escort you out,' he offers.

'But what about my viewers?' I whimper.

'The viewers aren't yours, they're the network's.' Len coos.

'Want to fucking bet?' My voice returns. 'Who's going to read the news?'

Everyone looks down. Of course. They've already discussed this.

Fergus places his hand on my arm. 'Come on, Liv, please,' he says gently.

'See you in court,' young buck says as he taps on his iPad.

'Seriously? You need some fresh material,' I snap at him. He shrugs. He doesn't give a toss.

'Good luck, Olivia, all the best,' Harriet says, too brightly, in PR overdrive. Her phone buzzes – 'Oops' – she checks it. 'You've reached a million views!' She announces this as though it's great news.

Winsome and Len nod as Fergus ushers me out to the lift.

'Tell me this isn't happening, Ferg?' I whisper, attempting to maintain some composure.

'I'm sorry, Liv.'

The doors of the lift open. Audrey, my bright, young mentoree, exits.

'Olivia. I'm so sorry.' She hugs me.

'You saw it?' I'm appalled.

She shuffles awkwardly.

'Are you here to escort me out and raid my wardrobe?' I try to joke. It falls flat. Even flatter when I see the look between Fergus and Audrey.

Audrey is twenty-eight, she's bright, ambitious, achingly beau-tiful, full of fertile eggs and ready admirers. She was so keen to learn, buddying with her in a mentorship has been a pleasure. Her wide eyes and her pert breasts peer up at me.

The penny drops.

'Right. You're here to see Len. You're filling my seat.'

'Tough gig,' offers Fergus.

'All the best,' I squeak tightly.

Then I glare at Fergus. 'Never talk to me again.'

I get in the lift, stare ahead blankly till the doors close, then collapse.

How did this happen? Wait, I should know that right? But I don't – one minute I'm spending my mental capacity on measuring furniture and hiding behind custom-designed fantasies, and the next I'm a pariah, an untouchable. A slut of the screen. A failure.

Rewind. This is not what happens to my life, to my family . . . to me.

3

I'M IN THE BACK OF AN UBER (NO MORE WORK CARS COLLECTING ME) watching sad tears of rain trickle down the side of the window. It's a solemn winter's day as the car travels down New South Head Road, past the shops and harbour-hugging restaurants of Rose Bay, past the private schools where girls with coloured ribbons and boys with hats wander near the entrances. For some reason I'm picturing the scene in *The Piano* where Holly Hunter punches the ivories in a maelstrom of passion on the beach, and refuses to be drawn away. Then her character's husband chops her finger off.

I'm reeling, tired, and I'm tempted to feel relief in the invitation to join the cesspit of defeat. You always think it won't happen to you. When success comes, you work so fucking hard for it, there's always the terror it will be cleaved from you but you tread carefully, you merge with the persona you created until you have no idea whose successful life you're living and then when you least expect it the gremlins of your underbelly rise and slay you and all that you strived for disappears in the time it takes to press share on Facebook . . .

We all have secrets. We all have a private box we hide from the world. And usually that box is locked tight and the instructions to unlock it are kept in a safe a long way away. We make it so hard to access those places, we make sure we perish before anyone else can open the box . . . or is that just me?

What was in Dave's box? Right now it feels like a jack in the box that sprang out and punched me in the face. Years of eating sushi side by side, joint washing, photographing each other blowing out candles and pretending to enjoy each other's hobbies has led to this.

Then you get drunk, stick a bomb under yourself and, in one fell swoop, explode the existence you spent a lifetime crafting.

Why did I spend all those nights with him burying myself in the latest *Gourmet Traveller* or pretending to sleep and all those times without him longing for him? Why? Every time he travelled I'd sniff his pillow, imagine him inside me. And then when he was home and we were in the vicinity for intimacy it's like the shop shut and my eyelids got heavy and all I wanted was to sleep.

Is this as bad as I think?

The Uber corners the final road to the drive where my house awaits. My house and a few dozen reporters.

Where is Dave?

Surely I can't be that interesting? The reporters – a few I know, a few whose columns I read myself, a few whose shows I watch – swarm around the car. They're happily turning against one of their own.

'Olivia, what happened?' A woman with a bob that needs a trim and heels with scuff marks asks.

I shrug and feel for my keys.

'Would you like to make a statement?' Paul, a journo from a competing network, offers. He and I have shared drinks at awards ceremonies in the past.

'Can't' is my reply. My hands are trembling from shock and the remnants of alcohol. I can't find my keys. Then I feel an arm around me. Hugo.

Ricky comes to the other side. Hugo and Ricky are two of my best friends in the world. Without a word, Hugo takes my bags, finds my keys and opens the door.

The press remains outside.

'Told you you should've got those security gates,' Ricky says brightly as I begin to blubber.

'Princess, what's happened? That was a hell of a news bulletin by the way,' he coos.

'You saw it too?'

'Sweet cheeks, everyone in the world has seen it. I personally found you spectacular. Especially the –'

'Too soon,' Hugo warns.

'Oh my god.' I make for the kitchen, unable to meet their eyes.

Though I guess your two gay male besties are probably a safer audience than most.

There's not a cell in me that doesn't feel exposed. Exposed, crushed and projectile-vomited out.

'I got fired.'

'We know,' Hugo offers gently.

'How?'

'The network issued a statement.'

'How come they're allowed to and I'm not?' I babble.

'You need the dragon mother,' Ricky says.

'Oh god no.'

'She's one of the best lawyers in the country.' Of course he would defend Karen, he loves her.

'She's Dave's ex-wife.'

'Who better to defend you than someone who's been there?' Ricky insists.

'She hates me.'

'Hate's too definitive an expression. Sure, she didn't love it when you and Dave got together, but she appreciates how good you are with Finn and she respects you as a professional,' Hugo reasons.

'How do you know that?'

They exchange a look.

'Hugo was panicking so I called her for you. She's on her way over. Martini?'

'It's 11 am!'

Ricky shrugs, unfazed. He's a leading cocktail-maker who has made a motza on his stock trades and investments. Hugo is the most sought after maitre d' in the city, an all-round gentleman. They met on Grindr three years ago and have been inseparable ever since. They're currently scouting around for a place to buy in Byron to run their brainchild – the ultimate gay wedding destination spa-bar-restaurant-B&B ... the concept keeps evolving and involving an increasing number of hashtags but it will undoubtedly include a designer fit-out, opulent pampering and a phenomenal menu.

'Consider it medicinal.' Hugo hugs me while Ricky begins slicing lemons, pouring ice into glasses and opening an untouched bottle of vodka.

I turned my phone off when I left the network and now I finally allow myself to switch it back on. There's a ton of messages. My work email and Twitter accounts have already been deleted, which is actually a relief. I don't think I could bear another savaging. Not for the next few hours anyway.

There are messages from Mum, Dad, Ava – my terrifying older sister – and my bestie Darcy, who appears to be oblivious to the drama. Finn, my sixteen-year-old stepson, has sent me a series of emojis, saying he'll call tonight. A text from Karen, but nothing from Dave.

Nothing.

Fergus has emailed me an 'everything I need to know about being fired and sued' note. His lovely wife, Hannah, has sent a condolence note. And that's it. A few emails on frequent flyer deals, credit card statements, and Pilates class discounts.

No Dave.

I call his mobile again. It goes straight through to voicemail.

'How can he not have been in touch, not responded . . . nothing?'

'Maybe he's on his way home?' Hugo offers with his signature optimism. 'Maybe he had a last-minute business trip?'

'He took all his clothes, his computers, his favourite pics.'

'His passport?' Ricky asks.

The boys follow me as I head into Dave's study, the place where he's spent the majority of the last five years burrowing into his business 'Homeontherange'. It has changed the way people buy, sell and rent houses. Owners list their properties for a fraction of the price it costs to have an agent. No crazy commission. It took a few years, and he'd had his share of setbacks, but these days Dave has a staff of five, some major investors and a plan to float the company at the end of the year.

Why would he disappear?

I rifle through his drawers while the boys watch. There's no passport. Is he having an affair? Does he have a second family I don't know about? Is there a bad investor who's scaring him, or fucking him? Any of these is a possibility, we've both been so consumed by our careers . . .

Weird how you can share a home and most meals with someone and never really talk to them. Dave and I are on different schedules. During the week I'm in bed by 8 or 9 pm and up between

3 and 4 am, depending on whether I need to wash my hair or not. Dave stays up late talking with potential overseas investors and clients so he's always asleep when I get up. It's made avoiding sex far too convenient. Sure, we squeeze hands, we place hands on shoulders and backs as we pass each other in the hallway of our lives ... Weekends are slightly better; we read the papers and brunch most Saturdays, watch Finn play footy or go to an event I'm meant to attend for work. When Finn is home we eat pizza and watch Netflix together.

Finn's a special kid. David and Karen were set for a ferocious custody battle in the family court when Finn called a stop to it by announcing his own terms and conditions, which included boarding once he was old enough (even though the school is only a few kilometres away) and alternate weekends and holidays. He's an unbelievably evolved young man, he's taller than me now, all grass grazes and braces. I adore him. Oh my god, please don't let Finn have seen the video.

Is this all a mistake? Did Dave actually tell me he was going on a business trip and I've forgotten about it and completely overreacted? He can't be too far away surely? Finn has school holidays coming up, we're going snorkelling in Fiji ...

The doorbell rings. Hugo and Ricky scamper to open the door to Karen.

Meryl Streep in *The Devil Wears Prada* has nothing on Karen Wu. The woman is totally, irreducibly, terrifying. She's Cantonese, with porcelain skin that she scrupulously keeps out of the sun. As a result, she has no lines. Neither do I, but I rely on monthly botox jabs. Her hair is as thick as it is luxuriant, and usually worn in a variety of styles. Today it's wavy and out, with a slight Bond girl glamour. Red glossy nails. An olive leather skirt and cream silk ruffled shirt, ridiculous heels, a cashmere cape. She smells of a fragrance she has especially made for her – Dave used to call it 'Essence of ball crusher'. She and Dave separated when Finn was just four.

I've tried to bond with her. We're on the board of several women in business organisations and charities together – but she's never let down her guard. She's never even smiled at me, not intentionally anyway. I've always wondered whether she was hoping for a reunion with Dave, one that my relationship with him thwarted. They were separated but not divorced when Dave and I met. She's dated a few men, not many according to Finn, but isn't that keen on any of them.

'He's overseas,' Karen announces as Ricky flits about preparing a martini. 'Dirty with an olive,' she instructs him.

Karen and I don't hug. We size each other up.

'Unfortunate. Very unfortunate.' I'm not sure whether she's referring to my current demise or my outfit. 'Nice suit, Carla Zampatti?'

I nod. So it's my demise.

'He's been in touch with you?' I ask, meaning Dave.

'He's taking some time out. He lost one of his investors, wants to reconfigure before they float the company.'

'Why didn't he just tell me?'

'He said you were separated.'

Clunk.

'He didn't tell me that.'

'He's commenced divorce proceedings.'

I cling to the kitchen bench so I don't fall over. Winded, I gasp for air before I gulp my martini.

'He hasn't spoken to you about it? Typical David.' Nothing surprises Karen Wu.

I'm staring at the kitchen floor tiles, they're granite, heated, we chose them together. We haven't had sex in two years. He's commenced divorce proceedings?

'He's stated separated but living under the same roof.'

'What does that mean?'

'Pretty much what it sounds like – he's been sleeping in a different room?'

The boys exchange another look.

'We're on different timetables. He has late calls –'

'He's created separate bank accounts.'

'Has he?' Oh my god, how can I not have noticed?

'And minimal joint social activity.' Karen takes a sip of her martini.

'That's because of work, we had Easter together.' As I say that, I realise how particularly lame it sounds.

'He's in Hong Kong. He's asked you to respect his request for space. And he's particularly asked that Finn not be used as a go-between. I second that request.'

I'm gulping for air, and fighting a throbbing rage that's urging me to yell, scream and tear the place and Karen apart – not that it's her fault, but there's no denying she's enjoying this. And then I realise what's happened.

'So he uploaded my message as a goodbye? Does he hate me that much?'

'He claims never to have seen it.' Karen has another sip.

'Oh yeah, right. Sure.'

My life is so completely screwed. How did that happen? This time yesterday I was in the studio after the show talking to schoolgirls about self-empowerment. I was bantering with Fergus about the Swans win, I was looking online for a new dress to wear to the children's hospital auction, I was reading the news, so confident of my place in the world. I was safe, I was happy, I was me . . . I think.

'My life is over,' I announce.

'Noooo.' Hugo places an arm around me.

The phone rings. I see it's Ava but I don't pick up.

'Yes, it is.' I finish the martini.

'It is a pretty spectacular downfall,' Ricky agrees.

'Thank you. Now if you don't mind, I'm going to slit my wrists. Or stick my head in the oven, or take an overdose. Possibly all three.'

'Don't be ridiculous,' Karen snaps. 'You have a lawsuit to deal with. You're being sued. You're being divorced. There's the property settlement to consider. You don't have time to suicide.'

'Let Dave have everything. I have no use for it now,' I say with a sweeping gesture that makes both the boys gasp with awe. They look to each other.

'So Bette Davis.' Hugo nods to Ricky.

'Bette Davis wouldn't be so stupid,' Karen keeps an even tone in the face of all this drama. 'You're not thinking straight. David wants half, not all. He's already listed the house – on Homeontherange – though we'll need to freeze that till we get your work situ sorted.'

I stop in my tracks. 'We? You'll represent me?'

'For your work situation. Unless you'd prefer someone else?'

The boys shake their heads in unison. Hugo points and nods subtly. Ricky mouths 'She's the best', which she is, she kept just about everything of Dave's without blinking an eye. Karen Wu is legendary. She makes the hardest bankers cry and bleed during property settlement negotiations.

'Aren't you more family law?' I query.

'I can do it all.' She polishes off the martini. Her lipstick remains untouched.

'You sure?'

'This will be just like a divorce. Besides, network negotiations get me hot.'

Who is this woman?

'How long was he planning this, Karen?' I venture.

She shrugs.

'Is it because we stopped having sex?'

'He didn't say.'

Hugo and Ricky lean in, keen to hear more.

'Is this the same as what happened with you and him?'

'Quite the opposite. We were at it like rabbits.'

This is news to me. Major news.

'Really, even after Finn was born?'

'The first month aside, yes. Sex was never our problem.'

'What was?' Ricky can't help himself. Hugo, sensing incoming danger, begins rustling around in the fridge and commences assembling some snacks.

'I don't like him.'

We let that one land. To be fair, Karen doesn't seem to like anyone; Finn being the greatly adored exception.

'Never have really. Nothing in common, except in bed. He was a gun in the sack, and I knew he was the right father for my child.'

A gun in the sack? Dave? My Dave? What have I missed? What have I done? What haven't I done? Yes, Dave was proficient and our early days were fantastic, but then – whether it was chemicals, hormones, life, age – it flattened out. And then flatlined. I know that drive-you-nuts-need-to-have-sex-now compulsion some couples have. Dave and I weren't like that, it was more like . . . well, to be honest it was more like brother and sister.

'So one marriage ended because it was all sex and no compatibility, and one because there was no sex. Nothing works. I'm going to bed. Forever.'

Before I get a chance to move, a text from Ava arrives. *On my way to pick you up. Mum and Dad want a family meeting. PS WTF have you done?*

4

I'M BEING FROGMARCHED TO THE CAR BY AVA, WHO HASN'T DRAWN breath since she arrived, not that I've heard anything she's said. A few journos and photographers persist.

'Eyes down, Olivia. No comment!' Ava says.

Ava, three years my senior, was born a girl scout. She loves organising people's fridges and people's lives. She's married to Darren (Derwood), her high school sweetheart and they have three children: twins – Bronte and Roman (I call them Chip 'n' Dale, they're ten now and very sweet, troubling but sweet) – and the latecomer, Ava calls him the closing down sale surprise, Bailey, who's three. All of her offspring share a large number of food intolerances and phobias.

Karen's words ring in my mind. All of them. She left me with the info that all my accounts are frozen until the work situation is resolved – i.e. I am being sued and will be bankrupted. Therefore, we can't have the house on the market. My only income for now will be the rent from my investment property – a studio apartment I bought in my twenties. It's in The Shire, where my family live. Dolls Point to be exact.

We approach the car.

'Not the front seat!' Ava shouts as she unlocks the doors.

I look up, bewildered, just in time for a camera to flash.

'You have to get in the back! I have something in the front already.'

I obey and get in the back, beside Bailey's child-seat. I sit on Thomas the Tank Engine and readjust.

'What's so important in the front? Nana's ashes?'

Ava rolls her eyes in the rear-view mirror.

'No, silly, it's my old school uniform.'

Makes no sense, but neither does anything else in my life at the moment.

'My old school uniform!' She repeats with big sister authority.

'I heard you, I was waiting for the why part. Are you going to a fancy dress?'

'Don't be stupid! It's because of the renovation.'

There's a pause here, which she thinks should be filled with my understanding. When that doesn't materialise, she continues talking as we head down to the main road.

'I had to clean out the closet. I don't know whether to donate the uniform back to the school or to charity, and since I was coming into town to save you, I thought I should bring it.'

'Well, if we're heading to the school you should take New South Head Road.'

'It's too late now. You took too long to get out of the house and we'll be stuck in traffic. Besides, I haven't decided yet.'

I'm still unconvinced why the uniform needs to be in the front seat, or why this is such a big decision. My parents put Ava and I through St Vincent's in Potts Point. Ava had a partial scholarship for her community spirit, I didn't, but I did top most of my subjects (except maths). We used to catch the train from The Shire and arrive in Kings Cross, passing the colour and action on our way through to the iron gates. It's a great school. We both liked it, Ava even more than me. In some ways her glory remains there. Maybe that's why she can't bear to let go of the uniform or have it take inferior place in the car. Obviously the same doesn't apply to me, which makes me want to annoy her.

'Instead of giving it away, why don't you put it on one night instead of your nightie and surprise Darren? Put your hair in pigtails and don't wear knickers.'

'Oh my god you're being completely unhinged, you know that?'

Bingo. Ava's face reddens and her already huge eyes widen.

'Just a thought.'

'A disgusting one.'

'He's your husband.'

'I'm not discussing my private relations with my little sister.'

'You mean sex?'

Ava puts some music on. Enya. She always plays that or k.d. Lang when she wants to soothe her rattled nerves. She sings the wrong lyrics in a wishful operatic voice that she knows annoys the shit out of me.

'Wail away, wail away . . .'

'Ava, that's not . . .' Ava stops me finishing my sentence by turning the volume up and continuing on.

'Wail away, wail away, wail away.'

Sisters.

No one in my family talks about sex. Ever. My parents are pretty strict Catholics who run an accountancy practice in Sutherland. Yep, riveting stuff. Ava works with them part-time. We were both too terrified of 'God's wrath' to commit any really errant behaviour when we were growing up. The worst that happened was when Ava and I went to the movies by ourselves one school holidays while Mum was doing the shopping. Ava thought '*The Blue Lagoon*' sounded nice. Mum, assuming it was a children's animation, agreed and off we went. I was eight. It was a revelation. I knew nothing about sex or periods, neither did Ava. I fixated on how bushy Brooke Shields's eyebrows were and Ava was moved to tears by Christopher Atkins's ringlets and white loin cloth, and the bulge within it. We had a lot of questions. Especially about him falling on top of her and making the baby. But we were clear how the baby was born. There was no stork involved and it wasn't her belly button. I asked Ava what she thought. Ava thought it was from 'the hole' the same 'hole' periods came from but a different one to where toilet action happened.

I had a lovely little hand mirror that I decided to put to good use when I got home. I wanted to see the 'hole' where the blood and the baby would come from. And I would have time to do it before dinner. Unfortunately, my father walked into my room to call me for dinner while I was lying on my bed, legs in the air, inspecting. He yelped my name in a way that made me know there was something very wrong and summoned my mother.

A family meeting followed and the full story of *The Blue Lagoon* emerged. We had seen a scandalous film that may well have damaged our moral fibre for the rest of our lives. Dad blamed Mum for not checking the ratings, then called the cinema and screamed at the box office manager for selling us the tickets. Some poor student got the sack. Mum yelled at Ava for letting us stay in the film. My hand mirror was confiscated and Mum began squinting, in the way she does when she's stressed, before saying 'Alban, I feel a migraine coming on.' Blinds were closed, curtains were drawn and Mum 'retired' to bed. We didn't see her till the next day.

I've never heard my parents argue. Just seen Mum squint and withdraw. Then Dad goes out and mows the lawn, tends to the roses or plum tree, or sits on his chair and stares at the TV screen.

The following day there was another family meeting. Mum had talked to our parish priest and taken instruction about how best to talk about the facts of life.

'When God wants a husband and a wife to have a baby to allow the world to once again see his glory and the possibility of original sin being overcome, he grants that it may be.'

'He allows the husband and wife relations. But it's in honour of the glory of the Lord,' added Dad.

'So the lord puts a baby in her hole?' I asked.

I was sent to my room. The use of the word 'hole' was banned and that was the last talk about the birds and the bees. Until now.

Ava and I disembark from her Prius. I can see Dad waiting in the hall, peering through the flyscreen door. He makes an abrupt turn to go and get Mum as soon as he sees us.

The twins, both dressed as Harry Potter, emerge. Bailey follows, holding Dad's hand. My parents adore being grandparents. They love Finn, but the fact I haven't given birth myself is yet another way I've failed them. Mum follows. Arms crossed. Squinting.

There are cheek kisses and awkward hugs from them. The kids, oblivious to my disgraced state, dance around showing their outfits off. It's near impossible to tell which one is Bronte and which is Roman, except Roman pronounces his l's as w's.

'Aunty Owiva, want me to cast a spew?'

'Yes!' I reply. 'Make me invisible.'

'That would come in handy about now,' Dad laments.

Roman provides some hocus-pocus. Sadly, I remain in full view for their humiliation.

The children are provided with screen-time and afternoon tea while the four of us assemble in the seats we've sat at as long as I can remember. Mum at the head, Dad to her right, me next to him and Ava opposite.

'Well, you cast a shadow over the kids' book week parade,' Mum finally manages.

'Please tell me you didn't see it.' I pretty much beg.

'Hard not to, Olivia. It's on every channel, every paper, the computer . . . but, no, of course I didn't watch it.' Dad says 'it' in a way that reinforces the fact that what I did was shaming, damning and reprehensible.

'It was meant for Dave. I don't know how it became public.'

'You looked like you were drunk. Were you drunk?' Mum asks and squints.

'A bit.'

'A lot.' Ava corrects me, a lifelong habit.

'Airing your dirty laundry like that. That's not how we raised you.' Mum provides a double squint. She's just minutes away from needing a lie down.

'Mum, Dad, I'm sorry. So, so sorry. Dave left and I didn't know what had happened, and I . . . I wanted him to know how I felt, to come back. But he's gone.'

'What do you mean gone?' Dad loves Dave. Everyone loves Dave.

'He wants a divorce.' I say it quietly, hoping it might miss their ears.

It doesn't.

'Why? Because of your terrible film clip?' It is more of a statement than a question from Mum.

'No. I sent him that clip when I got home after work yesterday and found he was gone.'

34

'Well it wasn't a very good incentive to get him back, was it? Oh dear. My head.'

'Poor dear Dave,' Dad says. 'He doesn't deserve this. You have to sort this, Olivia. You're married. Marriage is for keeps in this family.' Dad nods to Mum proudly. Ava puffs up too. Once again, I have let them all down. The black sheep.

'And it's not like you have a career to fall back on anymore.' Mum has never really rated my work. Sure, she's proud. They have a framed photo of me receiving my Walkley – it's somewhere behind the hundreds of framed baby pics of the grandkids and wedding day photos. I think they saw my job as a bit too showy, they would have much preferred me to have been a doctor, a nurse or a teacher. Or a war correspondent. Not someone with a lot of makeup reading the news. Besides, I can't compete with Roger Climpson, Brian Henderson or even Peter Overton. They're 'real' newsreaders. Dad used to like Jana Wendt. I think he may have had a bit of a crush on her, but he hid it behind the fact she asked 'sensible questions' in interviews.

'Poor dear Dave has deserted me, Dad. Goneski, wooshka, kaput, gone,' I say.

'Olivia,' my mother says in her tone. Hard to believe I'm forty-five.

'I have to go to the loo.' I get up and leave them to it.

Mum and Dad's home is like a living museum. Aside from a few upgrades on beds and lounges, there's been very few changes since the major wallpaper makeover of 1984. Landscapes, religious art and religious statues are the main staples. When I was growing up, I found them both terrifying and entrancing. There's a three-dimensional pop-up holy family above the architrave in the lounge room. Baby Jesus, Mary and Joseph all with halos. That sounds benign, except their eyes move, because it's on a rounded plate. All of them look slightly pervy. And slightly disapproving.

In my bedroom, I had Jesus on the cross above my door, to remind me of the sacrifices he'd made for me personally (that's what Mum always said). It scared me. I mean all that pain for a little girl born so long after he . . . went. How does that make sense? I also had a picture of a little girl praying. I thought she was the little matchstick girl and that she was praying for a family. I loved that picture and used to take it to bed with me and put it under the covers to keep her warm. Mum said the girl was kneeling to pray because she was humble (unlike me). I didn't buy it. I had a picture of a prince and princess on a unicorn that Ava bought me with all her pocket money for my sixth birthday. That's what I'd stare at as I was falling asleep – with the occasional concessional glance up to Jesus.

My poor family. This is about the worst that could happen to them. They're big in the church, and current paedophilia scandals and crooked archbishops will have nothing on what they'll cop by way of looks and whispers by their fellow parishioners.

Mum finds me as I'm heading back down the hall.

'You know your bed's always here for you.' She takes my hand, which makes me want to cry. I stop myself.

'I don't know what I did wrong, Mum. Well I do, but I don't. I mean with Dave, not the message. I know that wasn't . . . I think he's the one who posted it.'

'Why on earth would he do that?'

'To punish me.'

'For what?'

I look at Mum, I cannot bring myself to say, 'Because we haven't fucked in two years.'

'Because we haven't . . . there was a gap in our . . . relations.' Considering what the rest of the world has heard me say, it's pretty pathetic that's as close as I can get to exposing myself to my own mother.

'Every marriage has . . . was it because he wanted a baby?'

'He already has one.'

'Not with you.' She squints and puts her hand to her head again.

'Let's get dinner ready,' I suggest, reclaiming her hand as we head back to the kitchen.

5

LATER THAT NIGHT, I'M HOME, ALONE, AFTER SURVIVING POSSIBLY THE most stilted family dinner of my life. Any time conversation went towards the unmentionable, Dad would talk about the aphids on the roses and lemon tree.

I remember being little and sitting on his knee, being carried on his shoulders, holding hands wherever we went . . . and then around the time things began to sprout out of my body, all that stopped. He hated any mention of periods or tampons, was overwhelmed by the concept of two sexually active daughters. So me spilling my beans for the world to see is his worst nightmare as much as it's mine.

Shame continues to flush through my veins as I wander through my house.

Why did you do this, Dave? What are you doing in Hong Kong? Why do you hate me so much?

The house is empty, sterile, haunted almost. To be fair it's been that way for a while, even when we were both still here.

How did I let it go this far?

I switch the TV on. I've made my way onto the late-night news. I'm everywhere: a drunk, sad, desperate, ageing has-been, with modesty bars to censor my bits. Haunted just took on a new meaning. I watch her, the desperate woman I was yesterday. Who is she? Is she really me? She has eyes like mine, darting about, she has a voice like mine . . . oh dear god, it's like having your most cringe-filled drunken moment enlarged and blasted all over the world. In fact, it's not 'like' that. It *is* that. Exactly.

I wince and pull one of the overpriced cushions that sit on the underused couch over my head. My breath catches as thick tears of remorse and shame allow the scales to fall from my eyes. I hate myself.

I hear the lock on the door, I stumble to my feet; it's either Dave or someone about to perform a hate crime. I feel ready to lay down and hand them the kitchen knife.

'Olivia?' Finn, darling beautiful, innocent Finn, rounds the corner.

'Sweetheart, it's late, why aren't you –'

He overlaps rather than answer.

'Have you been crying? You never cry.'

Finn gives me a hug, one of those ones where love and the

39

desire to connect overwhelm teenage awkwardness. He's always been a great hugger.

'Have you, please tell me you haven't . . .' I realise how banal that plea is. Everyone's seen the footage.

'Not all of it, it's a bit . . .'

'Yeah I know.' I'm relieved he's happy to not go there.

'You made it for Dad, to bring him back,' he says gently.

It's too much. The only one who really gets it is my sixteen-year-old stepson. I put my hands over my face and begin to blubber. Ugly sobbing of loss and humiliation always involves a lot of snot.

Finn, like an expert parent, ushers me to the kitchen and pours me a glass of water, then hands me the tissue box. He waits patiently as a series of sobs and sighs chorus.

'You were trying to get him to come home.'

'I was, I . . . did you know he was going, Finn?' I can't help but ask.

Finn shrugs. 'I knew he had a trip, I didn't know he was leaving you.'

I nod and cry again. Finn hands me the refilled glass of water and puts his arm around me.

'You looked really pretty. In your clip. All the boys at school think so too. Especially Al. He says he's watched it fifty-six times.'

I try and nod but the thought of a group of pubescent boys who I've had playing in the backyard, and have cheered on at sports carnivals, finding my sexual musings 'pretty' is quite disconcerting. And as for Al, he's always been prone to lurking.

'Thank you' is all I manage. 'But please tell them I'd rather they didn't. Especially Al. It's a bit . . . what about their parents?'

'Al's dad says you're a dark horse.'

'Uh-huh. Oh Finn, I'm sorry.'

'I'm sorry Dad left.'

'Darling, are you staying at your mum's tonight?'

'Nah, I'm meant to be at school, but I figured you'd need some company.'

'Does school know you're here?'

'They won't mind. Family emergency.'

'Finn . . .'

I call the school dorm master. Finn was right, no one had noticed he'd taken his leave. Either that or I am now so unhinged, so persona non grata, they figured the best way to deal with the crazy lady is to go along with her. I speak fast and explain there's a home emergency and he will be returned before rollcall in the morning.

I text Karen. She's going to love this. She texts back that she needs to see me anyway so will be over in the morning to take Finn to school. And reprimand us both, I imagine. Finn heads off to his room and I to mine. I lay down and begin counting. Sheep . . . breaths . . . stabs of shame till this is all over. Then what?

I switch the TV back on in the bedroom. Big mistake. A late-night talk show with a panel of three, two of whom I've met, bemoan and blame me for all manner of atrocities in the western world. There's a delight in the outrage they express towards me. A vindication of their doubts, which till now they'd kept to themselves.

41

They show a biography of my downfall – from my humble beginnings as a copy girl, a junior reporter, fun times at awards ceremonies, memorable news reads and outfits, footage of Dave and me at a charity function – and then me today – a would-be Lady Di attempting to keep her peers, the reporters, at bay while sinking into the back of Ava's car. All of this is provided against the backdrop of a swirling soundtrack.

Again, there's that feeling. Is that me? Really? I'm guessing Darcy would call it some stress-induced dissociative disorder. Or a mid-life crisis. But I just don't understand how that woman on the screen, the one reading the news and the drunk one calling out to her husband, is me anymore.

Funny how your identity can leave you, just like that, one cold August Thursday. The previous morning when I'd left for work, Dave was still sleeping. There was no send-off. I wrote 'bin liners' on the shopping list. I heated porridge.

Was I happy then? What does happy mean anyway? I was busy. I was focused. I was possibly considered slightly uptight, but I was in control, a success, someone baristas made nice coffees for. And now? Now I plan to spend the rest of my life in bed eating Tim Tams.

There are no safe days, at any time the bubble of our seemingly happy existence can be punctured.

I crave oblivion yet I'm terrified of closing my eyes. Just as light creeps in I surrender to sleep. I dream I'm at an awards ceremony. They're pouring champagne, but I know it's not the right one. Fergus and John (one of my old mentors, dead now) sit either side of me, trying to tell me a joke they find hysterical. The joke is about a frog. They race to the punch line, which I don't understand because it's gibberish. They await my response, expecting me to fall about the floor laughing. I apologise, I didn't hear the punch line, could they repeat it? John pats me on the back by way of condolence, and says 'Well at least she's no fake' then they get up and leave me, while the rest of the table continues to laugh.

6

I AWAKE TO DARCY FACETIMING ME, AS PROMISED. 'SORRY, PETAL, YOU know how dodgy the reception is here. What's up? Wait, why are you still in bed? Why aren't you at work? You look, fuck me, you look almost human!'

Darcy Belmore, my dearest, oldest friend, is a widow and mother of two kids under ten. She doesn't have time for small talk.

She moved to Byron Bay following the death of her husband, left a career as a therapist to Sydney's celebrities to go and make kaftans that she sells at the markets and online. These kaftans are now being worn by Kardashians, but she refuses to make more than she wants, when she wants.

Life has changed for Darcy Belmore.

This rather extreme shift may have had something to do with the fact her beloved husband of twenty years was having an affair and on the verge of leaving her. His plan was thwarted by a sudden massive heart attack while on the running machine at the gym. None of which she knew till the day before the funeral when she was looking through his iPhone to ensure she'd invited everyone. At that moment Darcy realised the marriage, the life she thought she had, was a complete fabrication.

She got through the funeral service, hugged and thanked everyone, then went home and set Pete's clothes on fire, while the kids, Rose and Dylan, were with their grandparents. The next day she took Pete's mistress out to lunch. The mistress was as perturbed as Darcy. She'd thought Pete and Darcy were living separately under the same roof and had stopped sleeping together a long time ago. Now the life she'd been waiting to live with 'her' beloved was gone and a furious wife was sitting opposite her as she played with the grilled scampi on her plate. Darcy told me later she'd quite liked the mistress; she was disappointed not to find a 'hideous scrag' who'd stolen her husband away. She realised . . . Pete wasn't all that.

Her main fury comes from the sad fact that Pete is no longer alive, so she can't kill him.

Darcy is sitting before a mountain range, somewhere in the upper reaches of Mullumbimby, up on the north coast of New South Wales, slightly inland from Byron. There's a tepee in the background and a few logs around what looks like a campfire from the night before. She swears a kaftan (of course), her mop of wild red ringlets circle her cherub face, and she holds a delicate floral teacup in her hands.

'Where are you?' I ask.

'Just in the backyard, the kids are in the tepee. What's up?'

That's some backyard, I think, gazing at the ancient mountain bursting with a dense growth of banana trees.

Darcy, who clearly hasn't switched on the TV or been near her computer for the past day, has no idea about my dramatic descent into wanton notoriety. When I tell her the news, her response is a long, slow inhale, a shaking of the head, a slight smile on her lips and the words 'Fuck me'.

'I didn't fuck Dave, that's what got me into this mess. We haven't done it for two years,' I manage as the rest of my sorry tale pours out. Darcy still has a therapist's ability to be the world's best listener. She groans along with me, nods and helps me find words that fit what I'm feeling (like hell). I go on to tell her about the network, the potential lawsuit, the frozen assets. Her response? 'Get your arse up here. Today.'

'I'm a mess,' I moan.

'Come as you are' is her perfect reply.

Finn arrives at the bedroom door just in time to hear this. He walks over and waves to Darcy. 'I agree, she should go visit you and chill.'

Our conversation is stopped by Karen repeatedly ringing the doorbell. She yells out that there's still a load of press outside. By the time she's inside and the kettle has boiled, Karen has instructed me on not making a comment, providing a press release or mentioning Dave . . . and has informed me that the network's ratings have soared. And Finn has booked me on a midday flight to Byron.

Karen reprimands Finn for leaving school without consent, though concedes that there were extenuating circumstances – a stepmother who has lost the plot. Finn and I negotiate our way out of Finn being grounded, only via the fact Karen's heart isn't in it, otherwise beating her at anything is impossible. I try my best not to mention Dave. Karen announces she's passed all the necessary info onto him. He understands the assets have been frozen. I agree to make sure he's not taken to the cleaners if I'm sued. I also agree to backdate our separation to the last time we shared a bed. It's dreadful. I don't think I'm ever going to see him again. I ask Karen if he has a message for me. Karen blankly tells me he doesn't. He was sorry to hear about my strife with the network but that was it. Karen maintains he knew nothing about my video clip. He's looking into his IT and service provider. He'll get back to Karen.

'Why not me?' I whisper as Finn gets ready for school. 'Why can't he even talk to me?'

Karen shrugs. 'It's the way he works. He has to completely sever the bond.'

When she drops me at the airport, she warns me, 'It's going to get a lot harder and a hell of a lot worse before it gets any better.'

'You mean David?' I ask.

'David, the public and life in general. Yesterday you were the headline, today will be the escalating social media backlash and tomorrow you'll be the recipient of everyone's outrage. Just as well you're getting out of town.'

She pretty much pulls out in her latest model black Mercedes coupe as she says this.

I head in to the terminal.

It's a bit like Moses and the parting of the sea. But there's nothing miraculous about it. The entire airport terminal hushes and a united look of disgust meets me, or that's how it feels.

I check myself in. I'm pulled aside at security for a random pat-down. The female guard avoids eye contact. My bag is searched and it seems like there's some disappointment I'm not carrying a hand grenade or a giant sex toy.

I spend the flight (it's only an hour) staring out the window. The flight attendant collects my polystyrene cup and announces, 'Oh, it's you.'

'Who?' I ask, not as a joke. She laughs nervously in reply then quickly makes her way to her fellow attendants who whisper behind the trolleys with her.

Off the plane, I await my luggage at the baggage claim. There's a TV there too, which I keep my back to. I spot a well-dressed couple. The woman starts to smile before recognising me and tugging her husband's sleeve, she whispers in his ear and he throws a furtive glance my way. They move as far away as they can from me. I'm a social outcast, a leper. A fallen woman. Another group of women, looking like they've headed north to escape winter and domestic life, whisper, cluck, scold and giggle as they point to me.

I'm tempted to hop on the turnstile and circle with the bags, give them the freak show they desire. What stops me is an older lady, maybe a nun, with very thick glasses who peers up from her paper to look at me. A small smile forms on her lips and she nods ever so slightly to me before collecting her bag and heading on her way.

7

HOW IS THE AIR SO MUCH WARMER HERE, SOFTER IN A WAY? I'M IN THE hire car driving south from the Gold Coast airport, there's a scent of burning sugar cane and salt and cows.

I roll the windows down, listening to Neil Diamond. Anonymity remains a possibility on the highway.

No wonder people escape to here. I stare up at Mount Warning, sitting on my right; huge, imposing and majestic. The first place the sun kisses each morning on this northern coast.

I draw a breath, long and deep.

If you told me I'd be driving a hire car towards Mullumbimby singing 'Solitary Man' two days ago, I would have laughed in your face. Now life is steadily guffawing in mine.

Images from my video clip flash before me. I cringe, ducking slightly and lowering myself in my seat as I think of them.

Why did I do that? How come I exposed myself so sexually?

I'm not even that sexual. At least, I didn't think I was. Since *The Blue Lagoon* incident of my childhood, it feels like every time I embrace sex with gay abandon, I'm punished. I know this belief sounds like a residue from my Catholic upbringing, yet having this happen only affirms my theory.

Is Dave really going to let me go through this alone? How long has he hated me? How long has he been planning his escape? Was he waiting till his company was floated? When he lost his investor, did he just think, 'Stuff it, I have to go now, I can't stand to be with her one more minute.' What's going to happen with Finn? Will he fade out of my life and, in a few years, all I'll have is the occasional update from his Instagram account?

Am I really being sued?

Damn it.

I take the Mullumbimby turn-off. Mount Warning peers down, unmoved by my internal unravelling. I drive through the main street, past the health food shop in the old historic building on the corner. People sit with juices, yoga mats and matted facial hair. No one seems perturbed by my bringing about the end of western civilisation. I carry on, past a community hall offering salsa classes and life drawing, to the outskirts of town with the club and a stall next door offering a good deal on chook poo.

I keep driving, out along the road that eventually takes me up through the range to Darcy. The last part of the road is gravel and as steep as a rollercoaster ascent. Darcy bought the property in her teens for a song – it was always her plan to wind up here, but following Pete's death she sped up her plans, picked up sticks, and moved.

I'm not completely sure why she stopped practising psychology, she was such a brilliant therapist, but I think it had to do with not having anything left to give. And she felt embarrassed. She asked me once, 'How can I help anyone else when I didn't have a fricking clue what was going on in my own marriage?' She said men also made her angry, particularly men with marital issues involving monogamy. And killing clients or clipping them over the ears isn't great for business. Fair enough.

Darcy was the last one to foresee she'd become a kaftan designer whose work would be sought after by rock stars and televised real housewives over several continents.

Peter's death was nearly five years ago now. The kids seem remarkably resilient, and they love the property, which is a children's wonderland.

Rose is swinging on the main gate as I enter, hair dancing around her waist, not a care in the world. Seeing her instantly lightens my mood. Dylan jumps out from a tree to the centre of the road dressed as a zombie. He cracks himself up and disappears. Rose runs after him.

I pull the car up as Darcy appears. She walks straight up, opens the car door, pulls me out and hugs me.

'I saw it,' she says.

'Oh no.'

'I loved it! So proud of you.'

'For ruining my life?'

'No, for extracting the carrot that was lodged up your tushy. For being you.'

'That wasn't –'

'Yeah, babes, I think it was.' She rubs my arms.

'I was drunk.'

'You were real and messy and, oh god, it was fantastic. Have you heard from Dave?'

This conversation occurs in the time it takes to pull my bags out of the car, hug Rose and Dylan and head into the oversized shed that is Darcy's home.

It actually is a shed. Polished concrete floors, ceilings that go for miles, a hanging chair, a piano, beanbags, Persian rugs – it's like the Lost Boys from Neverland met up with a Scandi design guru (i.e. Darcy). It's relaxed and lively. I am so glad to be here.

'Earth to Olivia?'

I look back to her. 'Sorry?'

'Dave?'

'Nothing.'

'You're kidding? You'd think he'd head back on his white charger, grab you and race you off for a good going-over.' She sighs.

'Hon, that's *Outlander*.'

'Right.'

I look to my phone. No signal. I feel a huge weight lift.

Darcy has three tepees on the property for guests and Airbnb. She sets me up in one, then makes some tea before sending me for an outdoor bath.

In a far corner, behind a large sheet of corrugated iron, sits a huge, long, deep green bath from the '70s. The water is connected so the result is an outdoor steamy, sudsy soak while sipping one of her favourite chai mixes in a delicate china cup and staring out at the priceless view. My concerns are put into perspective by the majesty of thousands of trees and the peak of Mount Warning.

I get why she lives here and why so many people opt for a mid-life sea change up this way. You feel somehow protected and . . . quieter. I tilt my head back and look up into the early evening sky. The last of the day is retiring, her soft pink and lavender blanket trails behind the sun's departure. Nature . . . yes, please.

The chorus of birds, insects and soft quiet is interrupted by a loud, piercing screech on the other side of the corrugated privacy wall.

It's Rose.

'Mummy said you're having a bad hair day so I'm playing you my favourite song. Hang on a tick,' she chirps.

Rose recommences the screech, which I realise is her saxophone. She begins serenading me with the earnestness of an eight year old. It's tuneless and heartfelt. I realise she's trying to play 'Moon River'. Her simple kindness is so sweet. I kick my legs over the edge of the bath, allowing my head to be submerged, hoping to be born again.

8

LATER, ALL PINK AND WRINKLED FROM THE BATH, I SIT WITH DARCY AND a glass of wine as Dylan and Rose cover pizza bases with toppings.

'I know the last thing you want to be asked is what next,' Darcy ventures.

She's right, I'm still in the thick of 'what now?' And 'what now' cannot fathom the possibility of a 'next'.

'Stay here as long as you can.' Darcy tops up my wine.

'So good to be away from my life,' I admit.

I'm sprinkling artichoke hearts on a pizza base, much to Dylan's disgust, when a handsome brawny bloke enters through the sliding doors.

'Dr Ace!' The kids chorus in delight.

'Ace, hi.' Darcy smiles coolly but I know her well enough to see she's pleased to see him.

Dr Ace charges up to me. 'Olivia. Darcy told me you were coming. Thought you might need a hand.'

'What she needs is wine and space,' corrects Darcy.

I marvel at Dr Ace, it's like Bear Grylls just entered the building. He's tanned, ripped, not overly tall but clearly a pint-sized dynamo. Brown curls, baby blue eyes with long lashes, he looks around forty. I watch his smile as he looks at Darcy. Bingo.

He holds – oh my god, he's holding a talking stick as well as boxing gloves.

'Are they for me?' I ask.

He laughs. 'Can be, but right now they're for Dylan. I run the father and son workshops up the hill. Dylan and I have been bonding.'

Dr Ace speaks in statements, with a certain level of announcement in his voice. He has a broad Australian accent and his phrasing sounds like he could be the narrator of a show studying mating in the wild. I imagine boys and their fathers would be in awe of him.

'How 'bout a rumble, Dylan?'

Dylan leaps from pizza duties to pretty much jumping on top of Dr Ace. Soon they're rolling around outside, rumbling.

I look to Darcy who rolls her eyes and sips her wine.

'Don't ask.'

'You know I have to.'

'We met in town and I couldn't stand him. Then when Dylan was having trouble at school the principal suggested I enrol him in one of Ace's courses, and it was . . .'

'Ace?' I offer.

'Totally. Dylan spent the weekend making flying foxes, talking with men . . . rumbling. He loved it. When I thanked Ace, he invited me into his tepee for a chat and a chai.'

'And that's not a euphemism?' Dr Ace is growing more intriguing by the minute.

'Nope, he's pretty literal. Which drove me nuts. He told me I had a lot of pent-up aggression.'

I make a point of not commenting on that.

'What did he suggest for the cure?'

'Rumbling!' Darcy laughs, which makes me laugh too. The thought of tiny Darcy on the floor rumbling cracks me up.

'And boxing, and the fucking talking stick.'

'Seriously?'

'Yeah, he loves it. He'll try it on you.'

'I wish him luck.' I am nowhere near willing to hold a sandal-wood stick and share my secrets. 'I've already said way too much. So any romance in the rumblings?'

Darcy shrugs. 'He'd like it.'

'Yep, that's clear. But you've never even mentioned him to me?'

'After Pete, I was livid, I swore I'd never let anyone else get close enough to hurt me again. I like Ace, aside from all that patchouli, he's a good guy.'

'Are you attracted to him?'

'When we rumble sometimes I want to bite him,' Darcy offers. 'And I like him being here with us.'

'Well maybe that's enough?' I offer.

'If that was enough you wouldn't have wound up making that film. I want him and I'm shit scared.'

I put my arm around my strong, beautiful shit-scared bestie and we watch the rumbling.

Later, after pizza when the kids are asleep, Dr Ace turns his laser-beam focus on me.

'So, you've had a tough week, Olivia.'

'I've had better,' I concede.

'Would you like a rumble?'

'Ah no, thanks, I ate five slices of pizza and . . .'

Dr Ace nods then looks to the talking stick. I begin shaking my head and get up quickly.

'You know what, I'm exhausted, I'm going to head to my tepee and leave you guys to it.'

I can see by Dr Ace's expression he's sure he'll find his time with me. Still, I appreciate him not mentioning the footage.

Darcy equips me with candles, torches and lanterns.

'I've lit a fire just outside your tepee,' Dr Ace announces. 'Might be helpful for you to have a bit of extra light and heat tonight. You're at a liminal space. A threshold. A dark night of the soul means new beginnings, as long as you're brave.'

He nods solemnly. I smile, nod and back the hell out.

Darcy hugs me at the door. 'You can always come back in the house if you hate it out there. Pop in next to me or Rose.'

I agree but my feeling is Darcy's bed won't have a free side for too much longer.

I feel like someone who's been sent off for their rite of passage as I tread through the darkness to my tepee. I imagine Darcy and Dr Ace workshopped this before my arrival, so I try and find my inner huntswoman, my warrior . . . only to flinch when I turn and discover an owl staring at me. I'm pleased to see the fire as I approach the tepee.

Dr Ace is right, my dark night of the soul is well and truly here. I can't sleep to save myself and each minute takes an eternity to pass.

Awful truth after wretched truth pounces on me, and I attempt to become invisible beneath the bedcovers.

Dave did tell me he couldn't keep going like this. He said it a year ago and he said it three months ago and I . . . I ignored it. I guess 'like this' meant no sex. Or did it mean something else, something more? The fact our few joint meals were eaten in silence as we both checked our phones and updated our pages? The fact that when you continuously omit little things that happen in your day, they steamroll into bigger ones until you find you forgot to tell your husband you and your news crew were travelling to Perth for the week and he finds out via your Facebook account.

The fact I stopped asking and stopped listening to what was going on in his world. The fact I was acting like a wife without ever really being one. I don't like these facts. My shame builds to resentment. Did he have to just up and leave and upload my sex starved video clip on his way out? Who the hell does he think he is?

How dare he not be here for me to ignore him. I hate him.

I hear what sounds like a rumbling bear outside the tepee. I sink deeper. What the fuck am I doing here? I want to leave. First thing in the morning I'll pack up and . . . what? Go where? Home? To what?

I love working. I love my job. It's who I thought I was. What am I going to do with my life now?

There is a crashing of thunder and the inside of the tepee is lit up for an instant. Then it rains, or rather pours, heavy torrential north coast subtropical rain. Rain that you know can lead to mudslides and trauma.

It rains and rains and rains.

•

Drip, drip, drip. My eyes open to an ocean of green canvas. I'm sleeping under a bear rug. No one is beside me. I'm in a soaked children's tepee. My life has reached a new low.

They say life can change in a heartbeat, but how do you find your way back? I sent a love letter. It got the whole world talking and now I'm in a tepee in the hills of Byron, waiting for the storm to pass. For my lewd, drunken rant to be forgotten. Why has it garnered so much focus? Sex is everywhere. And nowhere near me . . .

Somewhere in the night, tears come and my howls for my old life, my husband, my job, merge with the storm.

9

BEFORE THE FIRST CRACKS OF LIGHT, DARCY APPEARS AT THE TEPEE. She passes me a teacup, hops into bed next to me and hugs me.

'Come on,' she says, throwing a blanket over my shoulders.

'Where?'

'Dr Ace just arrived, he wants to take us somewhere, show us something.'

I peer out of the tepee. I know this time, it's around 4 am, it's still dark. It's arriving at work, hair and makeup time. It's actually a magical time, there's a hushed reverence in a night who knows she's handing over to a day who hasn't yet begun.

'Why now?' I ask. But Darcy is already dragging me out of bed.

We arrive at a farm in Dr Ace's 4WD twenty minutes later. The farm belongs to his friend Atticus, a vet. Atticus's mare is foaling and Dr Ace wants us to see the miracle of life.

I feel like I've entered *All Creatures Great and Small*. The mare, Princess Cosette, is in 'the zone' when we arrive. Lying down, then standing. Atticus, who I must note is in possession of a cracking set of biceps, peeking out through a grey, stained t-shirt, smiles broadly like a dad-to-be as he pats the horse gently and whispers to her tenderly.

He nods at Darcy and me by way of a greeting. We nod back. Dylan stares in awe. Rose ventures off to get some more sleep in the hay.

There's a strange white balloon emerging out of Princess Cosette's backside, and in another moment a foot appears. Princess Cosette lays back down. I don't blame her. Another foot follows, then a nose and within ten minutes a whole new life is in the world.

'Gross, but cool' is Dylan's take on it.

Dr Ace undoes a hay bale and rakes it out, passing it to Atticus, who surrounds the mare and foal with it. Darcy looks euphoric. I have tears that won't stop.

Rose stumbles over sleepily and looks at me, concerned. I try the 'they're happy tears' line but she's not buying it.

What I'm feeling isn't a literal 'now why didn't I do that?' but a thing of family and belonging. What happened with Dave and me?

We wait till the foal is up and standing. It happens so quickly. Horses, it seems, really have the evolution thing down pat. Princess Cosette then delivers her placenta, much to the amazement of Dylan. 'There's more? Did you have that too, Mum?'

'Sure did, it's what fed you all those months.'

'So it's like a home delivery from a restaurant?' he asks earnestly.

'Exactly.' Darcy has a great ability to keep a straight face at crucial moments.

'Was Dad there? Did he help?' I see a flash of pain and tenderness pass over Darcy.

'Yes and yes, lots of cold washes and massages.'

Rose approves.

Princess Cosette stands to check out her pride and joy.

'We'd better give them some space,' Atticus whispers and leads us out. 'I'll make us a cuppa.'

Outside the stables, the sun is up and the farm has transformed in the first morning light. Whipbirds call, cows chorus and, though it's cold, it's nothing shy of magnificent. Dr Ace slows my pace as Atticus, Darcy and the kids walk ahead.

'How was that for you?'

'It was sweet, thanks for bringing us,' I say, realising I am using my pretend nice, slightly cold newsreader voice. I don't want to talk to Dr Ace right now.

'Pretty raw, pretty real and a total miracle,' Dr Ace continues on in an experienced facilitator way.

'Exactly,' I clip lightly.

'Probably a lot of feelings going on for you, Livvy.' He persists.

'Olivia,' I correct him. 'Yes, there are a lot of feelings but I'm not doing the talking stick with you.'

'Might help.' He won't back down.

'No!' I tread into a fresh pile of shit and realise I am yelling. Darcy and Atticus have turned to me.

'NO! It won't help so don't fucking ask me. Watching a foal being born won't get me back my job. I don't know you, I don't even know why I'm here. Just leave me alone!' I rage.

Rose and Dylan exchange excited 'Mum, Olivia's swearing and she's in poo' exclamations.

Dr Ace nods with satisfaction. 'That's it, Liv – Olivia, keep going.'

'Don't tell me what to do, Dr Fuckstick,' I scream. Atticus laughs at that then turns on his heel and heads to the house. It is an early twentieth-century farmhouse, old, white, a bit rambling.

'What is it you feel, Olivia?' Dr Ace is delighted now.

'Pissed off with you!' I spit. 'Darcy, we're leaving.'

'How?' Darcy replies calmly.

'I don't care,' I squawk.

'Okay, honey.' Darcy puts her arm around me, attempting to avoid my shit-sodden shoe.

'I'd be pissed off if I was you too.' I wonder if Darcy and Dr Ace worked this tag team therapy session out earlier. Day Two of Olivia in crisis.

'You've been left high and dry by Dave and by the network,' Darcy continues.

'I don't need to see a horse get born to feel my feelings.' I attempt righteousness.

'Kind of stirred them up though,' Dr Ace notes, pleased as freshly chilled Christmas punch.

'No, Dr Ace, you stirred them up.'

'That's just projection,' he breezes.

'No, it's you,' I retort, adamant, childish and smelling of poo.

'He can be annoying,' Atticus says. He has returned from the farmhouse and now hands me a pair of wellies. 'Put these on till you get your shoe cleaned up.'

'Thanks,' I manage to say, feeling ridiculous.

'Kettle's on,' he adds.

There's a pause. Dr Ace eyeballs me, daring me to go further down the road of self-expressive humiliation.

'Fancy a rumble?' he asks.

'Fuck off' is my reply.

'Fair enough.' There's another pause before I reluctantly laugh.

'Why don't you focus on Darcy?' I ask.

'Already has,' Darcy says, squirming at the memory of it.

'Besides, you're the one with the porno,' Dr Ace jokes.

Darcy inhales.

'Olivia made a porno?' Dylan is enthralled. How do ten year olds even know that word?

'Oh, you're the newsreader lady,' Atticus says. 'Nice one.' He nods, then turns and heads back to the house. We follow.

'I want to go,' I whisper to Darcy.

'Just a quick cuppa and we'll go,' answers Ace.

'No more talking stick,' he offers. 'Darcy, want a rumble?'

Atticus the vet's house is filled with a variety of pets. His practice is a few rooms off to the side. There's a huge fire in the kitchen. He looks like someone who can make their own woodfired pizza. He makes a very strong pot of green tea. He's very polite but I'm feeling so vile post meltdown, I avoid eye contact.

We leave Atticus to the horse and foal and head to Byron to pick up supplies, that's what Ace refers to them as, even though they're groceries as far as I can see.

There's a farmers' market that fills an oval. I keep my sunglasses on as I trail Darcy, who sniffs oranges and squeezes avocados. There's a few curious glances but no one says anything. I'm two-day-old news now. The kids head to a tree that is covered with other locals their age, and pass on requests for various treats.

Ace sings the praises of ginger butter, he's mates with all the stallholders. The market is a place of plenty and there's a quiet pride in the farmers' stalls. Being proud of what you've made, I get that. Well, I used to.

I decide to give Ace and Darcy some space to continue their farmers' market date and brave a walk on the beach by myself. As I'm passing the pub at the top of the main street, I'm stopped by a well-dressed woman holding a yapping Chihuahua. She smiles politely.

'Excuse me, you're Olivia Law, aren't you?' She grins so broadly now I figure she's my one remaining supporter.

'I am,' I reply, smiling back and holding my hand out to greet her.

She laughs at it. 'Yes, I thought you were. What a pathetic human being you turned out to be.'

'Excuse me.' I make to leave but she blocks my way.

'Your parents must be ashamed. You're a disgrace, an absolute disgrace, how you can even be out in public is –'

'Olivia.' A deep voice with a burly Scottish brogue drowns out hers.

'Over here.' A bald man in aviator glasses, tall, fit, around sixty, signals me over. I have no idea who he is. He stands from his seat, where he's been drinking a cappuccino and reading the paper, and heads over. He places an arm around me and kisses the top of my head.

'I should have known,' sneers the scary lady.

'We're over here, darling, I've ordered your latte already.' He throws a cold stare to the woman and her dog and steers me away.

'Do I know you?' I whisper as he directs me to a seat, which he holds out.

'Not yet.'

I sit. Once Chihuahua woman is out of the way, he offers his hand in a steely grip. 'Leo Montgomery.'

'Thank you for the mercy mission.'

'Piece of advice?' he offers in a non-irritating way. A good Scottish accent can do that.

'Shoot.'

'It's all in the attitude. Case in point.' He indicates his sunglasses.

'Rock star.' Then he lifts them onto his head to reveal two piercing green eyes, jade with mossy edges. He feigns a scared deer in headlights look.

'Not a rock star,' he says.

67

'Ummm . . .' I'm lost.

'Act like a fucking rock star! Don't give them the satisfaction of seeing, or even sensing, your fear. Loved your clip by the way.' He chuckles.

'Thanks, I think.' I feel naked once more.

'Oh no, don't thank me. I'm thanking you, just take it. It's the realest thing I've seen in an age. I know, I work in the industry.'

'Television?'

'Sex. I import toys and vitamins, and some porn.'

'Seriously?'

'You've heard of Kingdom of Come?'

'I've walked past the one in Paddington a few times.'

'Our flagship store. Anyway, that's mine. Though most of our business is online now.'

'I can imagine. Well, thanks for the save.' I stand up.

'You're leaving?'

'Yeah, I was heading for a walk. I have a friend who's going too – so I should go,' I babble.

'Five minutes. I want to hear about you.'

'Oh, I'm sure you have already.'

Leo laughs. 'Come on, stay for a smoothie, they have chia seeds.' He holds out the seat for me again.

I hesitate. Staying seems like a better option than being yelled at by someone again.

'Five minutes,' I concede.

'Deal.'

I sit.

'So you're here to skip the storm?' he asks. He has the papers in front of him. Old school. I catch a glimpse of an exposé of me in a news review article with the headline 'Outlawed'.

Leo catches me looking at it.

'Outlawed.' I moan.

'Badge of honour.' He laughs.

'Hardly,' I reply.

'Know what we do with this?'

I shrug. 'What can I do until it dies down? Apparently it's still in the rage phase.'

Leo takes the page and begins folding it. He neatly fashions a paper aeroplane and hands it to me.

'Let it fly, baby.'

I look to him, he nods. 'Right now, let it fly.'

I take the plane.

'Take off,' Leo calls. And I send it darting through the Byron air. It travels a fair way before it nosedives.

'Not bad, needs practice.' He walks over and collects it, then waves to a pair of nubile goddesses with thick locks and designer sarongs.

He returns the plane to me.

'Thanks. You live here?' I ask.

'I have a house up here. My winter circuit-breaker. You should come over.'

I consider for a moment what a Kingdom of Come house might be like. Before I can ask him, Darcy approaches.

'I've been calling you. Ace and the kids want to go for a swim at the tea-tree lake.'

'Sorry, I didn't switch my phone on.' I scramble for it in my bag.

Leo introduces himself to Darcy.

'He's Kingdom of Come,' I add as a plethora of emails download on my phone.

'Oh my god, I have three of yours!' She squeals appreciatively.

'Darcy!'

'What? I'm a single mum living on a property with no internet connection.'

'Which one's your favourite?' Leo asks.

'It depends on my mood.' She considers it for a moment. 'Angel's Wings has been busiest lately,' she says with a smile.

'That's one of our bestsellers. You know I make more money from women's sex toys than I do from porn?'

'No!' I'm astonished.

'It might be because so much porn is pirated off the net now. I also only import from certain production companies, mainly run by women.'

'So it's like fair-trade porn,' I ask, a bit sarcastic but also a bit curious.

'Not like, *is*. But, there's an audience for what you did, Olivia.'

Yeah, the kind who want to see me burn on a stake. Or the creepy kind.

'Okay. I've got to go now.' I stand.

Leo takes out his wallet and gives me his card. 'Come to the house, bring your lovely friend . . .'

'Darcy,' Darcy says, shaking his hand.

'Would it be a bit like going to the Playboy mansion?' I ask.

'I wish.' Leo laughs. 'I have a place in Sydney too. So come and visit, or meet me for a smoothie.'

He gives me a strong hug. It's not bad actually, though all I can think is that I'm hugging a porn king who owns the Kingdom of Come.

'He's cute!' Darcy reflects as we walk back to Ace's Uber-mobile.

'In a here comes trouble way.'

'I think you're capable of trouble with or without him,' Darcy quips.

'Evidently.'

We're driving down the highway as the last of my emails and texts download. There's one from Dave, a text. 'Sorry it's rough. I'll be in Sydney tomorrow. Need to talk. Let's have dinner. Best.'

My heart jumps and then drops. When did he sign off 'best' on a text? Never. Who is this man? Where is Dave? At least I get to see him face to face tomorrow. Surely I'll be able to get to the bottom of all of this.

Rose and Dylan are whispering solemnly to each other. Then Dylan pipes up.

'Mum, is Olivia going to jail for being bad?'

They look at me with equal parts disdain and pity. I edge closer to the window. Ace stifles a laugh. Darcy turns, takes her sunglasses off and launches in.

'No, Olivia isn't going to jail, and, no, she didn't do anything bad.'

'Well, why is she acting weird and hiding out in the tepee. She's a fugitive, isn't she? Cloud's dad says she's going to jail for not doing her job,' Dylan insists.

'And for being sexy,' Rose adds, widening her eyes.

'When we get home we are going to have a talk about the media,' Darcy mumbles.

'Don't go to jail, Olivia, you can hide in my room,' Rose offers. 'I like you.'

'I like you too,' I reply before returning to a few hate-mailers who've managed to uncover my personal email address. They do *not* like me. At all. I'll have to change my email address. Amazing how sex elicits such a response. If only people knew the irony, I haven't actually had sex for so long.

My eyes find an email from Hannah, Fergus's wife, saying she's appalled by how I've been treated and wants to meet up. Fergus is in the sin bin and she's making him forward some emails that have been going to my work email. *Read them Liv,* she adds, *you'll be surprised.*

I find the Fergus email:

Brace yourself, Livvy, it's all I can do to stop the network from broadening this to a class action lawsuit. It's not going to blow over.

As your mate, I'd suggest you settle ASAP. You didn't hear that from me.

Hannah threatened divorce if I didn't forward these on. She's been enjoying them. Way too much. Might be something in it.

There I was thinking it was all beeswax candles and shiatsu massages. Fuck me, I got that wrong.

Hang in there.
Fergus

I open the content he's forwarded me. There are five emails from different women of different ages. I gasp as I read the first one from 'Dorothy of Lithgow'. The kids shake their heads. Darcy turns to the back seat again.

'All right?' She asks.

I nod wide-eyed.

10

DISPATCH FROM THE INTERIOR

From: Dorothy Dwyer
To: Olivia Law
Subject: Ants
Date: 17 August at 9:51pm

You remember the ant song? 'The ants came marching two
by two, hoorah, hoorah.'

I've been interested in the world of insects for a long time,
and that's a particularly rousing ditty. I came up with this
story when I was a young girl, watching an ant crawl up
my leg one lazy summer's afternoon. It's remained my
old faithful, my go-to, for many a year, though I've never
mentioned it to my husband. He'd say I'd gone mad.
I think . . . Basically I'm lying back in the sun. I'm sixteen

again with legs forever that I've just shaved. A trail of ants
make their way up my leg. I'm not scared they'll sting. I know
from my studies that these are a special breed of ant; they're
incredibly rare and valuable. They continue crawling until they
enter the gateway to my promised land. So delicately they
proceed over my clitoris, tickling me slightly, arousing me,
as they venture further and further, making their way up my
vaginal wall. I look ahead and their line is infinite. I am going
to spend the rest of my life housing these tiny creatures.
They will have their colony within my euphoric folds.

Then, from nowhere, a very elegant explorer taps me on the
shoulder. He's travelled the globe in search of these ants.
He can see I am deeply aroused and asks if I will spread my
legs so he may gain a closer inspection of the ants in their
ultimate habitat. I grant his wish and his face morphs into
a huge grin of wonder and longing when he looks into my
secret inner world. He watches for hours as the ants flourish.
He asks if he may perform some tests to check the climate of
the new habitat. He does this with his erect cock that reaches
up to the ants. He doesn't hurt them, he brushes against
them as he fills me. He informs me my cunt has saved the
entire species. I come in a shudder.

Dorothy from Lithgow

11

'I HAVE A SURPRISE FOR YOU WAITING AT HOME,' DARCY ANNOUNCES proudly as we sit on the edge of the tea-tree lake in the afternoon sun.

'I've had enough surprises.'

'You'll like this one, trust me.'

Later, as the kids splash and play with Ace, whom I have to admit is awesome with them, I share the news of Dave's text with Darcy. She's not excited.

'Don't get your hopes up, babe, it sounds pretty official to me.'

'Yes, but at least he'll be able to tell me what's up,' I reason.

'Maybe.'

'And there's this.'

I show her the emails Fergus has forwarded. Darcy's face lights up as she reads them one after the other.

'Oh, hello, Deanna from Dubbo, she's a wild one! And as for ant lady!' Darcy is all smiles.

Unlike the barrage of hate mail, these five writers have expressed their support in the most unexpected of ways.

'You see what this is, don't you?' Darcy hands my phone back. 'It's the beginning of a revolution.'

'More like a few women who just wanted to show that I'm not completely alone.'

'Exactly. A revolution.' Then Darcy doubles over with laughter, the golden afternoon sun capturing her perfect red ringlets.

'What's so funny?'

'Nothing, nothing. Just the fact that you're the one leading it. You were always such a prude at school.'

'I wasn't.'

But Darcy's right, I was. After *Blue Lagoon* gate, I kept that part of me padlocked. I don't think going to a Catholic school in the '80s did much to help either.

'Do you remember how freaked out you got at church the day after Ella's slumber party?' Darcy says, chuckling.

I remember only too well. I was fifteen and our friend Ella lived on a farm on the south coast. She had fourteen girls over for a slumber party. I brought the latest *Cleo*, which had a questionnaire about being 'sexy'. One of the questions was 'How often do you masturbate?' In a world before Google and sex education, we were all in the dark. It obviously had something to do with sex, but what? We decided the questionnaire was asking how often we thought about sex. Much to the amazement of all the others,

I thought about sex more than anyone in the room – I'd pieced together *The Blue Lagoon* with a few things I saw on my way home from school at the Cross, as well as from *Flashdance* and a few late-night shows on TV. My prognosis? Sex was complicated, it not only made women have babies, it could also lead to them dancing like maniacs to reclaim their dreams. It meant a lot of staring, but it didn't always mean marriage. Men wanted it before and pursued it relentlessly, women wanted something after that the men had problems giving. Who knows why. So, yes, I 'masturbated' a great deal. When we added our scores up, I was head sex maniac, even though I'd never even kissed a boy.

The next morning at mass, the local priest, Father O'Malley, was not in a good mood. His footy team had lost the night before. Father O'Malley was known for hitting the whiskey and providing particularly sobering sermons the morning after. When he saw a row of fifteen-year-old girls in the front pew, and heard a little of our conversation, which was still rotating around my new status as queen masturbator, he had even less levity than usual. He reached deep into himself, and the scriptures, and withdrew a scathing sermon on the dangers of self-love and damned masturbation. Anyone who committed it would grow hair from their palms and the world would see what they were – vain, self-serving friends of the devil who would be expelled from the kingdom of heaven and face a life of humiliation and recrimination. A bit like me now. In the front row, tears began to roll down my cheeks, which urged Father O'Malley on further, his fury rising each time he peered down at us, and particularly

Ella's large chest, which had come about the previous school holidays (and, no, she wasn't stuffing tissues down her bra like me, it was all her).

Following mass, we filed out, flattened by the gravity of our – particularly my – situation. We walked back to Ella's in a woeful cloud of shame and silence. As we neared the gate, we faced each other and I renounced masturbation for good. Ella was concerned it was probably too late. I spent the next year staring obsessively at my palms any time I had a crush or sex entered my head.

And yet, now, here I am.

'I was a prude because I was terrified,' I confess.

'I know,' Darcy says. 'But now is your chance to turn it all around; to come out.'

'I'm not gay.'

'No, but you've been in the closet of your own sexuality – both Jung and Freud would agree with me.'

'Freud thought everything was sex,' I counter.

'Darling, pretty much everything is.'

Which brings me back to thinking about Dave.

'I think I was a crap wife. Good on an excel spreadsheet but, god, I never get it right.'

'You always get it right, that's why allowing yourself to be "wrong" has spread like wildfire. And it's giving you the opportunity to be truly right, which means being truly you,' Darcy says.

If I was Darcy's client I would nod and spend the next fortnight trying to work out what she meant and skip my following two appointments as a result. Since she's my bestie, we fast-track.

'What are you talking about?'

'Use those!' She gestures at my phone.

'The emails,' she continues. 'They're your defence. What you did wasn't terrible, it was a celebration of womanhood.'

It's moments like these when I wonder if Darcy has perhaps spent too long in Byron Bay.

We walk along Lake Ainsworth, grab fish and chips and then sit on the beach and play frisbee with rumbles (Dr Ace's idea, of course). Darcy is completely herself with him, slightly more girly because of the crush, but not too self-conscious. She's in one of her kaftans, no makeup, hair flying, and I've never seen her look more beautiful. I catch Ace admiring her too.

'You're lucky to have met her,' I announce, slightly schoolmarmish.

'Totally.' He grins.

'So what's your game plan?' I figure he's someone who respects cutting to the chase, no talking stick required.

'I'm into her. I'm taking it slow, she's been through a lot, and I've got a past with . . .'

'With what?'

'Falling hard and fast then fading out. I've been married twice.'

'Oh' is all I say and we keep walking. What is it with relationships? How is it we all manage to fuck up? We seek intimacy but maintaining it is something else. I like Ace – no, I'm not keen on the talking stick or rumbles or the feeling there's a team-building exercise coming at any time, but, as Dad would say, he's a good egg.

'I like that you're such a good friend to her and the kids,' I add. 'Maybe anything additional is a bonus?'

'If I don't kiss her soon, I'm gonna explode,' he says before my phone rings. It's Finn on FaceTime. I answer.

'How was your match?'

'Won and I scored a try.' Finn, still flushed from his game, glowing with triumph, sits with his friend Daisy. They're still at the park where the game was played. It's such a relief to see him.

'Dad's coming back for a few days,' he confides.

'It's okay, Finn, I know, he wrote to me.'

'You know.' He nods solemnly. 'That's good. You going to see him?'

'Yeah . . .'

Daisy and Finn exchange a look.

'What's up?' I ask, feeling a heavy pang in my gut.

'Your clip's been made into a mashup.'

'I have no idea what that means.'

Daisy, as tech savvy and life savvy as they come, fills me in. 'It's a blend of your sex tape with key lines like "That's how I want you to fuck me" on repeat with music backing. It's quite good.'

'Oh god.'

'They sang it in the crowd today when I scored a try,' Finn announces with some pride.

'Oh sweetheart, I'm sorry!' Why is this poor kid copping it all?

'He was awesome,' Daisy says proudly. 'At first the other team were doing it to heckle him and throw him off. But Finn like totally owned it.'

'Badge of honour,' adds Finn.

'And then he got everyone onside and cheering!' Daisy says.

'Better to own it. Besides, it's cool,' he says with a grin.

My god, I have a lot to learn from their generation about authenticity.

'Not the word I'd use, but thanks,' I reply.

'You should listen to it, Liv, it's good,' Finn says.

All I can see is the remainder of my life savings swirling down a drain as I sit in court with the network. Not to mention the never-ending damage to my reputation.

'Was Karen at your game?' I ask.

'Yeah, says you have a meeting with her Monday. Dad's staying at our place.'

Another stab. 'Oh . . . oh, okay.'

'Sorry, I didn't mean to . . .' Finn looks concerned.

'No, darling, it's fine. Be lovely for you to have some time with him. Daisy, how's your code cracking?' I ask as a circuit-breaker.

Daisy was actually born Douglas, she's one of the new wave of kids who is able to articulate their gender orientation from an early age in a way that both inspires and baffles me. Daisy was running around in her sister's frocks from the time she could crawl. She's continued to defy conservative expectations and regulations. She also has the backing of not only her family but also her friends. Since they're at an elite all boys' school it seemed that coming out as a candidate for gender transitioning was going to be a major issue, if not a deal breaker.

You'd think, being a computer nerd, Douglas would have been doomed to gang bashings and ostracism. Not so. Douglas was always so wickedly clever that people loved him. At the age of fifteen, when Douglas (as he still was then) made his announcement, all of his mates, including Finn, rallied so Douglas would be allowed to remain at the school till his final exams. They took it to their own student council meeting, and then to the principal. It made the news and was one of the headlines I struggled not to smile when I read.

Gender aside, Daisy is one of the smartest people I've ever met. I find her identity confronting and brave. I asked Finn if he'd feel attracted to her. Finn fell to the floor in a laughing fit. To him, Daisy is the same soul who helped him find the tuckshop when he first came to the school, the kid who helps him with IT and maths. Daisy is who he hangs with, Daisy is his best friend. Daisy identifies as queer, meaning she feels her sexual orientation is fluid. Finn is crushing on Taylor Swift and Willa Keatinge in Year 12. Girls like him and he likes them back.

Daisy and Finn are my contact to the younger world of sexuality – they're the ones who taught me 'Netflix and chill' was a euphemism, except I don't know if it still is, I think the latest is that it's a joke about the euphemism, anyway they're my barometer.

'Code cracking is good,' she replies. 'Olivia, you have to ride it out.'

'Or we could all move to Spain,' Finn suggests.

'You're only saying that because of soccer.' Daisy rolls her eyes.

'Still . . .' Finn fades.

'You'd better tell her.' Daisy nudges him.

'What?' There goes my stomach again.

'I heard Mum on the phone. The Women on Top business thing you guys belong to –'

'Yeah?' I'm not sure where this is going.

'They've kind of axed you.' He says it quietly, the way you do when it's something you wish you didn't have to say.

'Oh.' I feel like the child now.

'It's ridiculous,' chimes in Daisy.

'They said it's not the image they want to portray and . . .'

'What is it, Finn?' I know there's another whopper looming.

'They told Mum she's out if she's representing you.'

Bingo.

'What did your mum say?'

The pair look at each other and laugh.

'She told them where they could stick it.' Finn breaks back into his smile.

'Really?' That's a surprise, Karen loves that board.

'But she didn't want to worry you with it, just said you're probably going to have to step down from your charity gigs for a bit.'

A feeling of shame swells again. I don't want them to see it.

'Of course. I was thinking that too,' I say quickly.

'Sorry, Liv, sucks to be you right now,' Finn says gently. It's how we kid with each other when something's not going our way.

'Yeah, sucks to be me. I'll be home tomorrow. Come after school. You too, Daisy.'

'Ummm, Dad's asked me to . . .' Finn hesitates.

'Oh, don't worry. Another time.' I cover my disappointment. Finn looks worried but nods. 'You sure?'

'Sure,' I say too brightly.

'We say our goodbyes. As soon as the call is disconnected I have that hollow feeling again. Loss. Such an empty feeling, like being the last stale arrowroot in a forgotten biscuit tin of life.

I stare at the phone. What am I going to do? I scan some more emails. Women on Top is just one of six boards and organisations who've politely dumped me. The hardest one to accept is the Women of Wonder Words, which I helped found. But then who would want their twelve-year-old daughter with learning disabilities asking me for help with their reading?

It's all so conditional really, isn't it? You think you're working for these noble causes out of a higher sense of self and community, but they can be quick to abandon you. They're not like family, or friends, who stick by you no matter what. You're a figurehead, and if what you are changes – in my case into a wanton hussy with a potty-mouth – you lose a fair bit of your shine.

All of it actually.

How can you help anyone when you're busily drowning yourself?

So my identity as Olivia Law, chair of this and member of that, is as gone as my career and my marriage. And my Sunday lunches. I've never been one to navel gaze and bemoan my state, mainly because I've never had time. I figured there were two types of people: those who do and those who think about doing.

I was always the former. I know a lot of people move to the north coast to 'have a little think' about who they were and who they want to be, but I am not those people. Except now I am.

Oh god, who am I?

12

DISPATCH FROM THE INTERIOR

From: Shirley Fisher

To: Olivia Law

Subject: The Choir

Date: 16 August at 6.15am

Dear Ms Law,

I am sorry to hear of your recent misfortunes with your job. As I'm sure you are aware, your film clip has had a rather large audience. I am writing to thank you for it. I understand it wasn't meant for the general public, but I for one am grateful to have seen it. I have had my own fantasies for many years and always feared they made me less of a wife, less of a woman. But seeing you share yours so bravely has made me see that our fantasies are what keep us going. I hope you will find the strength and courage to continue. With that in mind, I am sharing one of my fantasies, something I've not spoken of to another living soul.

I live in England and belong to a choir. We sing carols every year. The hall where we rehearse is arctic. There's one bar heater but it does nothing. Most of us cannot feel our feet by the end of the rehearsal. And so I came up with this fantasy, to keep me warm, if you like. In it we're rehearsing. I'm a mezzo-soprano and I stand between Felicity and Agnes. I imagine our conductor has just made us sing 'Silent Night' and we are onto 'Deck the Halls'. When it comes to 'fa la la la la la la la la' we lift up our tops and rub our nipples. This eggs on the rest of the choir, who begin to caress each other, hands on treasure troves, soldiers standing to atten- tion and quite soon it's all on. By the time we get to 'Joy to the World' . . . well, it isn't just the good lord in heaven who is coming! It's an outright orgy. I do all manner of things I've never done in my real life to Felicity. I . . . to expand on your term, dine out on her, and she does the same to me, while Eric the tenor enters me from behind. Pounding me in time with his carolling. It's very naughty and very nice. And somehow the conductor goes on, oblivious. Perhaps because we're all singing so well. By the end we're a heaving, writhing mess, and no one is cold. We get back in our places, replace our clothes and hit our final note, then return home to our lives.

I arrive home to my husband reading the evening papers and he asks me, without looking up, how rehearsal went. I tell him it was most gratifying. He looks up and admires the colour in my cheeks. 'You do so enjoy your singing, Shirley. Well done,' he says. Then he pats me on the hand and I head off to fix supper.

I do hope sharing this helps you. You are not alone. And now, thanks to you, neither am I.

13

A SOON AS WE'RE BACK AT THE HOUSE, DARCY HEADS OFF FOR A NAP.
Ace hangs around, in the hope he'll receive an invitation to join
her, I guess, but the only one he receives is to help the kids with
a flying fox.

I flee the next round of talks and rumbles with Ace in favour
of a jog. Truth is, I want to go somewhere alone with a phone
signal and call Dave. Surely he'll talk to me. I miss his voice.

I jog down the steep slopes of Darcy's property until I connect
with the bumpy gravel road that takes me to the flat plains outside
Mullumbimby. The last of the afternoon sun intensifies the green
of the paddocks, the red of some of the bottlebrush, which is
blossoming early this year, the last blast of jasmine. I steady my
ragged breath, inhale, exhale. Here goes. I dial. The phone makes
the beeps of an international call – then fuzz and then:

'Dave? Dave, it's me, can you hear me?' I hear background noise of cutlery and diners, then his voice.

'I know, right?'

'Dave?' I yell.

'They totally rocked. For a live band to be that good after all that time.'

'Dave?' I call again.

And then I realise – he thinks he's cancelled the call. He's not talking to me. I should hang up. But of course I don't. I know that voice he does and I know that story (he saw the Stones recently). Combining these two bits of information leaves me with a dry mouth. I swallow. I keep listening.

More clanging.

'Oh thank you so much. This looks great.' A woman's voice. I can't hear what else she's saying. Then more Dave.

'You know, my soon-to-be ex-wife always insisted we share dessert, then she'd eat most of it. I tried to get her to order her own, but it was always, "No, let's share". It's so cool that you're happy to order your own. You're just so great.'

I scream as Dave, oblivious, continues delivering compliments to the muffled female voice that orders her own dessert. I hang up and tread right in a huge fresh cowpat.

Shit.

What are the chances?

I'm still scraping my joggers when Atticus approaches in his truck.

'You in the poo again?' He jokes. I fake a smile. He pulls over and gets out.

'Here, let me help.'

There's a few flies circling me. I truly am an untouchable.

For someone who is good at keeping a poker face I'm struggling.

'You okay?' He asks.

'Sure ... just ... it's a lot of crap and there's no phone signal ... um ...' I begin to cry into my shitty shoe.

'Here.' He gently takes the shoe off me.

'It's just shit,' he offers gently.

'It really is, it's all just so shit.'

'No, I mean, shit is part of life here, it's no big deal.'

'I'm not crying about the shit!' I wail.

'No, they look like global tears,' he tries to joke.

'It's all a mess, the phone and Dave and the goddamn fucking video. It's all wrong. This isn't me, this doesn't happen to me. Oh my god, this is shit.'

Atticus smiles to himself.

'It's not funny!'

'No, I know, it's just ... well, you know, Ace will be bummed he missed this.'

That makes me laugh.

'Film it if you like. I'm getting used to the world seeing my private moments.'

'I went through a divorce, nothing public or high profile like what you have going.'

'I didn't say divorce.' I correct him.

'No, I did, about me,' he says lightly.

'Sorry.'

'What I mean is, sometimes the only way to get clear of shit is to go through shit.'

'That's a lot of shit.'

'Divorce is.'

'So, how did you get through your shit?' I figure any advice may help. Judging from the dessert sharing, it's not looking hopeful for Dave and me.

'I ran back to Byron and bought a macadamia farm.'

'Sounds reasonable.'

'None of it was reasonable, or sane. I left a practice in Hunters Hill where I made a motza immunising lapdogs to come here and work with no sleep, temperamental nuts and a lot of cow drenching.'

'Glad you did it?'

'Absolutely.' He laughs. Then adds, 'The same rule for shit applies for sex.'

'This is one of the less poetic chats I've had.'

'Sorry, but it's true. Sex, like shit, is everywhere. I deal with a fair bit of both in my line of work.'

'I used to too. Well, via newsworthy scandals. Now I am one.'

•

Atticus drives me back to Darcy's, where I clean up in the bath. While I'm in the tub, a fairly decent tenor and a very good baritone start singing 'The Pearl Fishers' Duet' on the other side of the wall.

I recognise the voices at once. My two guardian angels, Hugo and Ricky, have flown up to look at a property they feel may be 'the one' and to check in on their flailing pal. Knowing they're around makes life more bearable, dare I say possible. I'm so grateful for them in my life. It's true that when the chips are down you find out pretty fast who your true friends are.

Since Hugo and Ricky's arrival a table with linen cloth and napkins has been set up outside. There are huge bunches of magnolias in vases. The boys have obviously worked their magic again. They buzz around with plates and glasses all filled with promising colours, smells and textures. Atticus and Ace marvel at the boys' flamboyant hosting skills.

Darcy sits at the head of the table and watches, delighted. Dylan and Rose, both enthralled, are set to work, helping slice, dice and ferry plates from the kitchen to the table. Atticus assists Ace in lighting a bonfire close by that ensures we're all tearing off jumpers as our cheeks pink with the warmth of the flames and wine.

'I didn't know I had linen napkins,' Darcy marvels.

'You didn't. We always carry a few with us just in case.'

'Of what? Impromptu dinner parties?'

'Exactly,' Hugo says as glasses are clinked and praise for the huge culinary feat is bestowed. Chilli prawns with coriander and a swordfish ceviche are followed by a duck and cashew curry, tomatoes roasted in mustard seeds and cumin, a beef rendang, and a meringue Hugo just 'whipped up' with lemon curd, and wattle seed ice-cream. It's one of those meals that reminds me that good food with friends is one of the greatest pleasures in life. For once I'm not concerned about calories or bloating, sugar poisoning or gluten overload, and the absence of my neurotic food obsessing pastimes provides the meal with so much more flavour.

'God, this is good.' Darcy sighs as her spoon scoops up another helping of meringue after the kids are in bed.

'Better than sex,' I say without thinking, mainly on account of the glass of shiraz I've just finished.

There's an awkward pause till everyone peals into laughter. Myself included.

'What's it all mean?' I ask.

'Got me.' Darcy puts her hands in the air. 'You're the one who started it.'

'It's you straight people.' Ricky speaks with authority. 'You are so rigid about sex and love needing to go together all the time.'

'But you and Hugo have that,' I say.

'Yes, that's because we've slept with everyone else on the eastern seaboard. We had an open relationship for the first few years and then, following our last threesome where our guest began nibbling on his own toenail clippings, we decided it was both easier and preferable to stick to exclusivity. Besides, he's already more than I can handle in the sack.' Ricky winks at Hugo as he says this. Hugo nods, quietly proud.

'But sex and love are a good match,' I argue.

'They are,' Ace agrees, throwing a shy look Darcy's way.

'Still, let's face it,' Darcy now on her third glass of wine is ready for a rant. 'How often are they really combined and for how long? And is it so wrong to have one without the other? What we fantasise about often isn't love – like, look at ant lady.'

'Ant lady?' Atticus asks. But Darcy wants to continue.

'This woman who wrote to Liv, she fantasises about ants crawling over her, and up into her.' Ricky and Hugo look entertained; Atticus and Ace look intrigued and a bit mystified.

'It's more poetic than that,' I offer.

'But that's the gist, and it's great! So, is she in love with the ants? No. It doesn't all have to be about love and it doesn't always work out when it is. I thought my husband and I had a solid sex life, but he was also having that with his lover and planning to leave me – so none of it makes any sense.'

'Maybe he loved both of you?' Atticus suggests.

'Or maybe the sex I thought was good wasn't what he thought was good.'

'Nah, you both know when it's working,' Ace confirms.

I raise an eyebrow at Darcy who stares into her drink.

'Maybe he wanted to have sex with more than one partner?' Hugo speaks gently. 'But then he fell in love. Sometimes love follows sex. I think it's something about oxytocin, women get doused in it.'

'I've had good sex with people I don't like, bad sex with people I love, it's a riddle I don't have an answer to,' I say.

'But great sex with someone you love, that's the best combo,' Dr Ace offers.

We all agree and quieten as we reflect upon our personal experiences. My mind makes a few round-the-world trips to different times and places. I have loved and been loved, been sexually swooned, but I'm not sure if I've had it all at the same time.

'Can we get back to ant woman please?' Ricky asks. 'I like the sound of her. I thought women's fantasies all revolved around Chris Hemsworth shirtless on a stallion.'

'That's *your* fantasy,' Hugo quips. 'But you, Liv, you're a vixen of the vagina.'

'Maybe we all are?' I ponder. 'Perhaps there's just a really limited perception of what we think is normal because of gender stereotypes and the media.'

'Fuck the media.' Darcy is on a roll.

'Well they're certainly fucking me at the moment,' I concede.

'So fuck 'em right back,' Ace offers.

'I'd love to.' I pause. 'How?'

'The emails!' Darcy yells.

'The ants!' Hugo encores her enthusiasm.

'You want me to try the ant thing?' I wrestle with a mental image. Sure, it's a bit sexy, but ants? Really?

'Share the ant thing.' Darcy and Hugo, obviously on the same wavelength, chorus.

'It's not mine to share,' I explain. 'It was really lovely of those women to offer me their fantasies to make me feel better but they're private, like my video was meant to be.'

'Maybe you could get their permission?' Atticus surprises me with this. 'They wanted to communicate, so perhaps it's a chance to de-shame.'

'They could remain anonymous,' adds Darcy.

'So what am I meant to do? Act them out?' I'm amazed how much excitement this idea is gathering. It must be the shiraz, maybe we should have played Canasta like Ricky suggested earlier.

'Not act them, read them!' Darcy slaps her napkin on the table in excitement.

'Maybe you could do it like a newsreader, that's sexy,' Ace says.

'You are all drunk or mad, or both!' I'm at a loss, a bit triggered and quietly intrigued, but I couldn't, I couldn't . . .

Could I?

'You've all gone crazy and I need to go to bed,' I announce, hoping to curb everyone's enthusiasm.

It doesn't work.

'You sit right back down, young lady,' Ricky orders.

'You know what I say . . .' Ricky, pouring himself another glass of wine, continues, 'Paint your drainpipes red!'

'Okay, we've ventured into drunk-speak,' I retort.

'What he means,' Hugo says, 'is instead of trying to hide the thing you're ashamed of, embrace it. Frame it with gold, love yourself sick with it.'

I consider the merits of this for a second. I have no idea where to begin or what to do but not hanging my head in shame, or taking up dog-walking in disguise as my future career, is appealing.

'I'll think about it, but in the meantime I have a pending lawsuit and an estranged husband to deal with.'

'Focus on *you*, Liv. There's no way round it, you have to go through it.' Ace uses his slightly preachy tone. Atticus and I roll our eyes to each other. I like Atticus, I guess if things go as badly, as I suspect they will, he may give me a job making macadamia nut butter or something.

I resort to my tried and true tactic when I want to change the subject with Darcy. I hand her her guitar, which sits nearby. I already know what she'll play.

'I love Bob Dylan,' Ace says as she begins the first chords of 'Just like a Woman'. We're all just tipsy enough to sing along.

I leave them singing that I, me, she won't be blessed till she figures out she's just like the rest, and head to bed. My mind is full of Dave and the call, Dave and sex, Dave . . . we have to work this out. A small voice that I've spent so many years squashing is telling me it's time to change, that the shit stops with me.

14

IT CONTINUES TO POUR FAECAL MATTER ALL OVER ME THE NEXT morning as I'm awaiting my flight. I'm front-page news, again, and trending, apparently. This time it's about the network pursuing me for damages and it looks likely a lengthy and expensive court case will ensue. I'm not sure why my story has caught on so much. Perhaps it's the enjoyment people get watching someone else's downfall, particularly a minor celebrity's.

There was a case a few years earlier, involving the sexual misconduct of a network executive, which was all over the news. The executive's network stood by him. Not so in my case. Is that a gender thing? A sex thing? Or an Olivia Law thing?

Olivia Law Outlaw at Large.

Back in Sydney, I'm prepped for this afternoon's mediation by Karen, though she only has marginally more information than the articles I've read.

'Why can't I have a press release?'

'It's part of the settlement conditions. You pass no comment.'

'It's making me look weak and guilty.'

'You are guilty. In relation to breach of your contract, in any case. The best thing you can do is lay low. The network are the ones with the money and the power.' Karen eyes me suspiciously.

'But you're the one who was excited to fight them.'

'Olivia, they could destroy you, which would destroy Finn. We have to play the long game.'

'What is that?'

'The best you could hope for is being able to read the weather on some regional outpost.' She speaks in a low, clipped voice.

My heart races.

'And the worst?'

'Crowd-funding to have your bunions fixed in your sixties and perhaps a guest role on a whatever-happened-to show.'

'So you've really thought about my options then? Thanks.' I feel ready to implode.

'Another thing . . .'

I await the next Karen Wu missile.

'Don't get your hopes up with David. I know you're having dinner with him tonight.'

Another bomb explodes somewhere in the wasteland of my soul. I know better than to ask. I just have to get through this meeting and then it will be night and I can talk to Dave and sort this out.

I hope.

We enter the meeting with Len, Fergus, Louie and Dewy – the lawyers, and a mediator. I'm informed the purpose of the meeting is to come to an agreement today to stop things proceeding to a full-blown court case.

It's horrific. Like the dream of the car crash or the puppy drowning that you can't stop. Fergus says little. He barely makes eye contact. The lawyers go through a series of injuries I have caused the network. Basically everything I mentioned in the video clip is used against me.

'What evidence do you have that any of these issues or events, Greece's economy included, is worse off because of Olivia's piece?' Karen asks.

'It was personal, a gilded memory, a fantasy!' I proffer, again and again. 'It was for Dave, not you, not my viewers. What about freedom of speech?'

'We're not in America,' Len reminds me smugly.

It gets worse. They want me to sign a shut-up-for-ten-years contract. A non-compete clause for five years with any major network. Three for cable. I'm to have five percent of my super. Due to our separation, they agree not to go after Dave. For now.

I am beside myself and I can see Karen is bubbling with bile.

'Is this how you silenced Isabelle Chan?' she erupts.

Indiscretions took place between Isabelle, a young reporter, and Wilson Bloom, the famous news anchor. Isabelle has since moved to Tasmania and runs an animal shelter and works as a receptionist at a local hotel a few days a week. Wilson continues to drive a Porsche, play golf and appear on his nightly current affairs show.

'That case has nothing to do with this.' Len's face reddens. Fergus studies his feet.

And then, I snap.

'It has *everything* to do with this. If I was a man, if I was Wilson, you'd be raising my bonus and slapping my back. You're using this, this, this ridiculous moment in my personal life to justify the fact a woman over the age of forty-five isn't who you want reading the news. You could have been supportive, you could have made it easy for me, instead you want to make me a cautionary tale to any other woman who dares to step outside of the non-existent parameters you've set! And hide it under the ridiculous title of being a "transparency policy". I'm not settling. Light your fires and burn me at the stake. I'm not shutting up for you ever again.'

I experience a moment of righteous exhilaration in which I see the tiniest smile pass Fergus's lips. Len studies his hands.

'I'm sorry you feel that way. A court case will ruin you. But if it's what you wish then so be it,' Len says.

'I'd rather be destitute than spend another hour huddling up your arsehole, Len.' Where did that come from?

'And you're wrong,' Karen adds. 'We won't lose this court case. You will lose it and your network's shiny reputation along with it.'

Len huffs. 'I look forward to you trying.'

'So do I,' Karen adds. She stands majestically. I attempt to do the same, but my chair is stuck beside lawyer number one's. It takes the memorable exit down a notch or two.

15

DISPATCH FROM THE INTERIOR

From: S. Muir

To: Olivia Law

Subject: Huge and Swinging

Date: 18 August at 5.00pm

If I had a cock, it would be huge.

I'd find it hard to keep my hands off it. I'd feel it rub against everything and I'd look at it all the time. Watch it shrink and grow.

Mainly grow.

If I had a cock, I'd want everyone to see it and I'd want to stick it in everything.

Everywhere.

In you.

No orifice would be safe. You'd hunger for it and call for it and I'd plunge it into you, surf you and you'd grip to the life-boat of my gigantic member.

If I had a cock, I'd wear tight jeans and rub cricket balls against it and say 'You ripper' as it awoke me every morning.

If I had a cock, I'd include it in all my conversations, speak to it directly and salute it.

If I had a cock, I'd hold it reverently as I pissed in patterns on the ground and then marvel at my masterpiece.

If I had a cock, everything would involve my precious, beautiful, long, fat, hard, throbbing veined, blood-filled cock.

Holiday plans, cocktail choices, political agendas would all rotate around it.

If I had a cock, I'd be you.

16

'THANK YOU,' I SAY TO KAREN AS WE DRIVE AWAY.

'Thank yourself, you womaned the fuck up.'

'But you were the one saying to accept it and to keep a low profile,' I counter.

'I was wrong. They were trying to scare us. I am not one for intimidation.'

'That's true.'

Karen narrows her perfect eyes before she laughs.

'Anyway, they're going to take you to the cleaners, so we might as well have our day in court to speak up about it. I liked your Joan of Arc reference by the way.'

'Thanks, except she led the French army to victory.'

'Well, perhaps you will too. For women.'

We pull into my driveway.

'Finn says he'll call round for breakfast, with Daisy. You don't think there's anything going on there, do you?' Karen demands more than asks.

'I think they're best friends and I have a lot to learn from them,' I offer.

She absorbs that.

'You know, you're not who I thought you were.' Karen stares at me unflinchingly.

'I'm not who I thought I was either,' I respond.

'That's a good thing.' She states it in a way that I know means it's the end of the discussion.

I get out of her car and watch her zoom up the street. She's pretty amazing. The fact she's only ever encouraged my relationship with Finn. The fact she liked sex with Dave but not him. The fact she's the best lawyer I could ever have represent me. She's a powerhouse.

I head into the house of empty. I'm struck by its starkness compared with the warmth and bohemian grace of Darcy's place. I miss the trees, the birds. I look around. It really is a shrine to the impossible dream. A temple of platitudes and sound bites, signifying nothing. It's never been really lived in and loved. There's no map of where or who Dave and I have been as a couple. None of the art reflects what I'm passionate about. It's all so muted, like my life for the past decade.

I guess I've finally taken myself off mute.

Finn's room is, of course, the exception. It offers chaotic

teenage possibilities through posters and papers, books strewn, unhung clothes. A few toys that have survived since childhood.

I sit on his bed and place his Peter Rabbit soft toy on my lap before falling asleep.

•

I awake to a dark sky. I check the time with a start and realise I have less than an hour to get ready and to the restaurant we've booked. Our favourite. Fortune. It seems apt considering I've lost mine and Dave's about to make his. And our relationship seems to be up for grabs to the highest bidder. A non-dessert-sharing bidder.

I look at my wardrobe, automatically heading to neutral, classy colours before I stop myself. I can hear Ricky calling 'Paint your drainpipes red.' And why not? I might as well go for gold.

I pick out a beautiful scarlet silk dress. It's off the shoulder, slimming, short without being slutty and it's been sitting in my wardrobe for an age. I bought it when Dave and I were in New York on holiday years ago. I thought it might spice things up . . . even back then.

I shower and dress, pick out heels that are higher than I usually wear, blow-dry my hair and, instead of straightening it, I let its natural wave rule the way. I finish with a red gloss lipstick. I've pretty much disobeyed all the newsreader rules I have followed for years. I look sexual, sassy. I check myself out in the mirror. I look like a different person.

You have to love a restaurant that turns a blind eye to daily scandal in favour of treating its guests well and making them feel completely accepted, included and part of the family. Fortune does that for me. It's a tiny restaurant in a back street in Woolloomooloo. Run by chefs who I think are the best in the country. It's bold but unpretentious, playful but not bossy. It's also where Hugo has been maitre d' for the past few years. He's still up in Byron but I'm met with the warmest welcome by Polly, the other front of house legend. Lucy, the head chef and owner, sends out champagne when I arrive with a message from her and her beloved French husband.

'They salute you,' Polly tells me. 'We're all with you. And damn you look hot, girl!'

'Maybe disrepute suits me,' I offer, nervous. Polly flicks her long glossy black hair over her shoulder; she has the deepest, sexiest female voice I've ever heard.

She purrs. 'I have some fantasies that make yours look like Sunday school.'

She winks and leaves me to the champagne. I watch her wiggle as she leaves and I grin. I bet she does. Dave enters. He looks well.

Too well for a man who has just separated from his wife.

He provides me with a dead fish kiss on the cheek. It's a lot less than my outfit deserves. I take a big mouthful of champagne to salve the stab I feel.

'You look different' is his first comment.

'I am different,' I say and wink. Dave clears his throat and adjusts his seat . . . away from mine.

I debate whether I should be straight-up and mention the pocket call. I decide to wait.

'How was Honkers?' I ask.

'Busy.'

'Lots of meetings? You found another investor?'

Dave hesitates. Then, 'Yeah, I did . . . thanks.'

There's a horrible pause that's as long as the night before getting your braces removed.

'Look,' I say at the very moment Dave says, 'Listen.'

We both back up and apologise.

I giggle politely.

'I'm sorry,' I say. 'For everything.'

'I shouldn't have let it get this far without talking to you.'

'How far has it gone?' My cheeks flush with vulnerability, which embarrasses us both. He looks away.

'Dave, the tape I made, it was to try and fix things.'

'I know. But I think it's past that.'

'It wasn't you, was it, who posted it?' There, I've said it.

Dave looks at me squarely. 'No. I haven't even watched it the whole way through.'

'But it was for you!'

'It's not. I can't. It's too painful. Sorry.' He utters in starts as Polly appears and silently pours champagne and places some pâté and Melba toast before us, then leaves.

'What does that mean?'

'Two years, Olivia, and before that it was minimal and . . .' He tapers off.

'Standard?' I finish his sentence. He nods, looking sad and hurt.

'What happened to us?' I ask.

Dave shrugs. Neither of us is comfortable with big emotions. Him even less than me.

'Things end,' he states, flatly.

'But this is a marriage, it – *we* – deserved some warning.' I sound like a stilted vice principal at her first assembly.

'Have you ever tried talking to you?' he says. 'You're never there. There's always something on, somewhere to be, some article you're reading. You're a master of digression.'

'Not about this,' I protest.

'You avoided any intimacy with me for two years and, really, in terms of marriage, I don't know if we ever had it. I've never even seen you pee.'

That stings. I always thought keeping bathroom habits separate kept the romance alive.

'Would it make you love me again if I did?' I can hear the rising desperation in my voice. 'Would it bring you back?'

'You don't want me back,' he counters.

'I do!'

'You didn't want me when you had me. You just don't want to be alone.' There's heat in his voice as he says this.

'That's not true,' I protest.

'Isn't it? Liv, I don't know if we even like each other.'

'We don't have to like each other, we're married, that's the point!'

He doesn't respond. He looks at the menu, we order French onion soup and coq au vin.

'I'm sick of feeling lonely,' he says quietly as I focus on my manicure.

'Well, let's not be like that anymore. We can be however, whoever, we want.' I am pleading again. Pitching for my marriage.

Dave processes this as he slurps, a trait I've found equal measures annoying and endearing.

And I realise, I'm rushing, panicking, not really listening to what's being said, and absolutely not sitting with any uncomfortable feelings I have about myself. I've gone into 'Choose me, like me, love me' mode, a place I've inhabited with ingenuity and dexterity all my adult life.

Our conversation turns to Finn and the network.

'Thanks for keeping me out of it.' Dave softens slightly as he says this.

'None of this is your fault. My bad.' I try for lightness though I desperately wish he'd say he's here in it with me.

It's clear he's not.

'The house is frozen, but they'll go after my share of it,' I tell him, though of course he knows this already.

'They're really going to town on you.' He sounds sorry about that at least. 'What's Fergus said about it?'

'Nothing, he's not allowed to.'

'I thought you guys were allies.'

'Me too. But he has a mortgage and kids' school fees; wouldn't be fair.'

Dave nods. There's a gap between us wider than a wind across the Nullarbor.

'What are you going to do?' he asks earnestly.

'No idea. I was hoping you'd help me figure it out.'

Dave looks torn but says nothing. We eat our mains, which, for all their flavour, I cannot taste.

'Let's not share dessert,' I venture. 'Let's have our own. I could really go the profiteroles.'

Dave looks positively startled.

'What?' I ask, playing it cool.

'You always want to share dessert,' he stammers.

'I like sharing it, but I know you don't. And it's not like I have to worry about watching my calories for camera anymore.'

'Okay . . .' He sounds unsure.

I lean in. 'Actually, I have a better idea. Let's skip dessert and go home and devour each other.'

Again, he looks stunned.

'I want to fuck you senseless,' I whisper in his ear. I place my hand on his thigh and move it up to his crotch.

Dave laughs nervously.

He does not say no.

We head home in an Uber and launch into each other. It's hot – the kissing, the urgency, the desperation to find each other again. Perhaps this whole catastrophe happened to get me to this place? To rekindle sex with my husband. I like Dave's smell. It's a bit like baby talcum powder, it's familiar and warm and safe. I nuzzle into his neck.

God, why did I stop doing this?

And then?

It's like some force field the moment we enter the house. Our home. Perhaps it's reality seeping in, but things seem to slow down. We both go to the loo – I leave the door open, but he doesn't seem to notice. Jet lag perhaps. I take a breath and head into his bedroom, naked. I lay on top of him and we begin. Our kisses are dry.

It feels . . .

Quiet.

Not in the sacred eye-locking way. It feels like the last gasps of air neither of us can allow in. It's so quiet, it's tragic. We move in the well-practised way of long-term partners. I'm on top and then him and then I'm on all fours with him behind, the same dance moves we've rehearsed for so long. There's no rhythm, no joy, all the passion in the Uber has morphed into a sorrowful dirge, a mournful salute to the sinking ship of us.

He stops.

'Did you come?' I ask.

'No.' He withdraws and every part of my body knows that's the last time he'll ever be that close to me again.

We sit side by side, silent for a moment.

'This is why we stopped,' I remember aloud.

'It's not working. It hasn't been for a long time,' he adds.

'Maybe we need to try harder, shake it up more?'

But Dave shakes his head and then tells me something that's excruciating to hear but needs to be said:

'Olivia, I don't love you.'

I nod.

'I don't want to have sex with you. I'm not attracted to you and I've –'

'You've met someone else.' I finish his sentence for him. He nods, tears form in his eyes.

'Has anything happened?' Of course I want to know, but, really, what does it matter? It's over. Over. Over.

'Not yet. But I want it to. I want to be free for it to happen. That's why I've been rushing things, the separation from you. I'm sorry.'

'What's she like?'

'Nice.'

Of course she's nice, I think. Dave's a decent guy and he's going to make some woman very happy. That woman isn't me.

'My parents will be distraught.' I try and joke but it feels horrendous. 'You're my family,' I choke.

'Finn's your family,' he corrects me. 'You and I are flatmates. I did love you once.'

'Me too.' We look at each other and exchange the grim smile of a funeral service.

I get up and head back to my room.

The last card holding up the castle of my old life has collapsed. I'm in freefall. I allow myself to weep, without distraction. I weep for the loss of my marriage, which, if I was more honest with myself, I would have known was over years ago. I weep for the time Dave and I have both wasted maintaining a charade. I weep because I have no idea how I'm going to get through this. And I weep because I have no idea who I am anymore.

And then I sleep, deep and sound in a way I haven't in years. I think that happens when you finally reach some core truth you've been avoiding for too long. The insomnia, the restless legs, the light sleeping are all cover-ups for not feeling comfortable in your own skin, not really surrendering to the depths of your psyche. I can't deny anything anymore. All is lost.

When I awake it's light outside. Dave has gone. Finn and Daisy are making pancakes and playing a kickboxing Wii game.

I shuffle out and they place fluffy Margaret Fulton style pancakes with maple syrup, banana and ice-cream before me. I begin bawling. They sit with their arms around me as tears drip into my breakfast. After a time, I stop and hear what the kids have planned for the day: footy, shopping, film. Finn goes off to shower and I begin stacking the dishwasher. Daisy approaches me tentatively.

'It wasn't Dave.'

'What wasn't?'

'I checked his email.'

'Daisy!'

'Sorry, I was trying to help. I hacked in. He didn't open your video till after it went viral.'

'So who then?'

'I dunno. Could be a fan or a random hacker. Want me to find out?'

'Is it legal?'

'Are you giving me permission to hack into your emails?' She asks, forthright.

'Yes.' I sound more confident than I am.

'Well, then it's legal.' Daisy grins.

I shower and dress with no particular place to go. No future to grab. There's been a deafening silence from a lot of my Sydney gal pals since the tape went viral. I'm not sure whether they're dodging me or giving me space.

I do what you do when you're alone, bored and lost. I clean out my handbag. I find the card from Leo Montgomery. I turn it over. And over again. I am now single, I reason to myself. He's in Byron so it's safe. And a little voice in me screams for rebellion. And so I dial.

'Hi, it's Olivia Law. You made me a paper aeroplane.' I splutter too quickly in a high-pitched voice into the phone.

'Ah, Queen Olivia. How're you holding up, kid? Great shot of you in the papers again yesterday – camera loves you.'

I'm so surprised, and I admit flattered, that I laugh.

'I'm . . . I don't actually know why I'm calling you.'

'Well if it's not for a new vibrator, my guess is it's for lunch.'

'Oh, gosh, well, actually I was just cleaning out my wallet and I found your . . . oh god I am boring myself. I have no idea what I'm doing.'

'Sometimes that's the best thing. How's the weather where you're at?'

I look out the window for the first time; it's a sunny day, way above average temperatures. 'Glorious,' I say.

'Don't suppose you're back in Sydney?' he asks.

'I am.'

'Well, that's lucky, I am too. What time shall I pick you up?'

'Excuse me?'

'I'm taking you to lunch.'

'Today?'

'No other day is closer.' He laughs. 'Besides, best tonic for the blues is being taken to a snazzy lunch somewhere great.'

'Did you just say snazzy?'

'I did. Give me your address. I'll pick you up at 1 pm.'

In an even greater surprise to myself, I agree. Then I rush back to my wardrobe and pick the best 'I'm going to lunch with someone I don't know but I'm doing it anyway' frock and coat. I go for a cream thin wool boatneck Scanlan Theodore number with a sexy zip up the back. Cream suede ankle boots and a camel-coloured cashmere coat. I leave my hair out and wavy again.

I call Darcy, who fortunately is in range. I tell her what I'm doing.

'Just in case he winds up being an axe murderer, I want you to know where it ended,' I tell her.

'What happens if you have a great time?' Darcy teases. 'Is there anyone I need to alert?'

I tell her about Dave and the bad sex. She groans in all the right places as best friends do.

'Liv, I think going out for lunch with Leo is a great thing. You're separated; you've just been pretty seriously rejected personally and professionally. You have nothing to lose and, who knows, the porn king might be good company. Can you see if he'll provide a few free samples? My Temple of O vibrator has nearly had it. Overuse.'

'How's Ace?'

'Celibate and tortured, like me.'

'How long are you two going to keep that up for?'

'Long as we can. I'm guessing there may be years of it ahead.'

'I don't recommend it,' I reply.

'When you coming back?' she asks.

And as she says it, I feel a big tug for Byron, for being back there with the trees, the quiet, the beauty and her company.

'Karen says nothing will happen for a few weeks. I need to work out what to do in the meantime.'

'You know what you should do.'

I rush off the phone before she reminds me. There's a car approaching my drive. An old – as in vintage – Bentley.

I walk out and admire the powder-blue vehicle. No wonder he was happy to pick me up!

'That's a lot of vibrators,' I say as I get in. He laughs.

'You look fucking dynamite. We'll need to take that dress somewhere to show it off.'

'Thanks, but I'm not sure I really want to be seen.'

'Don't let the buzzards get in the way of a good lunch, kid. Face it with a grin.'

'I was a buzzard once,' I attempt.

'I seriously doubt that.' We pass a harbour filled with boats and sails making the most of their spring preview.

'My husband and I broke up,' I blurt. 'Last night.'

'Jeez, you don't muck around. Respect.' He teases.

'Oh no, this isn't . . . I just thought Dave and I weren't, well, we tried and it didn't so I haven't . . . You invited me.' I finish, knowing how completely unhinged I sound.

'Relax, it's just lunch. You're free to leave at any time.' We turn a corner and fly up the hill to Edgecliff from Double Bay.

'Divorce is the father of all arseholes. I've had two.'

'You're divorced now?' I check.

'Well, I'm not picking out china patterns for the registry.' He grins again.

I look around at the families, the singles, the people with dogs getting on with their Tuesday. Shopping, errands, jogs . . . life goes on regardless of your emotional state.

We park and he offers me his arm as we walk down Woolloomooloo wharf. It's full of tables with people who lunch. We draw our fair share of focus as we stroll.

'Chin up, tits out, be proud,' he urges me. Then adds, 'That goes for you too, Olivia.' Which makes me laugh.

We take a table at Otto, an Italian eatery famous for its food and diplomacy. The staff know Leo. They know of me. But they smile graciously and seat us.

'You're doing great,' he tells me.

'I'm shaking,' I confide.

'I know. I would imagine a martini would benefit you around now.'

He's right. We nibble on ricotta with truffle honey on crackers and fresh prosciutto. I realise I'm starving.

Leo orders for us, which is a relief. And it's great. Pasta followed by steak and a matching red.

'I like sharing,' he announces. 'That cool with you?'

I smile, relieved I am not alone. Lunch passes and it is enjoyable. Better than enjoyable. Leo is full of hysterical anecdotes. He warns me it's because of his industry; I think it's more than that. He was a GP before he became a porn king.

'Why'd you stop practising?' I ask.

'I enjoyed writing prescriptions for myself too much. So I took myself off to one of those courses people with too much money attend where they pretend it's not just rehab . . . but it is.'

'And you had a porn epiphany?' I joke.

'I realised I wanted to make people happy. I, well, I've always loved women and I knew how many of my patients were sexually frustrated. I thought vibrators were an untapped market. And they were at the time. A lot more lucrative than medicine.'

'And the porn?'

'Porn's tricky. It can be great. It can be soul destroying. At least I have some input as to the standards and conditions.'

'So you're really a modern-day saint?' I kid.

'I'm about as saintly as the late Hugh Hefner.' He laughs.

'And do you have as many bunnies?'

Before he can answer a passer-by grabs my eye. It's Fergus, walking with a few of his mates. He looks straight at me. Takes in Leo. Nods and keeps walking.

'Friend of yours?' Leo asks.

'Was,' I mutter. 'Thought he was one of my best friends.'

'You need some tiramisu and some sticky wine,' Leo announces, signalling to a waiter.

I don't disagree.

More time passes and by early evening I find myself at Leo's under the guise of meeting his dog, Magnus, a French mastiff with the largest paws and smile I've ever seen.

'He's huge!' I say as the dark chocolate mass approaches me with a wagging tail.

'You know, I think I got him just so I could hear people say that with that tone of surprise in their voice.' Leo winks as he says this. I'm not sure if he's being funny or flirtatious but, after a very long lunch on the wharf, he seems both to me.

Leo's house is set just behind Taylor Square. An unassuming terrace from the front, it opens into sixteen-foot ceilings and then leads onto a beautiful garden. Antique leadlights capture the last rays of the day. The house is filled with bookshelves full of books and boxes and boxes overflowing with –

'Vibrators.' He catches my eye. 'Take your pick and take some for your friends.'

'Funny, Darcy made a request,' I quip.

'I'll talk you through the different makes and models when we get back but first I need to walk the dog.'

'I am hoping that's not a euphemism?' I say, slightly overwhelmed.

He chuckles, grabs a lead and indicates for me to follow him. Magnus springs to action, obviously keen to have a run.

The sun sets as we stroll around the back streets of Darlinghurst, past the National School of Art with its sandstone walls protecting the stories and experiences of generations of budding artists. Down past Saint Vincent's with its patients and visitors sitting outside, some inhaling their last cigarette, some making excuses not to leave their loved ones for a moment or two longer. Down Boundary Street with its old factories that have been resurrected as swish restaurants and showrooms for cars and couch coverings, and through to the beauty of Rushcutters Bay Park, where Magnus, finally freed of his lead, makes a dash for his canine mates in the expanse of green fields as the light fades and a short twilight makes way for evening.

Leo is easy company. A welcome relief from the stabs I have about work and Dave and the lawsuit. I receive a text from Dave, he's collecting some more of his stuff. He'll be heading back to Hong Kong in a day or two. So weird knowing he's here, probably just a few kilometres away, inhabiting a life that is now officially separate of mine.

His words echo again, 'You don't want to be alone.' Is that true? I was quite happy carrying on with my own life when I thought he'd be there alongside me if I needed him. I am guilty of not truly being interested in a great deal of his work, not truly sharing his passions, apart from Finn.

'Leo?'

'Yes, Olivia.'

'You think marriages end because of laziness?'

'I think marriages end for as many reasons as marriages last . . . though, in my experience, the end usually involves money, sex, addiction or the heavy hitter.'

'What's that?'

'Loss of love. That's what bites hardest.'

I nod and we keep walking.

'Ever thought that your love letter wasn't to Dave, that it's actually a letter to yourself?' he asks.

I'm not sure how to process that because it tugs at something so deep in me that I'm not prepared to acknowledge it yet. So instead I go for a subject shift.

'You've clearly had some very interesting relationships,' I say. 'Money, sex, addiction . . .'

'This coming from the naked orator of desire,' he teases.

'I have a question for you too,' he ventures. 'Your clip, your fantasy Have you ever really done that at work? I'm asking the question on everyone's lips.'

'That's what they're wondering?' I'm amazed.

'Well, quite a few.'

I laugh. We walk on in silence.

'Sorry, I shouldn't have asked,' he mutters.

'Not really,' I confess. 'Well, okay, yes. Once and a half.'

'Can you tell me about the half?'

'It was a slow morning, no one was around. I was at the news desk, adjusting my pantyhose, and I kind of found my hand down there.'

'Please continue.' Leo's grin is pretty much lighting the way home at this stage.

'Exactly what I felt,' I say and he laughs. We take a few more steps.

'I stopped as soon as my producer returned.'

'Damn producer. And the other time?'

'I'd had insomnia, more than usual, I'd had the flu. I had a migraine and I'd read that an orgasm was the best way to beat it.'

'So it was for medicinal purposes?'

'It was a long read, we'd cut to a political story, and I thought fuck it, no one will know.'

'Did you make it all the way?'

'I did. And no one knew. A few viewers wrote in that I looked flushed, but the network put it down to the cold I had.'

'Are you always that quiet when you come?'

I stop short at that.

'I guess.'

'Know what I think?'

'That I'm a deplorable?'

'Hardly. I think you're a risk-taker, and you need a big life.'

'That's funny, right now I have no life.'

'On the contrary. You've written a love letter and now you're saving yourself.'

'I don't know what I'm doing,' I whisper under my breath, though I know he hears it.

'You have a new voice which you will finally realise is your own, kid.' Leo links my arm.

'That's a nice thing to say. Thanks.'

'I can't take full credit, I'm paraphrasing from a poem. Mary Oliver, I think.'

'A porn king who likes poetry, who'd've thunk it.'

The streetlights are on as we wander back. Magnus, pleased with his efforts on the playing field, looks up at us each adoringly.

'He really likes you, which is saying something considering you're not holding any food.'

We arrive back at Leo's.

'I'd better go,' I say.

'I have a better idea. Stay.'

I must look shocked, though to be honest I feel tempted.

'Stay, I'll light a fire.'

It's on the tip of my tongue to ask if it's mine he'll be lighting. I don't want this day to end, and, well, hell, I'm single, so is he, we're both adults and I like fires.

I agree to stay.

'Whacko Magnus, we've got a friend to hang with!' He kisses me lightly on the lips and pulls me inside the house.

Once in he heads to his freezer and pulls out a bottle of vodka. He pours two shots and then he heads to his cd player, very old school. He puts Fleetwood Mac's *Greatest Hits* on.

I laugh but he grabs me and we start to dance, and before long more shots have been had and I'm a whirling dervish on the dance floor as we both pull out our worst dance moves, which seem better the more we drink. We start a fire, we dance more. Finally, between twirls and dips, we kiss.

'I need to pee,' I announce, slightly slurred.

'Sure, bathroom's up the stairs.'

'Do you want to watch me?' I say, surprising myself.

'I can if you like.'

'Not really, it's just, Dave says he never saw me pee.'

'That's about intimacy, not pee,' he says lightly. I shrug and head up to the bathroom.

When I get back down to the living room there's a heap of vibrators on the lounge. Not the image you expect as you debate commencing a romance, or is it?

'For your perusal.' Leo makes a magnanimous sweep of his hands. 'I know you're more of an organic girl,' he continues. 'But in the desire to offset any potential RSI, you might like to try a few.' He holds one up, it's pink, soft and unobtrusive.

'This is our bestseller. Woman in Denmark designs them. The Danes are really onto it. Seven speeds and it can fit in your handbag.'

'Wow,' I stammer.

He hands it to me. There's another that's a bit more complex. 'This one has a remote control, in case you're alone, you can lie back, relax and think of news-reading.'

He shows me a few more, then stops and kisses me again.

'There's a reason I'm doing this,' he whispers.

'What?' I ask.

'I'm wondering if you might like to christen one, with me. Stay the night.' We kiss again. I'm feeling warm and strong and . . . drunk.

'And there's something else.'

'Hit me with it.'

'I've had prostate cancer, it ended with surgery, so not a full prostatectomy but things haven't, I don't . . . function in a traditional way.'

Oh my god, out of all the gin joints! Karma is clearly at play again. After two years of not sleeping with my husband, I get rejected by him halfway through sex and now I have a new lover who is impotent!

'Will "it" ever come back?'

'No one knows. Hasn't so far. I consider it cock karma. You'll still have a good time. Trust me.' He squeezes my hand.

What I'm actually doing sleeping with an impotent porn king the day after my marriage has ended, and my professional reputation is in the gutter, is a question that someone with a significant amount of alcohol and superior denial skills doesn't spend a great deal of time contemplating. Besides, what have I got left to lose? Does non-penetrative sex count as sex? Oh the irony!

'Okay,' I whisper. We kiss again. He's a fantastic kisser.

'Can I ask, what do you get out of this?' I say.

He kisses me again. 'You don't know much about men, do you?'

'I know they like sex and they like to come,' I say, feeling like a slightly deficient campaigner for a lost cause.

'Men love pleasuring women, Olivia. They love seeing them turned on, adore seeing them come, more than you can ever imagine.'

'Serious?' I ask, slightly incredulous.

'Totally.'

'Well then . . .' I kiss him now and guide his hands to my breasts. Leo certainly knows his way around a woman's body. I'm guessing he's had more than a few in his time before, and possibly after, his cancer.

He undresses me slowly, watching me, marvelling at every curve and crevice.

I'm abundantly grateful for the kindness of fireside light. He kneels before me. I can hear my phone ringing. I try and ignore it as he parts the way. It keeps ringing. What if it's Finn? It's nearly 10 pm.

'Sorry,' I say just before his tongue touches my clitoris. I jump back and run to the kitchen bench to reclaim my phone. It's not Finn. It's Ava. Ava has a policy to never call after 7 pm and refuses to answer calls after 8 pm. It has to be a crisis.

'What's wrong?' Are my first words. 'Is it Mum or Dad?'

It's only then I hear the *doof doof* beat in the background.

'Baaaabbbeeee,' she slurs. I know I'm drunk but she's on a whole other planet.

'Ava? Ava, where are you, what's happened?' Magnus paws my leg, requesting a belly rub. Leo, now in jeans but no top, changes the music to Van Morrison.

'You're not the only one who can be naughty.' Ava squeals. She's as high as a kite.

'Ava are you at a hen's party or something?' Ava rarely drinks, though when she does, all three times I can recall, she hasn't known when to stop, and she has ended up in the bathroom and five days in bed with alcohol poisoning.

'Come out dancing with me, we never have fun anymore, no one has fun!'

'Where are the kids? Where's Darren?' I'm panicking.

'Hear that, Liv?' She sings along to 'Groove is in the Heart'. I can't get any sense out of her.

'1,2,3, I'm at the best club in town.'

'You're in Sutherland.'

'No, Darlinghurst, idiot. I'm the sister of a slut-star, know that?' She boasts.

'Which club are you at?'

'Oxford Street. Groove! Groove is on my harp . . . wooooo. Got to go dance. Coming?'

I'm already pulling my dress on as she hangs up. Leo passes me another shot.

'What's up?'

'Sorry, it's my sister, she's . . . well it's like hearing the German chancellor's decided to take an acid trip.'

'Big week for your family. Where are we going?'

'Every club on Oxford Street.'

'Excellent, I haven't done that since the '90s.'

I throw him a look.

'Early '90s.'

'Thanks, Leo. Sorry to ruin the moment.'

'Not like I get blue balls, kid.'

We head out, leaving Magnus with a bone. We search four different clubs till we find Ava in the middle of the dance floor at a gay club filled with trans folk who are providing her with a wide berth as she cuts up the dance floor in a would-be Salt-N-Pepa aspirational rap fashion. Ava and I were enrolled in ballet, tap and jazz as toddlers. Ava took it, as she did all tasks, with dutiful commitment. There isn't an ounce of rhythm in her being, but it never stops her.

I approach her.

'Livvvvv.' She throws her arms around me in a way she hasn't since she was twelve. She spins me around. Leo watches on, amused.

A few of the other people on the dancefloor point at me.

'Hello naughty newsreader.' A woman six foot four with a voice like gravel calls.

'Love your style, dirty bitch,' says another.

'Thanks.' I nod. 'Ava, let's go.'

'Nooo, I'm having fun. Remember fun, Liv?'

'Yes, I was actually reacquainting myself with it before you called.'

Ava can't hear me, she's on a rant. 'Why weren't we raised to have fun? I can be fun, see?' She dances again, knocking into some muscled, buffed boys who actually know what they're doing.

'Such fun,' I say. 'Let's go.'

'No.' She's like an overtired five year old around a platter of party pies. She won't be budged.

Leo swoops in.

'Hi, I'm Leo, would you like to come to my place and have more fun?'

Ava throws me a *who is this* look. 'Hell yeah' is her reply.

Leo takes her in his arms and swings her around the floor a bit. He's a great dancer. Ava is in heaven.

'Wheeee!'

He spins her right out of the club. 'Best night of my life,' she hollers.

Leo looks, and I feel, sorry for her. Leo chats amiably. Ava keeps slurring, 'I like him, ditch Dave and go with Leo the lion, he's fun.'

'Dave ditched me,' I tell her.

Ava loves Leo's house, she runs around with gay abandon, Magnus following her. She squeals when she spots the toys on display.

'Heelllooo . . .' She looks up, stunned.

'I make them,' Leo says.

'You're the Kingdom of Come?' Ava quakes.

'I am.'

'Halleluiah!' She yells.

'Ava, how do you even –'

'Are you kidding? I have four.'

Oh my god, my completely prude sister has four sex toys, my bestie has three. Where have I been?

'Well, no one has just one,' she says. 'You need back-up. Darren loves the High Roller.'

'That's a popular one,' Leo says.

'Where, what, Darren?'

'Up his bum!' Ava sings out gleefully.

The thought of this has me wanting to call it a night and never, ever, be near anything slightly sexual again. Ever.

'You think you're the only one, Liv?' Ava continues.

'But you hate sex!'

'I love sex! I just don't like talking about it, not with you. You have no idea how sexy I am.' Ava stumbles around a bit as she says this, struggling to take off her cardigan.

'I'm a sexy motherfucker.' She tries to look flirtatiously at Leo. 'You see, Leo, I was always the sexy one. Olivia doesn't like it, I'm the sex kitten, she's the brains. Meeoow.'

'Oh my god, that's so not true,' I argue. Leo laughs and pours a round of shots.

'Maybe we should have water,' I suggest.

'See!' Ava screams. 'The fun police. That's Olivia. Me, I'm up for it.'

'Ava, why are you here?' I ask her directly.

'Leo invited me, and . . .' She tries to whisper, it doesn't work. 'I think you should leave us to it, you're ruining my chances.' She winks at Leo. I don't know where my sister went but I desperately want her back. We've gone from the Sisters Prude to Sex-craving Hussies within a week.

'You've wrecked my life.' Ava's mood quickly changes gears.

'Me, I'm sexy Ava. I'm Darren's minx. You're sexless Olivia who looks like a Teletubby reading the news.'

'You think I'm fat?'

'Not a Teletubby, sorry, a Wiggle! A sexless, one coloured Wiggle.'

'I have to wear clothes that aren't provocative.'

'Nothing about you is provocative! Well, it wasn't. And then you go and ruin it all and I don't know who you are but I caught Darren jerking off to your clip on YouTube.'

'Ewwww . . .'

I definitely never, ever want anything sexual near me ever again.

'Darren is a sex god!' Ava proclaims.

Darren has as much charisma as a broken toaster. 'I'm sorry,' I say.

'You have everything of mine. All my clothes, my favourite doona cover, you got it all PLUS your own stuff.'

'I don't want Darren.' I shriek.

'I don't like you being slutty Olivia. I'm the slut. Hear me? Me, I'm the slut. I give you everything and I want one thing, just one thing that's mine.'

'Ava, you're not a slut.'

'I am! I am Darren's little whorebag. And everyone wants to fuck me!'

Leo cracks up.

'You can still be that. I promise never to tread on your territory.'

'Promise me I'm the slut!' She insists.

'I promise. You're the slut, you're Darren's whorebag.'

I cross my heart. Ava accepts this solemnly then studies her hands.

'Good,' she mutters. 'Now where's the loo? I need to vomit.'

Half an hour later and Ava is still communing with the porce-lain toilet bowl. Leo has been out on a mercy mission to buy ginger beer and Panadol. Nothing stays down.

'Oh god, oh god, oh please god make it stop' reverberates through the house between retches. I have to hand it to Leo, he has the perfect bedside manner. Even in her reduced state, Ava is still coquettish with him. Quite a feat with spew on your chin.

I call Derwood. 'She's with me. I'll bring her back in the morning.' I can hear an audible sigh of relief from Darren.

'We had a barney,' he says quickly. I try and block out images of him with sex toys and enjoying the video clip.

'She's safe, it's all fine, she just wanted to go dancing and let off steam.' There's a pause. Darren is only too aware of his wife's lack of dance floor agility.

'Oh dear,' he says. I round off the call and return to Ava, who is now lying across the bathroom tiles as Leo attempts to get her to sip some ginger beer. He places a cold washer on her head.

'You're a good sport,' I say to him as I sit down beside Ava and pull her hair out of the way as she lunges into the basin for her next round.

'You don't live in the middle of Darlinghurst without seeing a fair bit of action. You'd be surprised the guests who drop in because the nightclubs have shut or they're not in a condition to get in a cab.'

'I should get her back to mine,' I say as Ava hurls once more.

'Stay. I have a guest room. You two can sleep there. Or you can come upstairs with me?'

I look at my sister. It seems my moment with the porn king has well and truly passed.

'I'd better stick with her,' I say as Ava begins sobbing.

'I'm sorry, I'm sorry, I'm a horrible sister.' She weeps. I hug her.

After another half-hour, and half a Salada cracker later, Ava is able to leave the loo and lie down on the bed. Leo has retired for the night. It's nearly 4 am. Oh what a night.

'Sorry for upstaging you,' Ava says as I place another washer on her head.

'You didn't. I'm sorry about Darren, and for everything.'

She takes my hand and breathes deeply. It's probably the closest we've been since I was ten.

'You weren't going to go home with some random, were you?' I ask, a little unsure considering my sister's new self-appointed status as sex queen.

'Nah, that's why I went to the gay clubs. I just wanted to feel free for a bit. Thanks for coming.' Her breathing deepens and I know she's falling asleep.

I cuddle up to her and stare up at the ceiling.

When I was very little I'd sometimes creep into Ava's room if I was scared and hop into bed beside her and listen to her breathing. It's a bit like that all over again. I think of Leo upstairs above us. Now I'm sobering up, I'm not sorry what nearly happened didn't. Still, I do like him.

I'm in the soft fog nearing sleep when I hear a key in the door. Magnus, who has decided to sleep beside our bed, lets out a low rumble. I hear a door, the front door downstairs, open. Magnus growls.

I hear footsteps. Heels. Is this another of Leo's 'friends' dropping in after a big night? The footsteps stop. A small yap from another dog that makes Magnus growl more forcefully. Ava wakes up.

'What's happening?' she says.

'I don't know,' I whisper.

The light in the hall switches on. A woman's voice, very high-pitched and breathy, calls out. 'I should have known, you can't spend one night by yourself!'

Footsteps, belonging to Leo, clamber down the stairs.

'Who is she?' shrieks the high voice. 'Is she still here?'

Ava and I look to each other. Magnus barks.

The light in the guest room flicks on. The skinny woman who abused me in Byron stands in the doorway, Chihuahua in her arms.

'You're having a threesome with the news-whore,' snaps the woman.

Leo, in no mood, appears behind her. 'Margueritte, what are you doing here?'

'I came to forgive you.'

'No, you came to check up on me. You gave me back the key, how'd you get in?'

'As if I'd only have one key.' She chortles, adjusting her position in the hope of appearing more imposing.

'You two. Out!' she shrieks at us.

'Who are you?' Ava asks.

'I'm Leonardo's partner. And you're a pair of pathetic guttersnipes. Don't think I don't know what you've been up to, I've seen it all.' Margueritte nears the bed.

Magnus barks again.

'Margueritte, get out before I call the police,' Leo says very clearly. Margueritte ignores him and commences her cross-examination.

'Have a nice long lunch at Otto, did you? Enjoy the osso bucco?'

'You were stalking us?' I stammer. Leo rolls his eyes in resignation.

'I would hardly call it stalking. You were making such a spectacle of yourself. But then, that's what you do isn't it, Olivia Law? You're a tragic has-been who steals other people's husbands. Everyone hates you. Don't think I don't know exactly what you're playing at.'

'You hang on.' Ava, still ill and drunk, speaks with force. 'I don't know who you are but you have no right to speak to my sister that way.'

'So it's sisters you're sleeping with now, Leo?'

Margueritte pulls the covers off Ava and I, quite a feat without dropping the dog. 'Get out, get out, get out!'

'Gladly.' Ava attempts to sit up and fails. I help her. This is a new low in an altogether different way.

I have no idea what Margueritte's relationship with Leo actually is, but I have a feeling I'm in the thick of something that has nothing to do with me. The last thing I need is another headline, particularly one involving my sister and I being stabbed to death as part of some elaborate sex game.

'Leo, thanks for taking care of us,' I say, grabbing articles of clothing and handbags.

Margueritte looks vindicated. Then she smiles brightly. 'Can I call you girls a cab?' She really is a nutter.

'No, we're fine. Thanks,' I say.

'Don't go. You're my guests,' Leo says somewhat feebly.

'No, Leo, darling, they're interlopers. Users, opportunists. They have to go.' Magueritte now speaks as though she's just solved the murder of the week on a British detective show.

'You're an absolute lunatic,' Ava, more back to her usual self, says. 'And if you ever, ever abuse me or my sister again I'll get an AVO on you, or I'll knock your teeth out, depending what day of my cycle it is and how much sleep I've had.'

Ava speaks with a terrifying, calm force. Margueritte takes a step back.

I help Ava to the door.

Leo looks miserable. He mouths 'I'm sorry.' I nod and we head outside. Margueritte slams the door in our faces.

I feel something brush my legs. I look down and realise Magnus is beside us, staring up adoringly.

'Magnus.'

'Bring him with us, I'm not going back in there, nor are you,' Ava says before taking a few steps and vomiting into a nearby wheelie bin.

We finally find a cabbie on Oxford Street who takes pity on us and allows us to bring Magnus. At the house, most of Dave's things are gone and there's a brief note telling me he'll be in Hong Kong and I can use his car.

I have a shower and collapse into bed at 5 am. An hour later, Ava, looking very unwell, wakes me.

'The twins have their Little Athletics carnival. I'm meant to supervise'

Magnus jumps on the bed looking hungry.

I drive Ava home, with Magnus in the back before the peak-hour traffic begins. It's quiet in the car until Ava says, 'What was that? Who is he?'

'I'm not sure.'

'Did you meet him on Tinder?'

'No, in Byron. He's been sweet.'

'He can't be too sweet if he's with her.' There's a pause before we both crack up.

'It was pretty surreal,' I admit.

Ava continues to cackle. 'Most exciting night I've had for a while. But, oh god, get me home to my family! At least you got a dog out of it. I've been telling you for years you need a dog.'

As if on cue, Magnus attempts to join Ava in the front seat.

'Obviously I shouldn't have made the quip about dressing up

in your old school uniform for Darren. You guys clearly have your personal stuff sorted.'

'We do. Except for him wanking over my little sister.'

'Okay, so maybe that wasn't his best dance move.'

'I think I got jealous. I'm sorry. You had the fancy career and husband and house and the perfect stepson. I have kids with hives and a husband who won't say boo to a goose.'

'Well I don't have most of those things anymore. And even when I did, I think I've been . . .' It's now I realise what the truth is. 'I've been miserable but I didn't want to admit it. Dave and I, he was right. It's been over for a long time. I was just too stubborn to face it.'

'For what it's worth I like you better this way.' Ava then adds, 'I am still a bit pissed though, so I may retract that.' She nudges my arm and we continue on our way, Magnus between us.

I leave her with the twins dancing around her, Derwood holding Bailey and looking remorseful. I can see how glad she is to be back, even though she's still shitty with him. Derwood provides an embarrassed thank you and I head off.

I know Ava is sick as a dog, but I also know she will somehow galvanise and get through the Little Athletics carnival and yell and holler for her kids. And I'm in awe of that. She's an awesome mother and, really, a pretty fabulous sister.

I decide to visit Mum and Dad; I should catch them before they head into the office. I see them brace themselves through the front window as I walk up the front drive. Dad opens the door, eyes Magnus with a small smile and hugs me.

'How're you holding up?'

I'm surprised his first words aren't 'What are you doing here?'

Mum says it instead. 'What's happened now and whose dog is that?'

'I just went to visit Ava, that's all. I'm dog sitting,' I say lightly.

'At 7 am in the morning?'

'Magnus wakes up early. Magnus is the dog, not a man.'

They exchange a look.

'Better come and have some breakfast,' says Dad. He adores dogs and it's not long before Magnus has a bowl of water and a handful of scraps.

The small TV in the kitchen is on, with my replacement looking positively perkified.

Dad quickly turns it off. Mum makes toast. We sit with tea.

Finally, I rouse the courage.

'Dave and I have separated. Properly. It's mutual.'

Dad nods grimly. Mum studies the teapot, tears welling; she places her hand to her head. 'Oh dear.'

'I'm being sued by the network, I'll probably lose everything.'

More nods and silent tears.

'I'm sorry, Liv,' Dad finally says. 'You've been dealt a poor hand.'

'What will you do? What about the house?' Mum whispers, too appalled to allow her voice out.

'The house is frozen for now. I have the rent from the apartment to live off. Dave already separated our accounts before it happened.'

'Did you offer to have a baby or just a dog?' Mum asks.

'Mum, we don't love each other. Not like a husband and wife should.'

'So what next?' Dad asks.

'I'm thinking of going up to Byron and spending more time with Darcy for a bit. Just stop for a while.'

They both nod. Being rid of me for a while is clearly a good option. So I'm more than surprised when Dad pipes up and says, 'We might be heading up that way too. For a few days.'

'Sorry?'

'Your dad's bought a campervan.' Mum looks daunted.

'But you don't buy anything. And haven't you got your Christian islands tour with the church coming up?'

Mum and Dad exchange an awkward look.

'Not everyone has been very Christian in the parish,' Dad says tightly.

'I'm so sorry. This is all my fault.'

Mum rallies. 'We'd just as soon go and do our own thing anyway. Dad's been on about the campervan for years and if I never see Mrs Daniels again it will be too soon.'

I hug them both. They are seriously the last people I'd expect to become part-time grey nomads but I guess it goes to show you can't underestimate anyone. Ever.

I stay long enough for my parents to both fall in love with Magnus then we head home.

I pull up to find Leo and his Bentley in the driveway.

'Guess you've come to reclaim your dog?' I say as Magnus jumps out and runs happily between us.

'Actually, I came to apologise.'

'No harm done, though it might have been good to mention you're in a relationship with someone else.'

'I'm not.'

I throw him a look in response.

'It's not a relationship, it's the toxic co-dependent bane of my existence.'

'She thinks it's a relationship.'

'You've met her, you see what she's like.'

'Yes, twice. How – actually it's none of my business.'

'Don't suppose you have coffee?'

'I do but is you being here safe?'

He laughs. I don't.

'She's off somewhere else today. I haven't had any sightings anyway.'

He follows me inside as I set the espresso machine into action.

'I don't remember ever actually starting a relationship with her. She just kept turning up and . . . it was never agreed, never official. I just can't seem to shake her.'

'Perhaps you don't want to?'

'Oh no, I want to.'

'Then sort it.' Then I add, 'Which is pretty funny advice coming from the woman who attempted to save her marriage via a lewd late-night video clip rather than talking to her husband.'

Leo laughs at that. I take him out the back to sit in the sun, Magnus joins us with one of Finn's tennis balls, looking hopeful.

'Why is intimacy so complicated?' I ask.

'Because it's intimate,' Leo offers. 'Sex is only one part of it.'

'That's the part you're quite comfortable with,' I say, forgetting for a moment about his issues.

'Sex is great, but it's rarely simple, which is why my companies are such a success.'

'For a man with a few functional restrictions you don't seem short on opportunities.'

He lets out a loud, joyful laugh. 'That's true, but this is Sydney, the ratio of straight men to women is unfairly in our favour.'

So is this my future? Sharing an impotent man with a mad woman?

It's got to be better than that.

Leo places his hand on mine.

'Olivia, I really like you and I want to get to know you more, but I won't lie, I'm not easy.'

I nod. 'Perhaps it's better we keep it as friends while both our lives are at risk?' I am only half-kidding.

'Friends, I can live with. But I like the idea of lovers more. Oh, there's another reason I came. Are you interested in dog-sitting? Magnus is besotted with you, I trust you and I have to head to Melbourne and Shanghai to work on some new designs.'

'Sure, Magnus can stay, I like him too.'

'Also, I thought you might like to use my Byron pad. And before you ask, it's safe. Margueritte definitely doesn't have a key and I made my maintenance man change the passcode on the front gate this morning.'

'That's very generous.' I hesitate. 'I'm not sure.'

'You'd be doing me a favour. Magnus loves it up there, I'll pay for his airfreight.'

'Actually I'm thinking of doing a road trip. Are you sure?'

'It's a great house. Better with someone in it, and I'd like to do something nice for you, just so you don't think I'm a complete dysfunctional mess.'

'I don't think that. I do think you should change your locks on your Sydney home. And maybe let Margueritte know she's not your girlfriend.'

He nods, embarrassed.

'Not that I'm in a position to judge you. Or anyone.' We hug and Leo hands me the keys to his Byron pad and draws a detailed map of how to get there. He throws Magnus the ball and says his goodbye. Magnus watches as Leo opens the car door, but he doesn't try and jump in.

'Completely besotted with you,' Leo calls out. 'And it's totally understandable.' He waves and heads off.

I watch the car head down the street thinking how glad I am I've met him and what a great teacher he is. I do think we're going to be friends. My life has enough chaos without adding an impotent porn king to it.

Still, I like how real Leo is.

I head in and check my emails. There is another one from Fergus: *You're keeping some colourful company. Be careful. Hannah insists I forward these to you – doing so from her account. Delete this email, Len is on the warpath.*

I'm assuming by 'colourful' Fergus means Leo's business and the irrepressible Margueritte. I read the other fantasies. I'm inspired by these women's warmth and courage, and tickled by their sense of fun. I respond with my thanks and a question.

I call by school at lunch and pull Finn out of a basketball showdown. Daisy accompanies us. I tell them about my plan to head north.

'Cool, I'll come up as soon as school holidays start. Mum won't mind, she met this guy on 'Cougar Me Tiger' and she's into him.'

'Really? Is he nice?'

'Yeah, Dais ran a check.'

'Daisy!'

'Nothing too illegal – he seems okay.' Daisy and Finn nod at each other.

Finn runs off to grab his lunch.

'Daisy, are you sure about Dave?'

'I already told you.' Daisy rolls her eyes luxuriously. 'He didn't know anything about it.'

'Okay. I have a favour. Can you help me put something on YouTube?'

Daisy looks at me like I am a complete imbecile then agrees to help. 'You sure you don't want nude tube?' she asks.

'What's nude tube?' I ask. Another eye roll is followed by a brief description.

'No, no, not nude tube. No one's nude.'

Daisy and Finn walk me to the car – one of Dave's more recent purchases, a navy blue Porsche Macan.

Finn grins at me. 'Olivia Law back in the driver's seat. Suits you.' It's true, after years of being picked up by a driver or Dave driving me, I've barely been behind a steering wheel. That's all changing now.

I head home and load the car with my things, and then Magnus and I head off up the Pacific Highway on the long drive north.

Magnus has appointed himself co-pilot, sitting in the passenger seat, shifting position from head out the window sniffing the sunny day to lying down with his head on my lap and snoring.

As I leave town I note a giant billboard with my photo and the caption 'In Olivia we trust'. Someone has spray-painted a giant cock entering my mouth. Joy.

Karen calls as I'm just outside Newcastle.

'Got your message. You sure about this?' she says, referring to what I've decided to do.

'Can it make the lawsuit any worse?'

'Not if you remain fictional. Personally, I love it. The only way to turn this around is to be as public as possible.'

'I'm not sure it's going to take. I mean it will most likely only appeal to a few of the women like the ones who've emailed me.'

'Don't underestimate the sisterhood. Or yourself.'

'Thanks, Karen, you've been –'

I'm stopped by the sound of Karen giggling.

'Sorry, sorry,' she says, resuming her professional air. 'Matteo was just sucking my toe.'

'Matteo, your new friend from –'

'Cougar Me Tiger,' Karen says gaily then lets something akin to a growl out.

'I'm guessing that was for Matteo's benefit.'

'Drive safe, I'll book Finn a ticket for a few days after school breaks up.'

'Thanks.'

And she's gone, obviously to deal with her cub.

Magnus and I stop for a milkshake and a game of frisbee. Driving with a dog ensures I take a break every few hours. It's the longest time I've been alone with my thoughts that I can remember. The scenery becomes increasingly lush as afternoon descends. I move through playlists and albums I haven't heard for too long. I sing along, badly, though Magnus seems to enjoy it.

17

DISPATCH FROM THE INTERIOR

From: Ella Vinton

To: Olivia Law

Subject: Highway Man

Date: 19 August at 3.24pm

It's the middle of the night. Hot. The fan turns, slow. I've been waiting and trying to sleep. I'm starting to feel the heavy pull of dreams when I hear your car pull up, hear the ignition stop, the car door open and close. Your footsteps, tired and heavy. You head inside. You're walking to the shower.

I call out, 'Don't.'

You walk over to the bed. No lights on.

I pull you down to me. I want to smell all those miles on your flesh and the old rollies you've had between your fingers. My hands read your face, your lips, you take them in your mouth and kiss them before I reclaim them to travel down your torso and undo your jeans.

I'm starved of your scent and I'm in a rush to feel you inside me so I know I'm real. And as you do, all that other stuff – late-night calls, missing each other, countdowns – it all peels away. You start slow, on top, but I'm a fury of desire and I flip you under me and I devour you as I ride you, racing to you with every thrust, burning up the distance, meeting you, reclaiming you. I move back and turn and you take me from behind and I tell you you're never leaving again, and we're one hungry, angry fury of want. You pull my hair till my chin lifts and my mouth meets yours you ride me back to myself and I come long and hard and then we turn and fall onto each other. We fall asleep matted in each other's hair, sweat and cum.

You're never leaving again.

18

IF ANYONE HAD TOLD ME A MONTH AGO THAT I'D BE DRIVING TO
Byron, singing to Bruce Springsteen without a professional
prospect in sight and about to take up residence in the Kingdom
of Come country ranch as a dog-sitter, I would have had my
doubts. More than that, I would have laughed in your face and
run as fast as I could in the other direction.

Perhaps that's one of the good things about losing it all – the
upside of over, if you like. When all is lost, and you're still here
and the world still turns, you're humbled and bruised and raw and
there's a kind of bizarre exhilaration, and dare I say hope, in the
fact I'm a clean canvas.

And a road trip is the perfect way to ritualise leaving the past
behind.

We make more stops and share a hamburger that Magnus gets most of. I catch myself watching the sunset and being in the moment.

I reach the Byron hinterland and get lost for an extra forty minutes driving up the thin, winding roads in the moonlight. It's nearing midnight and I start to wonder if Leo made his property up.

I'm not one for noticing what phase the moon is in, but this one's a huge orb, shining brilliantly over what I assume is the ocean in the distance. I can't deny it's impressive. When I finally find the address, I pull up to an immaculate drive and press a code into a buzzer by the imposing gates. They open majestically, I let out a howl of thanks to the moon above me. Magnus joins in.

A paved road for another kilometre takes me to one of the most breathtakingly beautiful houses I've ever seen. The sensor lights activate on approach. Magnus, familiar with the environment, pants and wags his tail in anticipation of being set free to roam. I pull up and let him out and he runs in circles and under my feet.

I head to the door.

Open it.

It's magnificent.

The house is spread over one level, tasteful but warm, unlike my house. Huge canvases, books, open fires, ginormous couches made for napping and reading on.

I walk around like Goldilocks. It's expansive without being impersonal. Leo should forget porn and focus on interior design. The master bedroom is a light mint ocean green (similar to his eyes, funnily enough) with a huge beechwood antique four-poster bed and about a hundred cushions. An open fire and a huge lamb's-wool rug, which Magnus proceeds to roll around on adoringly, frame it. There's another daybed in a coffee covering that's as soft as cashmere. A walk-in wardrobe with only a few shirts hanging inside. A tremendous ensuite bathroom with a claw-footed bath leading into a divine garden with an outdoor shower.

I gasp in wonder. I'm in heaven.

I walk through more rooms back to the entrance with the huge living room and kitchen. One that could even entice *me* to cook!

I head out and unload the car.

'Thank you, Leo!'

Magnus barks encouragement so I figure I'll keep going. No one can hear me, I'm safe, the security gate closed properly so Margueritte can't pay me a visit. Not that she would, her focus is wherever Leo is.

'Thank you Magnus for keeping me company, thank you network for firing my arse, thank you Dave for leaving me, thank you Ava for getting drunk and loving me, thank you Daisy and Finn and Karen and Darcy and even bloody Dr Ace and sweet Atticus and Ricky and Hugo, thank you for putting me back at the start even though I'm midway through. Thank you, thank you!'

It's quite possibly sleep deprivation that's leading me to do this, but it feels great. I look up at the sky and I honestly feel grateful.

Magnus and I head in. I take a bath and head to the giant bed. It's like a fairytale but with bamboo sheets.

Magnus jumps up and settles himself at the foot of the bed, content.

I have the deepest, soundest sleep I've had in years. My eyes don't open until Magnus, now on the ground, licks my hand, summonsing me to let him outside.

I look at my phone. It's 9.50 am! This *never* happens to me. And god it feels good. There's also three missed calls from Darcy.

I call her back. She's in the car.

'I was going to visit you after yoga but I couldn't find Leo's house.'

I direct her with my scant knowledge of the area and my ability to find a house in the middle of nowhere in the middle of the night.

An hour later, she arrives. In the meantime, I find muesli in the pantry and, thanks to the maintenance man, fresh milk and juice in the fridge and provisions for Magnus.

The house is even more glorious by day. It's so posh it even has a name, though a lot of houses up this way do, all Sanskrit. 'Moksha' is no exception. Leo told me it means 'Liberation' in Hindu, which is pretty funny considering Leo's personal life.

Sun beams in through the windows. The property faces east. It's in a Dickensian-sounding village called Knockrow which has about four streets to its name and many properties up winding narrow drives.

There's a gigantic heated pool, so I decide to start the day with a dip. The property looks down onto Lennox Head via kilometres of sugar cane fields. The westside faces the mountains, which can also be seen way off to the north.

I call Leo after my dip.

'You failed to tell me it's the best house anywhere, ever.'

'Glad you like it, it doesn't get used enough. Enjoy. I'm about to go into a meeting to discuss dildo lengths.'

Darcy rings the front gate bell. Leo has to talk me through it, but we get there and Darcy bounces in minutes later.

'OMFG, are you serious? Wait till the boys see this, they'll cry. Maybe I should move in.'

'And leave the tepee palace?'

Darcy hands and hair are covered with coloured paints.

'Was this some sacred rite of passage with Dr Ace?'

'No, screen-printing! You've inspired me, I have a new pattern for the kaftans, I'm calling it *Olivia*. I brought you a sample.'

Darcy pulls a piece of fabric out from her bag, it's deep olive green with huge . . . I think they're meant to be flowers in magnificent bold colours – fuchsia, orange, yellow, red.

'They're orchids?' I ask.

'Orchids or yonis depending on your perspective.'

It's stunning and will look brilliant on the kaftans, I can see many a yoni being paraded around the homes of the glamorous kaftan-wearers of the world.

'Well?' She asks.

'I love it!' I say.

'It's a limited release.' Darcy smiles at the fabric proudly.

'Darc, all your kaftans are limited release.'

'Yes.' She muses happily. 'It's called having a life. You know Bergdorf Goodman in New York emailed me.'

'And?' I love Bergdorf Goodman, it's more like a film set than a department store.

Darcy shrugs. 'I'm thinking about it. I like my life with the kids and the property. I like being able to go to yoga and fall asleep at night not freaked out about getting through the next day.'

'I understand. It's the having it all dilemma?'

'No. I think the "having it all" dilemma is a patriarchal construct women have been brainwashed with.'

I stop at that. I love how Darcy frames things. She continues, 'Things are either as complex and stressful or as simple as you allow them to be. Your desire is your destiny.'

'Sorry?'

'I just picked that up in yoga class today. Pretty good though, huh? It's from the yogic bible our teacher keeps on about. It's like this: your desire leads to your will, which leads to your intention, or maybe that's the other way around, anyway that leads to your deed and *that* leads to your destiny.'

'Cool. Is your desire having your own kaftan line at Bergdorf Goodman?'

'I haven't decided. Maybe if I can control how many they have ... or maybe my destiny is playing beach cricket with the kids and swimming in this pool.'

And with that we make our way out for a skinny-dip, Magnus patrolling us as we dive in.

'What's the plan for your press release?' Darcy asks as she performs an aquatic dance manoeuvre worthy of Ethel Merman.

'I think what I'm going to film will serve as a press release.' I pull myself out of the pool and shake myself off.

'What do we need?'

'Paint, cardboard. I need to check Leo is happy for me to film it here, we can use his garage.'

'Brilliant, and you know Ace will help.'

'Can he still borrow his friend's camera?'

'All sorted, and an extra mic which I'll hold.'

'So I'm really doing this.' I wrap myself in the warmth of a fresh towel.

'Yup.' Darcy grins cheekily. 'No backing out now.'

I spend the rest of the day preparing, with Darcy's help. It's like an art and craft workshop, we create a makeshift set of cardboard, which will become the backdrop for my next foray into the world of confessional media.

We head into town and purchase supplies. I must be looking less and less like myself, or perhaps it's just Byron, because no one raises an eyebrow, though I'm in the paper again. Well I'm mentioned on page six. Dave's company has floated, there's a mention of it in the business section with some information on the fact it's completely independent of his 'estranged' wife. It also says a property settlement has been reached and the divorce will be legalised within the month. Oh the mirth.

Darcy drops in to see the kids for their science week projects at school and I take the time to walk Magnus on the dog-friendly side of Belongil beach. It amazes me that in the last days of winter, Byron is in full summer swing.

Bathers sunbake and head for lazy dips. A fire-twirler practises near the rocks. A few young men jam with guitars. It's like entering some kind of utopian Californian dream from the '70s. And in the distance stands the majestic, ancient Mount Warning, the sacred masculine site of the land's traditional owners. The women got the tea-tree lakes, where they would birth and heal.

The sand is pristine, the sea is calm. Magnus chases seagulls and splashes into the tiny waves with blissful abandon. I've found a ball thrower at the house, which he's crazy about. I call Leo.

'How's my favourite dog-minder?'

'Pretty good actually. We're walking on the beach.'

'I always intend to do that but rarely do. Everything at the house okay?'

'Superb. How are the dildos?'

'Lengthy. I'm at the airport now.'

'Hey, Leo, would you mind if I filmed something in your garage?'

'Will you be naked?' he asks hopefully.

'No, but I will be in it.'

'Ahh, going to use that voice of yours, good on you. Go for gold. Maybe one day tour buses will drive past the house to see where Olivia Law made her stand.'

'Tour buses would never find your place.'

'I like that about it.'

'Me too. Everything okay in your kingdom?'

'Chipper. I told Margueritte we weren't in a relationship. Me and her, not me and you.'

'How was that?'

'Let's just say it's a good thing I'm boarding a plane to China.'

'Have you changed your locks?'

'I – hey kid, my name's just been called, call you back later from Shanghai.'

'Travel safe.'

I hang up, put the phone away and look around. I think of what I am going to do, tonight, or tomorrow. It might make things worse, but it's hard to imagine how. I think about why I'm doing it and I feel stronger, more resolved.

A wet mass of fur brushes against my legs and looks up devotedly. I'm beginning to understand the therapeutic attraction to pets. They really are all about the joy and the love. You truly are their world. I know cynics would say it's because they know you're their source of food, but animals seem to have a huge capacity to love openly and unabashedly. Or am I loving Magnus because he can't talk? No judgement.

I lean over and hug him. He looks up at me happily again then starts walking in circles. I've learnt in the last few days what this means. He continues to gaze up adoringly as he unloads a rather massive bowel movement on the sand. A group of kids point and giggle. Thankfully I've got a bag and set to work. I've just tied it when I spot a very handsome body jogging towards me. Is he running towards me or am I dreaming?

He's golden, lithe, with fantastic calf muscles. I realise I am objectifying, I am having my own *10* fantasy, but without the braids. He smiles behind his sunglasses. That's nice, I think, attempting to put the bag of dog poo behind me, breathing in, standing tall.

Magnus barks for the ball. I raise the ball thrower, hoping to throw the ball far enough into the water to give me a moment to focus on the bionic man.

Instead I misfire and hit the jogger on the head.

Magnus barks.

'Whoops' is all I come out with.

The jogger rubs his head, half smiles (thank god) picks up the ball and approaches me.

'Those things can be weapons of mass destruction.' He hands me the ball with his lovely hands, his gorgeous forearms, his excellent biceps – wait, I know those arms.

'Olivia, it's me.'

He takes off his glasses. I do a double take. It's Atticus, the sweet macadamia-farming vet.

'Oh, hi.' I attempt to reconcile my lust with reality.

'What is it with you and poo?' He laughs.

'Sorry?'

He indicates the bag. 'More shit.'

I laugh. Oh god, how unsexy can I be? A stray fly begins buzzing around my hand. I flick it off. Magnus barks for his ball.

'Oh yeah, masses of shit, I'm just a big turd.' These words expel from my mouth before I have time to rein them in.

161

Atticus looks concerned. 'Are you okay?'

The fact I have morphed into a girly imbecile because I like his body hasn't gone unnoticed.

'I think I'm dehydrated' is all I come up with.

Magnus, tired of waiting, approaches.

'Hey fella.' Magnus immediately rolls on his back in the hope of a tummy rub, murmuring happily. I get it, Magnus, I think to myself, I understand completely. Why didn't I realise what a heart-throb Atticus was before?

'Want to get a smoothie?' he asks.

'Aren't you jogging?'

'I was but I break for turds.'

When did he get so funny? Or have I reignited my humour? Atticus throws the ball for Magnus as we stroll back to the car park.

'How old is . . . ?'

'Magnus,' I say with confidence. Then I hesitate. 'Four, maybe? He's not mine, I'm minding him for a friend. I'm a dog-sitter now.'

'Seriously?'

'No, well, for Magnus I am, no one else.'

'So it's not your next career?'

We approach the promenade.

'That one has acai smoothies.' Atticus points to the café where I met Leo.

'What is it with Byron and acai?' I ask as we find seats.

'Want my theory?'

'You have a theory on acai?'

'Living up here you tend to gather theories on a lot of things.' He smiles and raises his sunglasses. I think of Leo's joke, but in Atticus's case I'd have to say, 'Still a rock star'. Twinkly sapphire eyes, strong jaw, cheekbones I could kiss. I have to stop it.

'My theory is a lot of people come up here looking for the answer, be it meditation, diet, exercise, orgies.'

'They have orgies here?'

'So I've heard, and a thing called orgasmic meditation. Anyway, everyone's on the search for the thing that gives them peace, gets them closer to enlightenment I guess, and for some it's –'

'Acai?'

He smiles. 'Yeah, for a season or two. There's also a fair element of fickle up here.'

I look at the menu. Smoothies with blue green algae, macca, coco nibs, MSM, bee pollen, chia, acai . . . and then I see the price.

'Twenty-seven dollars for a smoothie?'

'Enlightenment isn't cheap. Not here anyway. What would you like?'

I follow his lead on an elaborate concoction that involves dates, banana and green things.

'So,' Atticus says casually when our drinks arrive. 'Ace tells me he's helping you with your next clip.'

I choke on my drink.

'Well he's borrowed a camera.'

'Yeah, Malcolm leant him that. Everyone's curious.'

'So no pressure then.'

'It's great you're expressing yourself.'

I feel the need to defend myself even though Atticus's tone is encouraging.

'It's a statement, of sorts.'

'You are a statement, of sorts.' He smiles and the day gets instantly warmer and brighter.

'Is there anything I can do to help?'

'There's no livestock or nuts involved, minus me,' I respond.

'I can always be relied on to make a decent sandwich.'

He offers. I think of his hands making a sandwich, oh butter me up.

'Or mind Magnus?' He continues.

'You're full of community spirit.'

'I'd like to help you, Olivia.'

A text from Darcy informs me she's on the way back to Leo's with more supplies.

Time to go. I head for my purse.

'I made you order and drink it, I don't expect you to pay for it too.' Atticus grins and picks up the bill.

Chivalrous too, heavens, I could swoon.

'Thanks so much. I'll see you soon,' I say as he kisses me on the cheek. I feel a zing.

It puts a spring in my step as Magnus and I head back to the car. Atticus, who are you? I wonder. Of course, knowing my luck, he will have a wife, fiancée, estranged lover, physical impairment, differing sexuality or incompatible sexual preferences, though he said he was divorced the other day. Wait, why am I thinking about sex with him? It has to be the jogging, the biceps, the fact I am a mad woman who fell off a cliff, landed, said 'Gee that was fun', ran back to the top and is about to jump off again.

Back at Moksha, Darcy and I get into our art department roles. Darcy has an old piece of cardboard we paint to make a backdrop. We use similar colours to the ones on my old news set, though a more surreal, Dali-esque version of it. Darcy is a talented artist and she muses over her efforts.

'What if we add a few of the orchids in?'

We look at each other and laugh. 'YES!'

Ace appears after lunch and helps us assemble a makeshift news desk where I'll sit and 'present' my piece. I borrow a stool from the kitchen.

'We're going to need more light,' Darcy announces, 'otherwise you're going to look ghoulish. Who do we know with some extra standing lights?'

'I can check with Atticus, he has a load of lamps when he goes out on call,' Ace says.

'Oh ...' I say before there's time not to say it.

'I mean he might, but he was in town, he may not be home ...' I'm going weird again.

'So I'll call him.' Ace picks up his phone.

Darcy observes me for a moment.

'He won't need to be here when we're filming,' she assures me.

'Oh no, I know, I mean, it's, well, you know ...'

'Sure.' Ace looks a bit confused. Even men who run work-shops about feelings can be sadly lacking when it comes to the subtle and at times bizarre internal negotiations and fluctuations of women.

Hugo and Ricky arrive and look around the property, clapping and pointing, in awe.

'Jasmine, huge jasmine bush in flower!' calls Ricky.

'And the paving around the pool – yes, yes, yes!' adds Hugo.

Ricky sets about making bruschetta with a broad bean paste he whipped up after finding some beans at the markets, with burrata, mint and tomato. Somehow he always knows just what to make and when.

Atticus arrives with the lights and then he and Ace attempt to recruit Hugo and Ricky for their weekly men's group. The boys decline this week in favour of filming my piece to camera.

Ace insists on a support circle before they take off, to wish me luck. Atticus and I exchange small eye rolls.

In the circle, Ricky and Hugo do their best to be subtle as they check their phones for messages regarding a nearby property they've placed a bid on.

'I'd like to honour our friend, Olivia, who is one hell of a brave woman,' rumbles Ace.

Butterflies commence in my tummy.

'Whatever happens, we're here to support you and not judge you,' he continues.

Darcy squeezes my hand. I sneak a peek at Atticus who smiles openly.

Dr Ace continues his sermon on high.

'Olivia is honouring her yoni.'

I look down.

'Her sacred goddess, her strong and brave vagina her coura-
geous cu —'

A text message sounds. Thank god.

'Whoops, sorry.' Hugo apologises before allowing a dramatic
inhale to fill the room.

'I was going with the pussy thing. Kind of.' Ricky attempts to
reassure me as Ace provides a very teacherly look of disapproval
for the technology and it's users.

Hugo places his hand over his mouth and looks at Ricky,
wide-eyed.

'We got it, we got the house. They said yes.'

'They said yes?' Even Ace is curious now.

Hugo and Ricky turn to us all.

'We are the proud parents of a 1920s farmhouse on two acres
in Skinners Shoot.'

'Skinner's Shoot,' Darcy says, 'it's fantastic there, how did
you manage that?'

'Ricky's been campaigning the owner for months.'

'We're going to finally have our own day spa, café, reception
centre and restaurant!' Ricky is shouting with joy.

Ricky and Hugo look at each other, alternating gasps of excitement and delight.

'Really?' whispers Hugo. 'It's really happening?'

'It is,' Ricky confirms.

They both have tears in their eyes. They really are a fantastic
couple. It's clear they've got the best friend and the hot lover

thing in one package with each other. Maybe next life I'll come back as a gay man.

Cheers and congratulations are had all round. Hugo's mother, Stella Supera, also known as, the wonder woman, facetimes him. I have a hunch her magic and sway helped make this happen. I try and stay out of shot since the board that Stella is chair of has banned me for life. I'm guessing she's on the hate camp, along with the majority of women I used to socialise with.

Ace gives up on the circle but wishes me luck as he and Atticus depart. I find it hard to meet Atticus's eye, he's not deterred though.

'Wishing you and your yoni all the best with your next appearance,' he says in his best Dr Ace voice, winking as he leaves. I lose my footing. I'm never going to be able to see this man again without blushing.

Darcy follows me inside to pick out a 'costume'. I've brought a few blazers up, all brightly coloured. I can't look at them without hearing Ava saying 'Teletubby' and 'Wiggle'. I choose a navy blue one.

'Awesome,' Darcy says. 'Wear it buttoned up with no bra underneath.'

'No bra? A cami then?'

Darcy shakes her head. 'You can't see anything. But it looks sexy. Lauren Hutton sexy.

Lauren Hutton is one of my idols. I love her face and her style. Darcy knows what to say to get me over the line.

She helps me with my makeup. Commanding me to go for it with the eyeliner and the lipstick. I have to admit, it's a lot of fun. After decades of my makeup having to be applied in a certain way, being able to play and apply it in a way I like, not in a way that doesn't offend viewers or elicit unwanted attention or tire their eyes, is freeing.

Finally, it's time for my hair. The most freeing moment of all. No hair straightener, no tongs. I wear it out, a mess of blonde waves still infused with salt air.

Darcy applies a dusting of powder so I don't look too shiny.

'Oh my god!' She pulls back like she's had an electric shock.

'What's wrong?'

'Your face just moved! Seriously, you just wiggled your forehead. Oh happy day!'

19

I SIT AT MY DESK. THERE'S A LIGHT IN MY EYES. IN THE SHADOWS I SEE Hugo beaming proudly and Darcy holding a mic and nodding her support. I swallow, hard.

'Okay, we're going for it. Ready?' Ricky, the self-appointed director of photography and cameraman, calls.

'Yep,' I reply. 'Here goes.'

Ricky flourishes his hands in 5, 4, 3, 2, 1 gestures and . . . there's the red light. I'm on.

Gremlins inside my brain snicker. *You've got to be kidding, this is a mistake, idiot. You've already hung yourself out to dry. You're too, old, ugly, fat. Get off.* To be honest, those voices have been there for all of my professional life.

Then Magnus walks past, looks up, wags his tail and heads to Hugo for a pat. Magnus will still need a walk and a feed regardless of what the world thinks of me. It calms me.

The world is not going to end.

A quieter voice inside says, *We can do this. Go on.* And that's the one I listen to.

'Good evening, I'm Olivia Law. Some of you may remember me from the news, others from my naked, drunk outpourings to my husband . . .'

Breathe, Olivia.

'When I was forced to leave my position so suddenly, I wasn't able to provide a press statement, other than the generic one from the network. But now I can. Well, now I'm going to.'

Another breath. *Get on with it for Christsake!*

'By way of another offering – you can call it a fantasy, a derailment or sheer lunacy, whatever floats your boat. Because right now I'm going to tell you what floats mine. And that is . . .'

Major pause. *Oh god, can I do this? Why am I sober? Think of the women who have shared their fantasies with you, this isn't any weirder. You're not going to die, you're not going to die . . . Oh god I'm going to die.*

Darcy waves and gestures to hurry up.

I dive in.

'I'm naked, I'm in the lifts at work. I've been summoned up to the conference room by the board – you know who you are. I'm nervous and my teeth chatter. Am I in trouble? Will I be expelled? The lift stops. Three women enter, also naked; they vary in shapes, sizes, age and ethnicity. We nod to each other. One of them has rope. Another gaffer tape. We all begin to smile. The lift stops again at the next level, and the next. At each stop

171

more women pour in. By the time we arrive at the top floor, the executive suite, the lift is packed. We're all touching, all naked and all armed.

'The doors open. We exit and march into the conference room. The young woman who's been taking your orders for coffee, turns, smiles and locks the door.

'At first you all scoff at this entrance, this stunt. You look to each other amused. Your breathing increases slightly at the sight of all this female physicality within your grasp.

'We get to work. We take your hands, which have all travelled to your crotches, of course they have, and tie them behind your backs. You're titillated by this and just the tiniest bit nervous. But you laugh to each other that it will just make your lawsuit against me bigger, make the ratings when you report this soar higher, and hasn't that young girl three from the back got great tits? Perhaps she can be chosen as the next up and comer? No she can't, we say in unison, as we cover your mouths with gaffer tape. Your laughter has stopped. You eye each other nervously. Where is this going? Where is security? Am I the only one who's scared? You wonder.

'I welcome you to our conference. The one that you're not running.

'We are.

'Each woman announces her name and highlights the way you've reduced, overruled or written her off – be it in a lift, a meeting or a "lively" debate. Whether you touched her up as you greeted her with your subtle frottage act or dismissed her opinion with a sideways glance to one of your peers. Insisted she defer to you. Ensured her pay was less than yours, or that of the male talent on one of your shows. You know who you are and you know what you've done. Women who have become invisible, the ones who were getting "too long in the tooth" or who are no longer willing to be coerced by you, stand tall and proud.

'And you know what we do?

'We begin touching ourselves, our hands travel down to our, as one of you once called them, "goldmines" and we begin going for gold. The rhythm of our fingers is synchronised. Our breath is a collective.

'Our sighs are not soft or suffocated, and they're not over you. They're over us and our united force. They're over us and our power and our abilities, regardless of the age of our ovaries or the size of our bras. It's better than a sword; each sigh, each flick is a testament to the truth that our identity is not dependent on you. Bullies are not lovers, they are not who we hunger after. Manipulation is not attraction.

'We get faster and faster and faster.

'Left, right up and in, over and over, around again.

'More joyous and frenzied.

'Wetter and wetter.

'And then – we come as one.

'And a huge fountain of our goddess juice squirts all over your stupefied faces.

'Landing straight in your eyes. It stings, you fear you're blind. You're not.

'The most amazing thing happens – the scales of misogyny, of judgement, of ageism and bullying, self-loathing and narcissism fall from your eyes.

'You gain peripheral vision as our love juice drips down your faces and you see there's more than you. You see the beauty of who each woman truly is. And you cry and bow your heads.

'We take the bowl of M&Ms at the centre of the table and we file out.

'And *that's* how I want to fuck you!'

There's a few beats of silence before I see Darcy's thumbs-up signal. Perspiration dripping down my face as I continue.

'I'm going to keep bringing you these updates and headlines. If you're over the age of consent and identify as female and you'd like your fantasy to be heard, anonymously or otherwise, email me at come as you are at mymail dot com. Until next time. I'm Olivia Law, goodnight.'

20

'AND CUT!' RICKY YELLS.

'Yes, yes, oh god yes!' Hugo calls out. 'That was brilliant. Now, can we please open some champagne?'

Darcy hugs me tight and tells me she's proud. 'Let's see what they do with that,' she says as Ricky uploads it to YouTube and Hugo fills glasses.

Ricky, a scandal lover from way back, also posts it to Twitter and Instagram and ensures he follows up with a lot of hashtags: #Olivialawasneverbefore, #newsreaderfantasythesequel.

'Maybe no one will see it, the public is fickle,' Ricky says, sounding worried.

'But she's done it, that's what counts,' Hugo says.

'Hello, I'm here,' I add.

'You certainly are and you're magnificent,' Hugo enthuses. 'Wait till Mumsie sees it, she'll love it.'

'No, she won't. She hated the last one.'

'That's not true, she loved it,' Hugo insists.

'No, she axed me from her board and uninvited me to the literacy outreach program.'

'Oh no she did not.'

'I'm with Huges,' chimes Ricky. 'She told us she loved it.'

'Well clearly the rest of the board didn't.'

'You just leave that with me.' Hugo smiles, though he looks ready to overturn a few chairs, or a few cushions anyway.

Darcy lifts her champagne saucer. 'To Come As You Are!' she calls as we clink.

'And Olivia Law at large,' she adds as we sip the lovely Pol Roger Hugo and Ricky brought over. I'm guessing Leo likes his bubbles. He has a lot of very nice champagne flutes and saucers. We use the saucers; they were supposedly originally shaped after Josephine's breasts for her Napoleon. Well, that's the myth anyway.

'Fitting to be drinking from a boob glass,' Ricky says, enjoying the champagne.

I look at my phone. I check the new email address. Nothing yet. A few more cancellations have been sent to my personal email.

Darcy can't keep still. As the boys settle into nibbles and bubbles, she takes her leave.

'Sorry, angel cheeks, I've got to fly. The kids need to be picked up.'

'Are you okay?' She seems on pins.

'Tickety-boo. I think I have another kaftan design in me . . . or something,' she mutters. 'Love you, love your work, love your sex chat.' We hug and she heads off.

I know the boys will be keen to head off to their own private celebrations too. They hang for another glass and more exchanges. All seems quiet on the YouTube front. On every front really. I watch them steal a quiet, intimate moment as I return from the loo. They're beside themselves with excitement.

'You two need to take each other back to your guesthouse and celebrate,' I announce, I don't want them to feel obligated to stay.

'Come with, we're going somewhere fabulous for dinner,' Hugo, ever elegant suggests.

'Thanks, but I think Magnus and I will lie low. It's been a big day.'

They kiss me goodbye and head off, arms linked, chatting merrily. That's another thing I notice about them as a couple, after years and years together they're still interested in talking to each other and hearing what each other has to say.

I walk Magnus and then sit outside in a swinging chair, looking up at the stars. I feel relieved to be alone, save for Magnus who slumbers blissfully on the floor beside me. Darcy's right. I did need to get that off my chest.

I'm already losing everything, at least I'll go to hell in a hand basket with my head held higher.

I take a breath that actually comes from somewhere deeper than the thin baby pool of my upper chest. A breath that's a relief, a breath that's a sigh. When you confront the scariest things, when you're faced with your deepest fears, they seldom destroy you in the way you've imagined. It's the walking on eggshells fear of the worst happening, the anticipation of the possibility of all being lost, that erodes you.

I want to set the record straight, to encourage and empower other women and, on a level that I don't fully understand about myself, it's to be free, to express my true self, whomever she is. Because she has been someone I've hid from for so long. And she is no longer willing to be silent. I think of the Mary Oliver quote Leo told me.

I think how lucky I am to have all the support I've been given. I really have the best friends; I couldn't have done it without them. Will Dave watch it? I'm not convinced he saw any of the first one – too painful, he said. My parents will be embarrassed, but hopefully they're on the road somewhere near Nelson Bay and are oblivious. And what of heart-throb Atticus, wait, why am I thinking about him? Then again, why shouldn't I? He's single, he's lovely, he seems like he might be interested and like someone who doesn't get hung up on the details. Actually, he seems damn near perfect.

Finn facetimes as I'm hopping into bed. It's nearly midnight.

'You all right?' I ask. 'Aren't you at school?'

'Mum's. I have an orthodontist appointment in the morning, so does Daisy. And no I didn't watch it, Daisy did, now we're counting views.'

Daisy grabs the phone. 'It's starting to trend,' she announces.

'Wow,' I say. 'That's awesome. What does it mean?'

'It means it's gaining traction –' She's cut off by Karen entering the room in a designer gown and matching slippers.

'What did I tell you kids about screen-time this late –' She sees it's me on the phone and her expression shifts.

'Well done, lady newsreader.' Coming from Karen this is akin to 'You've won the Nobel prize'.

'You'd better buckle up, the network is going to go ballistic. Nice imagery by the way. I'll call you in the morning.' I know with Karen this means 6 am. Precisely.

'One more minute then off. And Daisy you sleep in the guest room.'

'That's so stupid, Mum, we've stayed in the same room since we were five.'

Karen's iron appears. 'Finn, it may have bypassed your notice but Daisy is now a girl, a fifteen-year-old girl. Do you really think I'd let you stay in the same room?'

'But we –'

Karen holds her hand up. 'And you spend all night talking. So no. Daisy, tell Olivia about the course you've gained entry to.' Daisy blushes as Karen and her robe sweep out.

'What course?' I ask.

'Silicon Valley, or is it NASA?' Finn teases. Though he looks proud as hell.

'Shut up!' Daisy hits him then takes the phone. 'It's nothing just some tech geek course an IT company are holding on trend and early adapters and influencers.'

'And hackers,' Finn calls out in the background.

'That's phenomenal, Dais. Whose course?'

'Just Apple.'

'They asked her, invited her out of hundreds and thousands of geeks,' Finn adds.

'Okay that's enough. I rock. I know it.' Daisy says in a very clear 'boundary' voice that I doubt anyone would mess with.

'Well it's brilliant!' I say. 'When?'

'Next week, school hols, so I can't come up with Finn, sorry.'

'That's okay, this is an amazing opportunity. You should be proud of yourself.'

'Ditto,' she replies. 'Oh and good on you for including the trans community in your spiel.'

We say goodnight and sign off. I sleep like a baby and am awoken by a phone call from Ava at 5.45 am.

'Not bad' is her verdict. 'Could have had more sex.'

'Who are you and are you over your hangover?'

'Just. It's been hairy, and I may have been drunk but I remember bits, kind of, well not really, but I know we talk about sex more now, though it's still my area of expertise. Darren and I made our own film . . .'

'That's nice.' I do my best not to sound prudish.

'It's not something I can show you, for obvious reasons, but I've walked in on him wanking to it twice. My plan is that we make a series of them. I play all these different women –'

She continues to describe the films as I get out of bed and head to the coffee machine. The basic premise is that Darren's character, 'Mr ZZ', is trying to track down a number of females – a school girl, a Russian spy, an astronaut (with a round vase that was once for Mum's roses) and an erotic dancer who works hard for the money. Basically, whatever women Ava could get costumes for.

'Did you dance for him?' I ask trying to imagine and trying not to.

'Of course, I think pole dancing might be my next hobby. Wait, Bailey's awake. Say hi to Leo the lion.'

'He's not here, just Magnus the dog.'

'That's a shame, I think Leo would help you loosen up a bit more.'

'Ava, I've just made my second video clip about sex in a fortnight. How much looser do you want me to be?'

'Like I said, I'm the sexy one. Mum and Dad should be in Byron in a few days. I'm tracking them.'

Of course she is, I think as I hang up to take Karen's call.

'Have you seen it?'

'What? I haven't even seen my face in the mirror this morning.'

'Some days when I first wake up I think that's lucky,' she quips.

Oh my god, Karen just quipped! I wish Dave was here to witness this, or do I?

'Olivia, did you hear me?'

'No, sorry, what?'

'You're viral and people are loving it!'

'Seriously?'

'Well, not everyone. There's a protest outside the network this afternoon.'

'Who?'

'A church group who think you need to burn in hell and a few women who are taking a stand over the network's treatment of women, of you, backing you.'

'Really?'

'Get online and take a look. I have a conference with them in a few hours. Personally, I think your latest offering has scared the shit out of them. Oh, and one of the young reporters has made a complaint against Len for touching her up in the lift. There's a strong chance they won't want to wait for a court date.'

I hang up and absorb that. Take a breath and get Magnus some breakfast and me some coffee . . . Then I do something unlike me. I don't check my messages or YouTube. I leave my phone on the counter and I take Magnus for a long walk. Or he takes me for a long walk.

I still have so many questions. Most are about my marriage. What day did it start to go wrong? Was it after the first two years, which is when scientific studies show our love hormones drop and we plummet off our pedestals. Something tells me the issue is even deeper, and more fundamental in the connection between Dave and I, and, to be brutally honest, I think it is within me.

When I met Dave it was on – swept off my feet on. But all too quickly we both started acting like we were playing roles, if that makes any sense. I was determined to be the perfect wife, to never lose my temper, to always look great, to have my own life . . . all the things I'd heard were so important. Recent events aside I haven't been known as a warts-and-all person. I thought it was selfish to spew emotions like a Balinese volcano. But perhaps it would have been good to reveal more than I did. It's an easy mistake for people to think you're one way if that's all you're presenting them with. Not to say I'm fake, I hope I'm not, I just find it hard to let my guard down. Especially when sex is at play. I was never that confident with it. I'm much more relaxed in my friendships, like with Darcy, Hugo and Ricky. I feel comfortable with them. And Finn, of course. But Dave? No, I was probably too busy trying to be Olivia the wife and hiding my real self from him to really let go.

My fear of being too much made me far too little in the end.

If we hadn't gotten married would it be different now? What if I'd had a baby with him? These are things I need to sit with.

And now what? I've shown people my most untamed side, inadvertently at first but then as a means of exonerating myself, and I can't lie: it felt great. Sure, I will never be invited to another social event and people will most likely cross the street to avoid me. Or spit on me. But my true friends are still there, they even helped me, and I'm not dead. In fact, I feel pretty good. Perhaps growing up is really about getting over the need to be perfect and to have everyone like you. It's about liking yourself instead. And to do that, to truly do that, you need to know who you are.

All this on a glorious late winter's morning, already there's the hopeful feeling of spring in a few of the trees who've decided to reveal their commitment to the next season via tiny green sprouts. There are some wild orchids growing along the drive as we approach Moksha once more. They remind me of Darcy's kaftans and, well, yonis. Or yonis remind me of them, both ways work. For someone who has never seen herself as sexual, my life has certainly become all about it, even though I'm not sure I'll ever have any sex again. When the opportunity was there I didn't take it, now I want it it's not there. These are the swings and roundabouts of a life I guess.

My phone's ringing on the counter as we re-enter the house. It's Leo.

'You're a star,' he says. 'And may I add, pwhoarrr.'

'And that's your professional opinion?' I jest.

'Absolutely, quote me whenever you so wish. Have you seen how many views it's had?'

'Not yet.'

'You're something else, Olivia Law. How's Magnus, is he keeping an eye on you?'

'He is, we're great. Love your house. Thanks so much. How's your trip?'

I like how easy it feels talking to Leo, perhaps our near-sex, no-sex moment has cleared all that awkwardness out of the way. Maybe it's because I unfairly see him differently because he's shared his vulnerability with me. Perhaps it's because he's so comfortable with revealing his flaws. No obsession with perfection there.

'Funny you should mention it . . . Margueritte hasn't attempted an ambush on you has she?'

'No, was she intending to?'

Leo tells me that he had to rush off the phone during our earlier conversation because Margueritte had shown up at the airport, with the intention of 'catching him out' in his affair with me. A pretty spectacular showdown ensued which led to Margueritte being escorted out of the Qantas club by security. And Leo taking an AVO out on her.

'Good on you. You can't be looking over your shoulder all the time.'

'Thanks. I think it was my fear of being a sissy, I mean being impotent and then having to get protection from my crazy non-girlfriend. Still, a cheese knife and a smashed glass in the hands of a lunatic can help you overcome your vanity.'

'Sounds scary.'

'Just intense. Plus my daughter insisted I ban Margueritte for life because of what she did after the airport scene.'

I'm hesitant to ask, but do. 'What did she do then?'

'She managed to get into my house via the garage and took my favourite painting. The Olsen.'

'Ouch.'

'My cleaners found a note. It said, "I consider this partial settlement".'

'Did you tell the police?'

'Naah, she can keep it if it means she leaves me in peace.'

'You said the note said partial?'

'That's why I wanted to doublecheck. It's like Fort Knox there and you have the new security code, still I'll get my maintenance man to check on it. I want you to feel safe.'

'Thanks.'

'Magnus isn't a fan of Margueritte either, and no one gets past him.'

We continue chatting a bit longer.

'Don't be scared to keep being bold, it's actually your signature strength,' he enthuses.

When I talk to him and when I'm with him, it's not the crazy tingles I got with Atticus yesterday, but there is a weird feeling of relief. Maybe it's because he's seen it all and done most of it too; he's not about to judge me for my quirks.

'Hey Leo, thanks for your support. It really helps.'

'Think nothing of it, kiddo.'

'When are you back?'

'Next week. My daughter's making me do a music festival with her in Tokyo first. I will be the oldest one there by at least two decades. So, tell me, what's your plan for the next one?'

'Clip? Well there have been some pretty interesting fantasies coming in.'

'I'll bet. Female sexuality, the biggest mystery of the universe, and the most appealing. If you keep going at this rate you'll start getting offers from sponsors.'

'You mean I could get paid to be a ranting mad woman?'

'Absolutely.'

We round off the call as Darcy rings from the front gate.

When Darcy enters her hair is pretty much standing on end. She's wearing the same kaftan she had on yesterday with a gorgeous full-length burgundy woollen wrap over it. She looks radiant but there's something . . . I look to her hands expecting to see them smeared with paint, she looks like she's been up all night.

'I can't talk yet,' she announces.

'Where are the kids?'

'At Nippers training then play dates. They're a bit over the markets, we'll pick them up on the way back.'

She looks at me in a way that's nothing short of haunted. I wonder if it's a grief relapse?

'Darcy are you –'

She puts her hand up to stop me. Then, without talking, she strips off and dives into the pool. She re-emerges moments later.

'Oh thank god, thank god, thank god,' she murmurs.

'What's wrong? What's happened?'

She ignores me and dives under for a lap. I decide to get into the spa so strip too. I leave her to it.

She meets me in the bubbles a few minutes later.

'It's all your fault,' she says gravely.

My stomach lurches. 'What's happened? What did I do?'

'I was so worked up after you recorded your piece last night. That's why I left here so quickly.'

'I thought the muse was calling.'

'It was, just not the muse of kaftans.'

'Oh?'

She derides herself silently some more then it all comes pouring out.

'I got home, I cooked like a mad woman, cleaned the house –'

'You cleaned your –' I overlap, cleaning is not Darcy's forte.

'Shh, let me get this out.'

'Sorry.' I zip my lips and shut up and listen.

'I cleaned, I washed, I frigging vacuumed.'

My eyes widen at this but I bite my tongue.

'It wasn't enough. So I headed to the studio. I designed, I printed. I stitched. I sewed. I came up with three new versions for the Olivia range.'

I nod, determined not to interrupt her.

'Then ... I just couldn't stop seeing the flowers, the yonis. I used my vibrators. I used my hands, but it wasn't cutting it, so I ... I ...'

I'm bursting inside but remain mute.

'I climbed on top of the shed to where I get that bit of phone range and I called Ace.'

I nod, trying my best not to smile because I'm beyond thrilled for her.

'He got there in record speed. Left a tribal men's pipe smoking or sweating or something.'

'And?'

'I was a woman possessed. We did it everywhere, I mean everywhere! All night. There isn't an inch of me that wasn't devoured. I howled like a banshee. It's a wonder the kids didn't wake up. Olivia, he's amazing. Maybe it's because it's been building up for so long or because it's been literally a lifetime since I've been with anyone, but ...'

She pauses as the bubbles around us continue to gurgle.

'Oh my effing god!' She finally allows herself to smile and laugh wildly until tears roll down her cheeks.

'Darc, that's the best news ever, that's amazing!'

She stops laughing.

'No, it isn't. It's terrible.'

'How? Why?'

And then she starts to sob into the spa.

'Because now I've ruined a really great friendship.' She continues after a moment, 'Outside of you, he's my bestie and now I've scared him away.'

'He hardly sounds scared away. He's probably performing a ritual in your honour as we speak.'

'But he told me he was a womaniser in his past and me ... Oh god, Liv, look at me. I'm the woman who thought she was happily married. What a joke that turned out to be. I have no radar of what's working and what's not.' She puts her head under the bubbles for a moment. I yank her back up.

'But that's different,' I say.

Darcy shakes her head. 'No, it's not. Pete and I had great sex and yet, while he was building cubbyhouses with the kids and holding my hand, he was planning on leaving. And he did. He dropped down dead.'

'Darcy, what you went through was devastating but it doesn't mean it will be the same with Ace.'

Darcy stares at the bubbles.

'You don't know that.'

'True, but I don't not know it either and neither do you.'

189

Darcy cries a bit more. I put my water-wrinkled hand over hers.

'There were a few times last night when it was just so special with Ace but once or twice I thought, what if he has a heart attack like Pete did, I mean he really was going for it, his face was red, he was sweating.'

'Well, it's unlikely but at least he would have died happy?'

There's a pause then we both laugh.

'Oh it's this sex thing. You know what women are like.' Darcy looks up to the bright winter's sky for the answer.

'What are we like?' I ask, curious.

'We're biologically programmed to get all gooey and lose our power once we start sexing them.'

'I don't think that's true.'

'Oh yes it is. When a women has sex all this oxytocin gets released, she wants to snuggle, she wants to talk childhood pet names and top five films. Men just want to head out to their next conquest.' Darcy recites this as a mantra.

'I think that's a bit of a limited view.' We get out of the pool and drip our way into the house, shivering, and head to the linen closet.

'You weren't a relationship therapist for twenty years with a dead cheating husband,' Darcy reminds me as she drips water onto the tiles.

'Granted.'

'In any case, I made Ace leave. I couldn't have the kids seeing him there in the morning.' Darcy shakes her ringlets onto the tiles in a show of protest.

'Darcy, he's at your place just about every day anyway.'

'I'm not exposing them to anything unless I know he won't run,' Darcy insists as I open up the closet. We find ample towels, all fluffy and fresh, as well as quite a few boxed vibrators.

'They must be for the house guests.' Darcy marvels.

'Have I mentioned how much I like Leo?' She continues.

'You like the perks, you don't know him.'

'Oh my hunches are pretty sound.' She narrows her eyes and smiles.

'So why don't you trust them with Ace?'

'My hunches are sound with other people's relationships, not my own, clearly.'

Before I can argue with her, my phone pings with what sounds like a lot of messages.

'Your love letter!' Darcy cries.

Cloaked in towels, like playboy bunnies, we race to the kitchen counter where the phone still sits.

I freeze.

'What if it's terrible?' I say.

'If it's terrible we'll deal with it. You told dragon lady what you were intending on doing, didn't you?'

I nod obediently. I'm terrified.

'And you didn't name the network or anyone, so you're no more libel than you were before.'

'Karen says someone else at the network has made a complaint about sexual harassment from Len.'

'Great. If there's one you can be sure there'll be more.' Darcy can see I'm procrastinating. 'Okay, it's time to look at the phone.'

'And Leo said it was good.'

'Like I said, Leo is a legend. Had enough of stalling yet?'

'Just about.'

'On the count of three, one, two –'

I turn the phone over, there are fifteen new messages, twelve missed calls. But I go straight to YouTube – 314 000 hits!

I scream. Darcy grabs the phone and screams too. We hold hands, jump up and down and keep screaming. Magnus jumps around us, keen to be part of the action.

'Quick, check the emails,' Darcy says.

I do. There are nearly a thousand emails from women who have sent their fantasies in.

'Oh my god, you won't need to read a novel for like a year.' Darcy beams.

It's beyond anything I've imagined. So many women have connected to the video and have shared their own offerings. I scan a few. They're all so different, so varied – from candles, to caterpillars, bulldozers, threesomes, foursomes, lonesomes, revenge fantasies, romantic fantasies . . .

'It's going to take days to go through them.'

'And more, because they'll keep coming.' Darcy sounds thrilled.

I can't believe it, I cannot believe how quickly things can change if you show up and stop hiding.

'Let's look at the press . . . No, wait, we need to get on the road if we're going to the markets. Get dressed, we're leaving in five.'

Darcy seems to have snapped out of her sex fog momentarily and we both head off to shower and dress. I reappear to find Darcy back in her kaftan and wrap with her hair on top of her head in a topknot.

'There's some press all right. You check your messages, I'll drive.'

I hand her my keys, farewell Magnus and we head off.

There are a few articles online – one opinion piece by a well-known right-wing commentator who discusses my stunning fall from grace; my desperate attempts to remain visible in the 'fading light of my career'. But most of the articles are discussing sexual harassment, gender bias in promotions and the disparity in pays between sexes. It's so much bigger than me. One article reads 'Olivia, we're with you sister, that's how I'd like to fuck them too!'

I listen to my messages. It's mainly journos asking for comments, particularly about Len. One from Karen telling me to post another missive because it's making the network sweat and panic.

There's another cancellation to a fundraiser I was going to talk at, of course they don't want an oversexed pariah supporting research into childhood diabetes. But then, miracle of miracles, there's a message from Stella Supera, Hugo's mum.

'Olivia darling, I've been meaning to call. I want to applaud you. I think you're just fantastic. Please disregard that silly email about the board. I'm the chair and I am personally re-inviting you. We'd be lucky to have you. I actually have a luncheon up on the Gold Coast this weekend. Any chance I can convince you to come and talk about the female gaze and the media?' She pauses and then cracks up laughing. *'Men with peripheral vision – love it! Also, I'll be up to see Hugo and Ricky's new home. So exciting. They're in a tizz about hessian this morning, crazy kids. Okay my darling, that's all. And Olivia? Never underestimate the power of women who admire you. Oh and I've sent you a fantasy, anonymously of course. Kisses.'*

I play the message again on speaker so Darcy can hear it.

'This is like that moment when Harvard say they're interested in printing your essay on family dynamics and law reform,' Darcy marvels.

Stella Supera is one of the chief social doyennes of Sydney. She holds sway.

'It's a game changer,' Darcy continues. 'Awesome. Oh god, I have to stop and pee, I think I have a UTI.'

Quite a few stops and a cranberry juice and a dose of Ural later, we arrive at the market, full of rainbow flags and countless stalls upholding the philosophy of 'make, bake or grow'. Everything from ginger elixirs to tie-dyed baby clothes, hats, massages, palm readings, reiki, gluten-free vegan brownies, samousas, world music with the shakuhachi, antique books, resin vases, and enviro-friendly household cleaners are on display. We wander around, Darcy pondering over various coil pots at a pottery stall.

'Darcy, you're sniffing a pottery vase.'

'Am I?' She places it down trance-like then takes out her phone. Misery clouds her face.

'What?'

'Nothing. No messages.'

'Do you and Ace usually message each other?'

'No.'

'Well,' I say.

'Still.' She moves to a pottery coffee cup. Sex fugue is back. Or oxytocin fugue.

There's a gooey sludge ball she's promised the kids that seems to be the go-to gift of the day. Hordes line up for it.

More messages ping on my phone.

I wave to Darcy, indicating a place on the hill where people are congregating, eating their lunches, listening to music and chilling. 'I'll grab lunch for both of us and meet you there, okay?'

Darcy nods grimly. With each passing hour she's becoming convinced her moment of passion with Ace was a bad idea, she will never have sex again and will spend the rest of her life as a single mother with a messy house, fabulous kaftans and quirky pottery purchased at the markets. She has also decided her moment with Ace is most definitely my fault.

I find a place in the shade and bite into my lamb kebab, made with local lamb, homemade pita, hummus and tabouli, it's delicious. I sift through more and more messages and emails. A text from Ava announcing Mum and Dad are in Coffs now so they're only a day away. Ava has found Leo's property on Google maps and sent it to them with directions that are as detailed as a secret code from the CIA. Dad's 2008 *Gregory's Street Directory* won't be able to compete.

Another text from Karen. Fergus is taking a few weeks leave. Len too.

I watch a news bulletin online about the protest outside the network. There's about ten men and women holding banners about family values and my face with devil horns drawn on top. There's also a very vocal group of women with signs reading 'equal job, equal pay' and 'workplace safety means no groping'. The news reporter mentions me and there's a tiny slice from the YouTube clip – 'we cover your mouths with gaffer tape'. But the report is more about the young woman who has come forward. And the five others of varying ages and jobs who have followed her in speaking out.

I look up; Darcy is still in the sludge ball queue. And still checking her phone. I am going to kill Ace if he's flaked out.

There's another message from Karen with flight details for Finn. And a text from Atticus inviting Magnus and I for an afternoon stroll and raw carrot cake and chai at his favourite café. I hope he's joking about the raw carrot cake, but I text back yes.

I have a date! I have a date with the hot macadamia-farming vet. Yahoo!

There's something in the air, a smell, quite nice, quite . . . it's pot, a group of twenty-somethings are sitting around sharing a joint. I'm slightly scandalised before reminding myself I am at the market and that's what people do here. So I finish my kebab and lie back.

I enter a dreamlike state thinking of all the different fantasies women have sent me already, the different voices; I've only scanned a dozen but the worlds . . . I imagine each fantasy is a step I tread on as I descend into a crystal cave of my imaginings. It's calm and there's water nearby and I can hear Finn laughing. Someone else is laughing, really laughing hysterically, having a ball. I walk through a light-filled corridor searching for the laughter, I know that woman's laugh. It's so familiar . . . it's . . .

'Olivia? Olivia, wake up!' Darcy's shaking me.

My eyes open. I'm back at the market.

'What?'

'You were laughing so loud, I couldn't wake you.'

'Oh.'

I try and sit up. I notice the colours are more intense on the rainbow flags and Darcy's topknot is shining so magnificently in the sun. I move to touch it.

'Liv?'

'Huh?'

'You're stoned.'

'What? No.'

Darcy nods and laughs. 'I've only been here a few minutes and I can smell it. You've been inhaling for half an hour.'

'Really?'

Darcy nods again. 'You're a big ole Byron stoner.'

'But I have to have raw carrot cake with the hot vet.'

'Atticus?' She looks curious.

I nod.

'He won't mind. He doesn't judge anyone.'

'But I want to look pretty.'

'You look great, stoned but great.'

'How's Dr Ace?'

'Nada. Come on, let's get you home.'

We head off. I feel like I'm walking through soft fluffy clouds, everything's just a little bit slower and a bit further away. It feels very nice, though I could definitely eat a few more kebabs.

Darcy vetoes my plan to stop for more food and drives me home. I face plant for a few hours till Magnus licking my hand wakes me up. All I can think of is carrot cake. And the hot vet's arms, of course.

21

WE'RE WALKING ALONG THE BEACH, MAGNUS IS IN HEAVEN.

'You look lovely,' Atticus says. 'Do you usually dress this well for beach walks?'

Sprung.

I spent half an hour debating what to wear. This could have been the remnants of inhaling organic grass at the markets or more likely it was me trying to be perfect. And what do you wear for a beach walk carrot cake date on a slightly cloudy afternoon in August? I know the beauty of Byron is you can wear anything, but I'm not about to have chai with Atticus in activewear. I settle on some trousers that can be rolled up, a light pink cashmere jumper with a silk top underneath and a scarf. Okay, I over-dressed. I use the line about comfort as Magnus jumps up on me and implants sand everywhere.

I ask Atticus about his life, trying not to seem like an interrogator.

'Well you know it really, the nuts, the veterinary practice and me.'

'No kids?'

'Not yet.'

I inhale sharply. Byron is full of nubile goddesses with ripe ovaries and young uteruses. Strange he hasn't partnered off with one of them.

'Kidding.' He smiles. I exhale.

'I love kids but I don't think they're part of my plan.'

'Oh . . . what is?' I do my best to sound casual. I fail.

'Well right now it's to take you for carrot cake.' Atticus smiles and ups the momentum.

Nice dodge, I think, before remonstrating with myself for needing to know a stranger's plan. I mean, what's my plan? (Aside from eating the biggest piece of cake I can get my hands on. I hope it has a cream cheese icing. I'm still so hungry.)

'I think I may be a bit stoned,' I confess. 'I'm sorry.' I explain the passive inhalation situation, which amuses him.

'You seem like you're good at keeping a fair bit of drama around you.'

'I know it seems like that given the last few weeks of my life but it wasn't like that before, in fact it was the opposite. I was the least dramatic person I knew, outside of Dave.'

'So do you think this is circumstantial or the real you?' The question is innocent but it bites me because it's what I've been wondering too.

'I'm not sure,' I venture. 'I can't go back to what I was, but I also think this is a heightened time. Maybe it's somewhere in between?'

He absorbs that as we keep walking. Why do I want his approval? Isn't that the very thing I need to get away from? Where is the cake?

We sit at a sweet café in the sunshine. It seems café hopping is quite the pastime here. Bronzed beauties stretch over smoothies, yoginis discuss deep and important issues over chai, a few business-looking folk rush through coffee meetings, ladies who lunch debate gluten-free options and a few prams overflow with toddlers declaring their enjoyment of babycinos. All is well with the world.

The chai is fantastic. I watch Atticus's hands. They are very good hands. Sure they spend a fair bit of time inside animals but they are saving hands, nut-picking hands, handsome hands.

'Enjoying the chai?' he asks.

'Best ever.'

He smiles, I smile. We smile. He has great teeth. Why am I obsessing over them?

I try to re-engage my brain and ask about his veterinary practice.

'A lot of livestock, a few lamas, and a heap of pets.' Atticus is definitely content with pauses between words. I need to be more like that.

The carrot cake arrives. There's no creamed cheese. There is a cashew butter icing which isn't bad, but I can't see myself engaging with it as part of my future.

'So your clip went well?' he asks. Still smiling.

'Yes, it's getting a heap of traction. I don't know what that means but I think it's great so many women are sharing their fantasies.'

'It's awesome. Well done you.'

We clink chai cups. We're cute. I wonder if cake and dessert sharing are a natural part of his life or if his ex-wife trained him? Who is his ex-wife, are they still friends? Did they have great sex?

Stop it, Olivia.

'I haven't watched it yet,' he admits.

'Oh that's okay, you might think I'm a complete fruit loop when you do and ban me for life.'

'I seriously doubt that.' He holds my eye contact and I am an instant blushing, blithering mess but determined to stay engaged.

And then a dark shadow crosses his face. He looks up. Then looks to me.

'Stealing someone else's husband now? You really do keep busy.'

It's Margueritte. She's sporting a tight black halter-neck top, spray-on jeans, stilettos and a withering expression.

'Am I?' I reply. Atticus looks at us both, at a loss.

'Atticus, this is Margueritte, she's an art collector,' I say calmly, though her presence has made my body go into a distinct fight or flight mode. This may have something to do with the fact she's a lunatic. Not many people make my skin crawl, aside from Len in the lifts at work of course, and now Margueritte. I read somewhere you shouldn't make eye contact with sociopaths or engage them in any way, so the fact our eyes are locked and I have entered into a verbal exchange is probably not highly desirable.

'How dare you bring your whoredom to my favourite café. I was having a lovely time with all my friends.' Magueritte indicates a woman behind her, in activewear holding the Chihuahua, who is now wearing a pink diamanté t-shirt. The woman half smiles apologetically. I have a feeling she's been pulled into this inadvertently.

Margueritte continues. 'And you come and ruin it with your loose morals and your guttersnipedom.'

'Hang on,' says Atticus.

'It's okay,' I say to him.

Margueritte is on a roll. 'And as for Leo, you can keep him. You're clearly obsessed with him.'

'I am?'

'That's why you're staying in his house, flaunting yourself on the internet; it's all about Leo, but he doesn't love you. He'll just use you as his sex slave and then discard you. I've been through it all before. He always comes back to me.'

'Is that why he has an AVO on you, Margueritte?'

She pauses before increasing in venom. 'You think you're so clever, but you're a nothing, a has-been, a sad and pathetic bisexual who doesn't wear underwear. Everyone hates you, *hates* you, everyone is laughing behind your back.'

'That's enough.' Atticus stands, as do I. Margueritte has been yelling loud enough to attract the attention of the entire café. The manager approaches.

'I think you'd better leave,' he says to her.

'Oh, don't worry, I'm leaving, you bet, I don't need you,' she spits.

She steps in for a final attack. I'm pretty speechless. 'I own half this town, I have rental properties all up the coast, I have children and I am sitting pretty, you – you have nothing but a part-time dog, you're a dog-minder and he doesn't love you.'

I've had enough. Magnus growls.

'Margueritte, it has nothing to do with me. I'm not a threat. The only threat to you is yourself. And your determination to confuse stalking with love. If you *ever* approach me or my part-time dog again, I'll get my own AVO on you. Not only that, I'll get my sister to come and sort you out.'

Atticus is staring at me, mystified, as we walk to our cars.

'Pretty impressive,' he says. 'But who is she?'

'I don't even know her. She's a lover or ex-lover of my friend Leo. She's just wanting to hate on someone. Sorry.'

'You handled it well.'

I'm actually shaking and feel like I might vomit.

'Sorry she hijacked our carrot cake. I'd like to make it up to you,' I say.

'Not sure I can handle the drama.' Atticus smiles but there's more than a joke in his words.

'But this isn't . . . like I was saying before, this isn't me.'

He nods but is unconvinced. It highlights his perfect jawline.

'Please, let me make it up to you, let's have dinner.'

'I'd like that,' he says warmly. 'How's tomorrow night?'

I nod enthusiastically before remembering.

'Sorry, my parents are coming to stay and I wouldn't want to inflict that on you. How about tonight?'

'Tonight?' He looks wide-eyed. 'That's keen.'

My heart drops. Idiot, what was I thinking, why'd I say that?

'Sorry,' Atticus continues. 'That sounded harsh, it was meant to be a joke. Sometimes my humour misfires.'

'It's cool.' I try not to look rattled. I feel ridiculous.

'No, I'm really sorry. You've just been pulled apart by that mad woman . . . Tonight is good. I go to a sacred acoustics circle. Do you mind coming to that with me and then we can eat somewhere nearby after?'

'Love to.' I have no idea what sacred acoustics is, but it sounds nice.

'I'll pick you up at six then.'

'Great.'

He kisses me on the cheek and Magnus and I head off.

I look at my phone, as well as an insane number of messages, I have under two hours to get home and get ready!

22

THE OVERHAUL BEGINS; I RUN THE BATH, OPEN THE WARDROBE AND
seek inspiration from the small range of outfits I so hurriedly
packed.

I check the 'Come As You Are' emails – the number of women
writing in has doubled. The YouTube clip has hit nearly one million.

Darcy calls. 'Nothing, nada, zilch, zip.'

'No . . .' I think of the number of ways I will berate Ace when
I get my hands on him. I'll give him more than a rumble.

'Come over for pizza and Trivial Pursuit with the kids.'

'Oh Darcy, I'd love to but . . .'

'What have you got a hot date?' Darcy jokes.

'Kinda, I hope so, maybe?'

'What? Who? When? Where?'

I fill Darcy in on the details. There's a pause.

'Darcy?'

'Yup, sorry, range went out. You're going to sacred acoustics and dinner with Atticus. Sure you wouldn't rather come over here, it will be more fun.'

'What's wrong with Atticus, or is this an aftermath of Ace?'

'Atticus is lovely. I just . . .'

'What?'

'Nothing, just not sure he's your match. Now you're going to hate me.'

'I won't as long as you tell me what I should wear to sacred acoustics.'

Darcy informs me that sacred acoustics involves lying down and listening to a large gong in a yoga studio. I think that sounds kind of sexy. Though clearly right now I think the ingredients on a packet of chicken chips is kind of sexy. After two years of nothing then a bad, abandoned something with Dave, a near miss with Leo and over 2000 sexual fantasies to read, I am more than toey.

I wash my hair and dry it with the curls in. I choose a boat-neck easy-fitting baby blue woollen dress with a full skirt. With ankle boots I can easily take off to listen to the gong. And a soft rust-coloured scarf. I also wear my sexiest bra and knickers, just in case.

Atticus picks me up right on time. He looks nice. How is it that men only need to have a shower and iron a shirt and they're considered dressed up? Whereas women spend hours doing the most bizarre things to themselves, waxing legs, bleaching mo's, tinting eyelashes, applying eye shadow that matches our outfits. Atticus wears a loose-fitting cream linen shirt and jeans with a cord blazer over the top. He looks comfortable and sun-kissed and very, very good.

'I have a yoga mat for you, and some blankets.' He informs me as we drive down the winding hill to the venue.

You have to hand it to Byron, with more yoga schools than anywhere outside of India, they know how to do them well. This one is on a property just out of town. Lanterns and huge stone sculptures usher our way. There's cubbyhouses for shoes and lemon tea and mint water. Hordes of yogis and yoginis fill the space. Stretching, providing full body hugs and massages to each other. There's a lot of sandalwood. At the front of the room sits a massive gong.

Atticus places the two mats side by side before he's hugged by half the room. He returns.

'Now lie down,' he instructs. I obey. This could be the best date ever, except for the fact we're not alone.

Atticus flicks a beautiful Aztec woollen blanket over me and tucks me in.

'Very important you're snug,' he whispers.

'As a bug.' I watch his magic arms tuck the blanket all around me. Oh this is good, very good.

Then he lies beside me. It's a bit like nap time at preschool.

The lights go off and a deep voice sings a hymn in Hindi (I think), everyone else oms along.

And then the gong begins. The first strike sends ripples through my body. It's fantastic. I get why they call it a sound bath.

Okay so now I am meant to just let go. Let go, Olivia. Breathe in. Breathe out.

Let go.

Oh god, did I put my phone on flight mode? What if I fall asleep and start to snore, or what if Margueritte turns up with a gun and shoots me? Would Margueritte actually own a gun? Probably not. I should call Leo but I don't want to worry him. Will Magnus be okay till I get home? What if something happens to Mum and Dad on their way up and they can't get hold of me? Is Dave going to marry the Hong Kong dessert lover? Will he invite me to the wedding? Is this why he's rushed the separation through? Maybe she doesn't believe in sex before marriage as well as not sharing desserts and she's perfect and I'm – what was it Margueritte called me – a pathetic whore. Am I? Has Ace been to see Darcy and why can't she imagine me and Atticus together? I really need to start replying to the emails and choose a fantasy to read next time. Is one clip a week enough? Are they going to drop the lawsuit? Will I get my super back? Oh god, where am I going to live and how?

'Olivia?' Atticus whispers, touching my hand. I jump up and yelp.

'Shh,' he soothes. 'You were groaning, are you okay?'

'Groaning? Sorry.' Oh god I was groaning, and not in the good way.

'So relaxing, isn't it?' he coos.

'Aha,' squeaks my tiny, high-pitched lying whisper. 'How long does it go for?'

'Loads of time yet. Ninety minutes.'

'Goody,' I fib again as he closes his eyes.

Ninety minutes? Ninety minutes of a fucking gong gonging and nothing else? What am I doing here? This is a terrible idea, I'm not going to last ninety minutes. Perhaps I could sneak out and reply to emails, but I don't want to offend Atticus.

I sneak a sideways glance at him. He looks blissful, his perfect light brown curls framing his Michelangelo inspired face. I try and breathe him in. Okay, I really am pathetic. I study his hands, oh what those hands could do to me. I feel their warmth as I place mine closer, accidently on purpose brushing against them. Electric shocks pierce through me. No reaction from him. Damn. That could have been sexy. I reluctantly close my eyes again and begin counting gong strikes.

'Two hours (they lied) and about 7000 gong strikes later, Atticus and I are sitting in a pretty restaurant on the site of the yoga school. It has outside heaters and a vegan menu.

I begin wondering how many slices of salami pizza Darcy has left.

'What'd you think?' Atticus asks. 'Great isn't it?'

'Well this is lovely,' I say, squinting to read the menu in the dim candlelight of the table lanterns. I don't want to pull my phone out and use the torch because there's a clear 'No Mobile' sign on the wall.

'What's good?' I ask.

'It's all great.' Atticus beams in his post-gong gloriousness.

I pull the lantern to me and hold it over the menu. It is a farm produce menu and it does look good – stuffed capsicum, eggplant fritters with pesto . . . no steak. I'm just about to decide when I sneeze and drop the menu on the lantern and set fire to it.

'No drama then.' Atticus laughs as he helps me put it out and a waitress called Santosha practises the law of tolerance and places us at another table.

Why am I such a mess? Is this the real me? I can hear a conversation from the table beside me; it's about kinesiology and inner children. I study Atticus, does he want to talk about kinesiology? The gong? To be fair, it got better, well, I fell asleep so that helped a bit. It's the kind of thing I could do once every three months, or every six. Oh who am I kidding?

'What do you think about the foreign minister's response over the coal dispute?' I say, ready to talk about something that isn't a gong, a yoga pose or sex. Unless Atticus wants to talk about sex, then I'd happily participate.

'Oh I don't watch the news,' Atticus informs me. 'That's why meeting you is so funny, everyone was talking about the lady newsreader scandal but I had no idea who you are.'

'No news?' I find this refreshing and perplexing.

'Nup, avoid it completely.'

'Oh.' I mull on that. 'Why is that?'

'I just think I contribute more to the world by getting on with my thing and meditating for peace.'

I know I'm meant to say 'That's very admirable'. Instead I say, 'That's sexy.'

Atticus, rightfully, looks confused. I backtrack. 'Sorry, sorry, I meant it's attractive that you're so self-contained. Does it ever make you feel a bit disconnected?'

'From what?' Atticus asks. 'War, scandal, corruption?'

'Current affairs, being part of the political debate.'

'I avoid politics too.'

I love politics.

'But you vote?'

'When I have to.' He shrugs. Amazing. He's really not interested.

The fact I find this hot rather than concerning must be connected to my hormones, or the gong. Both maybe.

The rest of dinner passes amiably; with me watching the way Atticus's mouth moves as he talks, mainly about meditations, macadamias and animals. I lose the thread quite a few times because I'm too entranced by his physical beauty.

'You're going to sleep so well tonight,' he reassures me as we get in his ute to drive home. I am secretly hoping (very hard) that that may be because he's going to be sleeping with me.

We arrive at my house. He stops at the driveway.

'Thanks for taking me to your people,' I say, jokingly.

'Anytime,' he says.

'Would you like to come in for a nightcap? I have bancha tea and Magnus would love to see you.'

'Better not, but thanks.'

Smack. The slap of rejection. Again.

But then he leans in. I close my eyes. Perhaps this is a taking it slow thing, which would be healthy and good, although it will also mean many more vegetarian meals, discussions on meditation and I have a fair hunch we'll be heading to partner yoga sometime soon.

But a good kiss, a good kiss can be remembered for a lifetime.

He kisses me . . .

On the cheek.

'Oh,' I say before I rein my bruised ego in.

'Olivia.' Oh god here comes the rejection speech. I don't think I can stand it.

'I really like spending time with you but I think my life is going down a different track to yours.'

Paths, tracks, what is it with him and navigation?

'I don't know where mine's going,' I blurt.

'I think you do, but you're a bit scared. You're a very powerful woman.'

'Is that a bad thing?' It feels like it must be bad if it has scared him away.

'It's a great thing, and attractive, but I think you're trying to fill some kind of hole inside yourself.'

He continues. 'And that's why you're attracted to me but, really, there is no hole.'

'No hole?' I repeat.

'No hole.'

Not one that he'll be entering, I think, as he hugs me close.

'What's your path, Atticus?' I ask.

He hesitates, pauses and then says, 'I'm studying to be a Buddhist monk.' He confides with a quiet pride. 'Only Ace knows, and now you.'

Boom. Hat-trick – the deserter, the impotent porn king and the abstinent Buddhist monk. If they walked into a bar it would be the beginning of a great joke, one that is, of course, on me.

'Are you sure?' I ask.

'I've been studying for years. It was part of why my marriage ended.'

'Oh.' I digest this for a beat. 'You know, in Japan the Buddhist monks aren't celibate.' I figure it's worth a shot.

'I know. But this one is.' He indicates himself.

I nod and, wanting to die, open the car door so I can crawl inside. He places his hand over mine, then lifts it and kisses it.

'Just so you know, you're very beautiful and very, very sexy.'

Not sexy enough, I think but manage to say, 'Thank you. You too. Night.'

He waits until I'm inside and then drives off in his celibacy truck. Of course he's a gentleman. A lovely Buddhist monk gentleman.

Magnus at least is beside himself to see me.

'Thank god for you.' I give him a pat as we head out to stretch our legs and try and make sense of the night.

23

THERE'S AN EMAIL FROM FERGUS. *WHAT'S YOUR BYRON ADDRESS,*
Hannah has something for you.

Karen calls at 10.30 pm. 'You know you have Finn arriving
tomorrow?'

I tell her that yes, I do.

She tells me she's only heard from the network once today,
they're busy putting out fires. Five new cases of sexual harassment in the workplace have emerged.

'Your clip has certainly put the cat amongst the pigeons.
I recommend putting another one out as soon as you can. The
more agitated the network are the better for us.'

'But the next one won't be about the network.'

'That's okay, just stay visible. You're doing well.'

I decide to bite the bullet and ask about her private life. 'How are things with your new friend?'

Karen is quite happy to share. 'He's a sex god with abs like a washing board; he speaks five languages, is a ski instructor and made me eggs Benedict for breakfast, and plays soccer with Finn. How do you think they're going?'

I sigh as I look through the door at the empty king-size bed.

'I'd say I should get the details of the site.'

'You need to focus on work. Oh and Dave still wants you to have half the house. He also checked with his email provider, there was nothing in the receiving of your message – a hacker would know how to forward it without it including his name. He said he's sorry he can't be more help.'

'That's decent,' I mumble.

'Like I said, decent guy, just not for me . . . or you.'

I take that in.

'Have you met his –' I start to ask before she cuts me off.

'Girlfriend, Bridie, she's sweet. They're well suited.'

I swallow.

'Did you think Dave and I were well suited?' I ask.

'Never.'

Thanks, Karen. I hang up and get into bed. Alone.

Magnus curls up on the floor beside me and begins snoring.

I call Leo. There's background noise.

'I'm at the music festival,' he yells into the phone.

'Having fun?'

'That's one word for it. Amy's having fun, mainly showing how old her father is to her mates.'

I laugh.

'Magnus is snoring.'

'He's in love then. It's official.'

'And Margueritte approached me at a café in town.'

There's a pause.

'Are you okay?'

'Sure, she certainly likes a chat,' I joke.

'I'm sorry you've been exposed to her, Olivia. I was talking to my therapist and she said you've achieved more with me in a few weeks than she has in five years.'

'Oh, what's that?'

'Shaming me into quitting a very bad habit.'

'You're not going to go back to her then?'

Leo laughs loudly. 'Do you know this is the happiest I've been since I met her. It was one of those toxic things which you don't realise is so bad because you're too involved. Frog in water scenario.'

'You see a therapist?' I'm curious, perhaps I should see one too.

'Trust me, I've needed one. Between womanising, prostate cancer and navigating fatherhood, I need all the support I can get.'

I begin to yawn. Something about Leo is so relaxing, maybe because neither of us is trying to be anything other than what we are.

'Boring you?'

'Chilling me. I got stoned and went to a sacred acoustics session.'

'Kid, you're definitely getting into the Byron vibe. Just don't get too soggy.'

'Huh?'

'You know, it's great there, I love it, but there's only so many conversations about kinesiology and aura cleansing I can have.'

'Mum and Dad and my stepson are coming up tomorrow.'

'Great.'

'Mum and Dad are in a campervan.'

'Casa mia casa tua. They're all welcome.'

'You're a good guy, Leo,' I say, my eyes closing.

'Just don't let anyone else know, okay?'

'Deal.'

I hang up and within a nanosecond I'm asleep. I don't know whether it is the pot, the gong, the vegetarian food or having Magnus by my side and a nice bedtime chat, but my feelings of sexual rejection abate and I curl up and sleep, the epitome of contentment.

24

I AWAKE EARLY AND DRIVE DOWN TO LENNOX HEAD TO WALK MAGNUS along Seven Mile Beach. The pink of a new day beckons as we stride along and Magnus dances at the waves' edges. I grab croissants from the local bakery and head to Darcy's for a debrief.

'You're kidding, Ace hasn't even popped in for a rumble with Dylan?' I'm now officially outraged for my friend.

'He's completely disappeared.' Darcy moans. 'Oh why didn't I stick to Leo's toys, they're so much simpler.' She pulls the inside out of a buttery croissant and dips it in strawberry jam.

'How was the gong show?'

'Long.'

Darcy laughs. 'And Atticus?'

'Celibate.' I moan.

Darcy nods. 'Makes sense, he's never with anyone, I wondered if he was gay.'

'Nope, just spiritually committed. Can you believe it? I'm like the Goldilocks of sexual derailments – not into me, not working and not gonna happen with anyone.'

'Didn't Goldilocks find the bed that was just right?' Darcy tops up our teacups.

'Half her luck. I just have to resign myself to the fact my life is going to be about helping women reclaim their sexuality while not having any myself.'

'Swings and roundabouts,' says Darcy, 'things will turn and turn again. Have you decided which fantasy to read next?'

I tell her a few of the ones I've read. Darcy's eyes bulge.

'My god women are awesome.' She sighs. 'I still like the ant one to start with, it's gentle and sweet, it would be good for your audience to see a range.'

'Agree. I have to race. Finn's due at the airport. I'll see you all tonight.'

'Ah yes, family barbeque with your parents. Be good to see them. Life certainly has gotten more interesting since you've come to town.' She hugs me.

I head off down the road and straight to Ace's. His truck's there. I spy a group of boys around Finn's age sitting in a camp circle with breakfast bowls in their laps. They're still waking up as Ace, definitely a morning person, holds the talking stick and informs them of a range of activities in the day ahead.

I walk straight up. He flinches as I approach.

'Liv.' He quakes. A few of the boys nudge each other. My notoriety around teenage boys continues, oh joy.

I grab the talking stick from his hand and announce, 'You can rumble for the next five minutes. Go!'

Overjoyed to be free of washing-up duties, the boys yell and call and head off to the sawdust-covered ground close by to rumble.

'What's going on?' I ask Ace.

'What? Nothing, I've had back-to-back workshops then I gave a talk at the hospital yesterday.'

'So busy you couldn't send a text or make a call to say thank you for the best night of my life?' I demand.

Conflicting emotions battle it out on Ace's face, a bit of shame, also excitement over his memory of the evening of love.

'It *was* the best night of my life.' He reflects.

'Well dingbat, tell her that! Why are you sabotaging? You know what Darcy's been through. You cannot mistreat her.'

Ace, chastened, nods. 'I know, I know, I didn't mean to, she's the best, I'm just . . .' He trails off.

'What?'

'Scared shitless.'

'Ace, we're all scared shitless when it comes to intimacy, that's why it's intimate. How do you think she feels? Or have you been too busy being a lost boy and building clubhouses to think of it?'

Ace looks at me blankly. I tap the stick lightly on his head.

'You're the one running workshops teaching boys to become men. Men treat their women, or their men, well. They honour them. They do not take off with no contact for two days.'

'But she was the one who kicked me out. And she never listens to her phone.'

'She does after a night like you two had. And she kicked you out because she was scared of being rejected and of the kids thinking there was something going on if you weren't solid.'

I pause to catch my breath. Ace kicks a non-existent pebble on the ground.

'Are you solid?' I ask.

Ace takes a breath and meets my stare. 'I'm solid.'

'Well let her know that. Come to my house for a barbeque tonight. My stepson and parents will be there. Do not bring the talking stick.'

Ace nods.

'And send her a text, will you? Thank her.'

Ace nods more enthusiastically. 'I will.'

'Stop being a wimp.'

'Olivia, you should come and teach some workshops to the young men on how to treat a woman.' A bit of his Aceness is already returning. It's kind of nice to see him being more human and less workshop eagle.

'I'd love to.' I hand him back his talking stick and head back to the car. Ace regains his composure and returns to the rumbling teens. I'm grinning as I drive along the dirt road back to the world beyond Ace. I think he and Darcy will be a fantastic couple.

I arrive at Ballina airport just as the small Regional Express plane lands. It's a lovely rural airport, harking back to another time. I scan the front pages of the paper. Nothing. Page three is about the network attempting to settle several cases of sexual misconduct out of court. And an exposé of various board members. I get a mention as being in hiding, possibly on the north coast, and reinventing myself as a figurehead of female sexuality – a princess of pink porn, with the help of Kingdom of Come guru and founder, Leo Montgomery, whom I've been romantically involved with and spotted around town with. Jesus, where do they get this stuff?

Oh, of course . . . Margueritte.

The cabin door opens and passengers disembark off the tiny plane. I spot Finn and try not to embarrass him by waving too much. Which is hard. My heart leaps at the sight of him, though he doesn't look very happy.

He greets me with a huge hug. I can smell something on him, alcohol? His eyes are red.

'What's happened?' I ask him.

'Nothing,' He says mopishly in a way that implies everything is, in fact, wrong. I figure he will talk when he's ready.

'Are you hungover, Finn?'

'Dunno, maybe.' He looks out the window as he speaks. I decide a hamburger and milkshake are going to be my best allies in getting him to open up. We stop at a small takeaway shop.

Munching on the burger and sipping his chocolate milkshake, while watching the tide go out along Shelly Beach, he opens up. Finn has been so exemplarily, I know kids his age experiment with all kinds of things, but Dave, Karen and I have all kept a very solid collective eye on him and, to date, there's been no misdemeanours, apart from a few abandoned geography assignments that were remembered and completed last minute. One fist fight defending a mate when he was ten. And of course the ongoing desire to not have to clean his room or wake up early. Oh and eating all the biscuits and leaving the packet in the fridge as a means of torturing the rest of us. So this is something different.

'I went to a party,' he starts. I command myself to listen, to imagine Finn has the talking stick. Do not read the riot act of the damage booze can cause to young minds, I tell myself.

'It was at Russell's, there were a few hundred kids there. It was pretty wild.'

I am choking on the words 'were Russell's parents there?' when he answers.

'Mr and Mrs Edwards were overseas, Russ was meant to be at his grandma's.'

I nod.

'I told Mum I was going to a party, but she's so into Matteo, she didn't ask too much. So I went and Daisy had a bottle of gin.'

'Oh, gin,' is all I say.

'There was heaps of other stuff there and we didn't do any of it,' he says reassuringly, which makes me worry more. I know this had to happen at some stage, when I was Finn's age I was experimenting with Vok Advocaat and Passion Pop at a slumber party. But still, this is Finn.

'So Dais and I drank the gin.'

'Did you like it?'

'Not really, I like vodka more. But it's better than wine.'

I realise we are only just scratching the surface.

'Did you get in trouble from Karen, is that why you're upset?'

He shakes his head and looks traumatised again.

'It's okay,' I say.

'No it's not,' Finn blurts. 'Dad and you have split, he's with Bridie and he wants to marry her.'

'I know,' I say softly.

'Did he tell you?' Finn has tears in his eyes.

'I kind of figured it out. He's the marrying kind. Keep talking.' I encourage.

'Mum's with Matteo, which is good, and you're here and not working and everything is changing.'

'It's a lot of change in a short time,' I affirm.

'And I kissed Daisy.' Clunk. There it is. I do my best to keep my face neutral but my mind is racing. Is he gay, is he trans, is he . . . ? What's happening?

'It was our last night together and the girl I've been crushing on, Mila, was there and ignoring me. When she finally talked to me, Daisy looked mad. So I asked her what was up and she said Mila wasn't into me, she was just using me so the guy she was into would get jealous.'

I'm doing my best to keep up.

'Anyway, I realised she was right, Mila is hot but she's a bit of a bitch. And Daisy was upset and I asked her why and she said she'd been into Mila too.'

'Daisy's a lesbian?' None of this makes sense.

'She's not sure. Anyway we were laughing about how random it all was and I said how much I'll miss her while she's away and we were both drunk and we . . . kissed.'

'Wow. Okay.' I hold my breath then ask, 'How was it?'

'Weird. There's the boy who was my first friend at kindergarten who is now a girl but still my best mate and – but I don't see her like I see other girls, she's just . . . Daisy.'

He feeds a few of his chips to a persistent seagull.

'Do you want to kiss her again?'

He shakes his head. 'But I don't want to stop being friends. Please don't tell Dad, or Mum. Promise.'

I think about it for a moment.

'I want you to promise to always let us know where you are and if there's an adult present.'

He rolls his eyes.

'I mean it, Finn. You're so precious. And I know you feel like an adult but you have a lot of growing and changing going on.'

'So do you,' he retorts in self-defence.

'True. And I'm so glad and honoured you trust me.'

He nods his head.

'My advice would be you tell Karen about the party, she knows everything anyway and if she finds out you'll be seriously in trouble.'

'I guess.' He hesitates.

'And I think you and Daisy will still be friends. But maybe have this break to chill a bit. You're also very tired. And no more gin. Deal?'

He nods and I hug him.

'Are there any other kids my age up here?'

'We'll find some somewhere,' I say as we head back to the car. I know Ace will be just the connector Finn needs.

'Your clip was awesome btw.' He grins.

'Oh Finn, I didn't want you to watch it.'

'I know. I didn't watch all of it. I hope Dad sees it. It's mad.'

We drive home via the Ballina fish co-op, which Darcy and Leo have both raved about. We buy a load of prawns, flathead, scallops and Moreton Bay bugs to prepare for the family barbeque. We call Karen on the speakerphone and Finn fills her in about the party. She's surprisingly restrained. She also has another meeting with the network lawyers this afternoon.

'How serious is it with Leo?' she asks.

'He's a pal, that's all. Why?' I wonder if she thinks he's a bad match too.

'Just wondered if we could get a friend's discount, love his stuff,' she purrs.

'What does he make?' Finn asks.

'Exercise balls for pelvic floor strength.' Karen knows that will put an end to Finn's curiosity. She's right. Man she's good.

We get home and Finn and Magnus rejoice at their reunion. Finn marvels at the house. 'This is mad.' He chooses his room, has a swim, helps me shell prawns and then face plants on the couch for a nap.

I retire to my room with the papers and spend a few hours

reading fantasies. I'm at a particularly raunchy one when the front gate buzzer rings. I hide my iPad under the pillow and answer.

I'm more than a bit surprised to hear not Mum, not Dad, but Fergus over the intercom.

'Your material is good, but your lighting is shit,' is all he says as I press the buzzer for him to enter.

25

FERGUS AND HANNAH, HIS BEAUTIFULLY ELEGANT, BIRD-LIKE WIFE, SIT opposite me at the outside table over chai.

'What's this shit?' Fergus makes a face as he drinks it. He actually likes it, he just can't miss an opportunity to tease.

'Chai, silly.' Hannah and Fergus are one of the oddest couples I've ever seen, and yet they're perfect for each other. Where he's brash and impulsive, she's refined and intuitive. Rather than cancel each other out, they harmonise and they're one of the few couples I truly see as admirable.

'I love what you've done,' Hannah enthuses.

'Yeah, and that's why we're here basically. She wouldn't stop going on about it.'

Hannah and I ignore Fergus and she continues.

'Fergus loves it too, that's why we're here, we want to help.'

'I'm guessing Len doesn't know you're here.'

'Nup. I've taken the week off. There's a heap of crap going down, you really upset the shit cart.'

'We think it's great, don't we?' Hannah talks with quiet firmness.

'Yeah, reign of the dinosaur is over. They should never have fired you. That replacement's no bloody good.'

'I'm sure she's fine, Ferg,' I correct him. Audrey is a good newsreader.

He shakes his head and pulls a sucking-on-sour-lemons look as he feeds Magnus a biscuit under the table.

'He misses working with you,' Hannah says.

'Get off,' Fergus growls, which is his way of saying 'yes'.

'I miss working with you too,' I reply.

'Well let's bloody get on with it then.' Fergus fires up. 'I'm not here, neither is Hannah, and this never happened but we're going to produce your next clip. Got a fantasy?'

'I've got nearly 4000 of them, but there's one about ants I think will be good.'

'If you've got fucking 4000 you should be doing them daily. Saturate the market with them.'

'Okay.'

'We film a heap of them then release one a day for the five days we're here. You'll end up with sponsorship or an offer for your own show within a fortnight.'

'Really?'

'Nah, no idea really, but what else are you going to do up here, study Sanskrit and tattoo a picture of me on your forearm?'

'How'd you know?' I counter. 'Do you want to stay here?'

'We're booked into a spa at Newrybar,' Hannah says, 'this is actually a holiday too. I love it up here, Fergus only came so he could work with you.'

'Aww, Ferg.'

Hannah nudges him. 'Go on, pumpkin.'

Fergus turns to jelly when Hannah calls him a pet name, all his bravado melts and he resembles Magnus receiving a belly rub.

'Olivia, I'm sorry.'

I start to say 'It's okay' but stop. If Ace has taught me anything it's to give people the space to say what they want to get off their chest.

'You're like a kid sister to me and, even though you drive me nuts, I hate not working with you. I should have backed you up from the word go. I was worried about my own job and, to be honest, seeing you . . . like that . . . was confronting for me and I wimped out. I regret that and I apologise. I want to help.'

He finishes, grunts and gives Magnus another piece of biscuit.

'Thanks, Fergus. I'm really glad you're here.'

'Hug now, you wallys,' Hannah orders.

We've never really hugged but we give it a go.

'Oh and Hannah brought her cello, she's got your theme music sorted.'

'Really?'

Hannah, excited, places her arm around Fergus, who puffs up at her touch.

'There's a harpist in the symphony, Zoe Wylde, she's an extraordinary composer, does all sorts for Hollywood. She absolutely adored your piece to camera and we were talking about it and she composed this piece for you, it's a play on your old news theme.'

'Not enough to be an issue,' Fergus says.

'It has its own exquisite melody, she says it's her musical version of a sexual fantasy and her gift to you.'

I don't know what to say, I know my nostrils are flaring and my eyes have tears.

'None of that,' quips Fergus. 'Darls, grab the cello and let Liv hear it herself.'

'Yes. Great idea.' Hannah kisses her husband and heads to the car. Fergus looks around.

'Not too shabby.'

'It's Leo's, he lent it to me in exchange for dog-minding.'

'Sweet deal.' Fergus whistles.

'Why did you warn me off him?'

Fergus shrugs. 'Just trying to protect you, toots. He used to be quite the party boy and he's been going out with a right maddie.'

'Margueritte. He has an AVO on her now.'

Fergus nods. 'Just didn't want you getting mixed up in their mess. And I'm sorry it didn't work out with Dave.'

'Me too. Leo's been a really good support though.'

'Fair enough.' He pauses and then adds, 'I was a bit scared too, to be honest.'

'Of Leo?' He is kind of imposing.

'No, of you. You told me to never speak to you again.'

'Oh that. I was hurt.'

'Mates?' He looks vulnerable.

'Absolutely.'

Finn emerges from the house and Hannah returns with her cello.

Finn is more than pleased to see Fergus, who he's known since he was little and calls 'Uncle Ferg'. Fergus dotes on him. And Finn has always had a huge crush on Hannah. She gathers him in a huge hug and he blushes blissfully.

'Uncle Ferg and Hannah are helping me with my next video.'

'Cool, what's to eat?'

Hannah performs the piece. It's both sexy and cheeky, whimsical and haunting. It's perfect intro music. And it plays brilliantly on the urgency of current affair and news soundtracks. I send a thank you message to Zoe Wylde, composer extraordinaire.

The front gate buzzer rings again. The parental unit has arrived.

26

I PUT IN A CALL TO HUGO AND RICKY AND ASK THEM TO BRING EXTRA supplies for the barbeque. I leave a message for the monk in waiting. I figure my bruised ego will survive his presence at the barbeque and he's a nice friend. So what if we don't have sex? I don't have sex with anyone!

Mum and Dad look ready for a long bath, a hot meal and a lie down.

'Dad's hip is giving him gip,' Mum says. 'All that sitting and driving. Honestly this nomading is tiring.'

'You're a nomad?' I ask, as she starts Leo's washing machine.

'That's what your father calls us. I'm glad it's only part-time.' Mum always adds the detergent and waits for it to get sudsy before adding the clothes. She inspects Leo's machine as part of her quality control regime.

'Do you like the campervan?'

'Oh, it's fine.' Mum adds the clothes. 'It's your father's passion, he's a bit obsessed with it, you know.'

'More or less than the garden?'

Mum considers this for a moment. 'Slightly less but he's enjoying the infatuation.'

Infatuation is a very provocative word for my mother to utter. Must be all those hours on the road.

'And what about you, dear, have things calmed down?'

'Kind of, they're . . . evolving.'

'I see.' She hesitates, looking unconvinced. 'Any chance the network might take you back? I wondered, because of Fergus being here.'

'None. Fergus is here as my friend, and he's helping me with my . . . relations project.'

Mum refocuses on the laundry, it's easier than showing me her disappointment, I guess.

'Yes, I heard about it.' Of course her hand travels to her forehead. 'Oh I do hope that new shirt of Dad's doesn't run. It says it's colour safe, but really you can never be sure.'

And that concludes mother–daughter intimacy chat number two, though I am sure the coming days will hold more questions and dashed hopes (hers) about Dave and my fallen future.

How is it mothers make you want to stamp and scream, 'I am actually valid, I am doing okay, for a pariah' and at the same time have you longing for them to validate you without your needing them to?

Atticus texts he's out on a call and can't come to the barbeque. Hugo and Ricky arrive and take everything up a notch, or five. Suddenly the prawns are on skewers, the scallops are ceviched. The fish is garnished and wrapped in foil. Wine is opened and poured. They're just magic with their hosting skills. Mum and Dad watch on in wonder.

'I could use both of you at home,' Mum jokes, a rarity and a lovely surprise. Dad takes great pride in firing up the BBQ with Fergus and Finn assisting.

Darcy, Ace, Rose and Dylan rock up. Darcy has that glow again. She pulls me to the side as I'm setting the table.

'He texted not long after you left.' She speaks in an urgent whisper.

'That's good. What did he say?'

'That it was the best night of his life and he was sorry for the radio silence, and he couldn't wait to see me again and could he pick us all up and drive us to yours.'

I know there's more to come.

'And then what?'

'Then he rocked up after his camp of sixteen year olds left, before the kids' bus got back from school.'

'And?'

Darcy nods, smiles, shakes her head all at once, 'He and then I, we, totally mind-blowing . . .' She drifts off before adding, 'I have to get some more Ural!'

'Did you tell him how you're feeling?'

'That's the funny thing, he told me first, he's as shit scared as me that he's going to stuff up. So silly, huh? What's the deal with Fergus?'

I fill her in. She's excited about the music. She heads off to her Ural supply and I set the table.

It's one of those delightful nights that if planned would never be quite so special. We eat and drink and laugh. The kids swim in the pool and run around with Magnus. I look to Finn and he has his carefree smile back once more. What a relief. He tells me Daisy texted to say she landed, she's going to facetime him tomorrow but called him an idiot for worrying and is into a girl she met on the plane.

'Do you think that's real or she's saying that to make you feel better?'

'Both,' he concedes. 'I'm just glad we're still mates. Oh and who is the girl in all the pictures?' He indicates some framed photos Leo has in pride of place as a feature wall.

'That's Leo's daughter, Amy.'

Finn nods and grins. 'She's pretty.'

'She is and too old for you.'

'No one's too old for anyone, haven't you figured that out yet?' He teases.

'Yes, but not for you.' I pause. 'There's one thing I do think I've learned lately,' I venture.

Finn waits for it, sensing a lecture.

'Talking about it is better than not talking about it.'

He smiles his beautiful smile and nods then heads back to the pool and bombs the kids and splashes the adults.

27

MY NEW 'CREW' AND I ORGANISE TO MEET IN THE MORNING FOR A production meeting before we film the next fantasy.

As I'm getting into bed there's a text from Leo, checking in to make sure Magnus is taking care of me and there's been no further crazy lady sightings. He's heading back to Melbourne then Sydney. The man can travel.

I call him and tell him about the workout his house is getting.

'Dad says the BBQ is like brand new.'

He laughs. 'That's because it is. I haven't been there long enough to fire it up. Is it okay?'

'The Bentley of BBQs apparently.'

'Sounds like you've got a great team around you.'

'I'm lucky to have them,' I say. 'Even my stitched-up parents. Dad asked what you do and Finn said you work in the women's fitness industry.'

Leo cracks up at that. 'Well, it's not a lie. And the fact you're the common thread with them all, the linchpin, indicates to me they feel just as lucky to have you as you do to have them.'

'Maybe you'll meet them one day.'

'I'd like that.'

There's that feeling again I have with him, of relief. I start yawning.

'Oh here we go,' he says. 'The countdown till I send you snoring.'

'I don't snore, thanks very much.' I know full well I am prone to the odd wheeze and groan.

'Magnus told me that you do. Before you go, I've forwarded your clips to one of my colleagues.'

'Oh no, Leo, I don't want to make porno films.'

He laughs more. 'Not for that, but like I keep saying, you've got such a strong voice. It deserves a broader audience.'

'Who?'

'Let's just see if they respond. Trust me?'

'I'm sleeping in your bed, so yes I trust you.' I rub my eyes. 'What is it up here that makes me sleep so well?'

'Maybe you're unwinding or maybe it's the oxygen I had imported, it's the Bentley of oxygens.'

I fall asleep running through the day, glad Magnus is on the floor beside me. Finn is slumbering safe and sound in the room next door and I'm even glad Mum and Dad are in their little campervan out the front. Dad's already set it up like a campsite, putting the awning and the deckchairs out.

28

DISPATCH FROM THE INTERIOR

From: Carol Hughes
To: Olivia Law
Subject: Grand Designs
Date: 20 August at 7.29pm

I've long been an admirer of *Grand Designs* and its host.
And although it's a successful franchise, it's Kevin whom I
like best. Kevin and his deep voice, his penetrating stare, his
gentle flirtation and superior knowledge of construction.

I imagine he comes to our house, we've just finished a major
renovation, the road to its completion has been treacherous,
filled with young upstarts who won't listen to me, and my
husband Greg is the worse for wear. He's been up all night

putting the finishing touches on the 120-year-old shutters that face the sea. Everything has been immaculately repaired.

I've sanded and scrubbed, I've painted and polished, I've paved.

Kevin turns up in his breezy way.

'What have we here, Carol?' he asks.

His camera team follow him around as he marvels at our renovation: the skylights, the repolished walnut floors, the atrium at the centre of our abode, the exterior panelling that offers a scale and a look sympathetic to its environment and respectful of its past but located with confidence towards a bright future.

Then he walks up the narrow stairs, which we've made a feature with art lining the walls, to my 'retreat'.

'Oh Carol,' he whispers as the cameras go into a close-up. 'I didn't think you had it in you, but this is really something.'

'Isn't it,' I say as I lean against the banister. He places his arms either side of me, his strong hands clutching and brushing against my hips.

'Tell me what you used.'

'An all-natural veneer, Kevin,' I whisper.

He turns and faces me, the crew continue filming.

241

'But before that, you sanded it right back.' He moves one of his hands under my dress and brushes it up my thigh.

'Yes, I sanded it back, just like that.'

'And what was underneath?' He asks as my hand goes to his jeans.

'An antique intricate design from around the seventeenth century,' I say as he sighs.

'And what did you do with it, Carol?'

'I treated it with painstaking care, Kevin.' The boom operator lifts his microphone to capture my sigh.

'Cleaned it and oiled it, rubbed it all the way down.'

He begins to move inside me.

'And then came the varnish, Carol?'

'Yes, Kevin, then came the varnish.'

He gets faster.

'How many coats, Carol?'

'Seven, Kevin, one after the other. I coated it, thicker and thicker . . .'

Faster still.

'Until I reached a full gloss that reached my – ahhh.'

We come at the same time as I say, 'Satisfaction.'

'You're a marvel, Carol.' Kevin looks to me then the camera.

'I am, thank you, Kevin.'

'Greg must be so proud.'

'Oh he is, he is.' And as I say this Greg stands with the crew, smiling.

'It's a secret gem, this tiny unassuming south coast house is nothing short of magic thanks to its loving restorers, Greg and Carol,' Kevin says as we all smile and wave to camera.

29

IT'S EARLY MORNING. I AWAKE AS THE FIRST LIGHT TOUCHES THE NEW day. Magnus is still asleep but as soon as I get up to creep to the loo he's by my side. So I throw my dressing-gown and slippers on and head out quietly. Magnus and I do a walk around the property, taking in the startling beauty of the new day as the sun climbs up over the stretch of blue ocean in the distance. Birds start their morning song. All is well.

Except, as we creep past the campervan, there's something odd, something . . . it's rocking, gently. At first I fear it's about to fall down the hill and I make to yell out. I stop myself as I realise the swaying is steady and rhythmical. I rush inside, grab my phone and call Ava.

'Ava, the campervan's moving. It's swaying. I think Mum and Dad might be, could be having relations?' I stutter, stupefied.

'Of course they are,' Ava replies. 'They're always doing it.'

'What? No they're not.'

'Yes, Olivia Evelyn Law, they are. They have sex all the time, you just never realised.'

'But no, they were always so uptight about it.'

'Just because they didn't like talking to us about it doesn't mean they didn't like doing it, a lot.' I can hear her munching on toast while she talks.

'How much?'

'Usually three times a week.'

My mind is exploding. 'But how?'

'You know how, you're making a career out of how, and Darren and I just made the best new film, we're really hitting our stride.'

'Ava, how did you know this and I didn't?' I stammer.

'Because you were too little when I realised and my room was closer to theirs than yours.'

'Why didn't you tell me?' I'm completely incredulous as I head for the coffee machine.

'I wasn't going to talk to my little sister about our parents' relations.'

And then it hits me.

'The dishwasher.'

'Exactly,' Ava chirps.

When I was six, before the evils of *The Blue Lagoon* incident, my parents got a new dishwasher. It was around the same time *Close Encounters of the Third Kind* was released, which of course neither Ava nor I saw, but we were both consumed with thoughts of UFOs, the possibility of alien invasion and the potential to be zapped up at any time.

Late one night I heard a low rumbling noise. I saw a red light dancing in my bedroom and I was convinced I was about to be taken. Panicking, I tiptoed to Ava's room and woke her. She followed me out to the hall to see the red light. Ava informed me it was the new dishwasher and went back to bed. I followed her. From then on whenever I heard the rumble I knew Mum had a load of dishes on. Sometimes the dishwasher went for a long time. Sometimes she put it on in the middle of the night.

'Oh my god, they were having sex!' I'm stunned.

'Totally, they're like rabbits. Where do you think I get it from?'

I hang up and wander back out into the yard, stunned. There, shining brightly in the morning sun, rocks the little campervan that could. The very fabric of my existence is forever altered. My stitched-up, prude parents are love gods.

Later that morning, following a breakfast where Mum and Dad repeatedly ask me what it is I'm thinking as I stare at them, stunned, attempting to come to terms with their new identities, Finn calls out to me, 'Dad needs to talk to you.'

I catch the exchange between my parents. 'Not going to happen,' I say as I head into Finn's room where he's Skyping with Dave on his laptop.

'Hey,' Dave says in the way he does when he's trying to sound casual but really it's official.

'Hey.'

'There's a buyer for the house.'

There's a pause as he rallies himself. I help him out with it.

'It's you, isn't it? You and Bridie.'

Dave nods.

'It will be easier for Finn,' I say.

'Yeah. Bridie really likes the house, which surprises me, because I'm not sure I do.'

'Maybe it just needs to be lived in a bit more,' I offer. 'You and I seldom seemed to get around to doing that.'

'I know.'

'Would have been nice to hear from you about your sudden, impending marriage. Is she pregnant?' May as well get the whole damn thing in the open.

'Not yet, but we're actively trying.'

That sounds medical. Dave is trying to have a baby with someone else.

'I didn't think you wanted more?'

'I wasn't worried about it, and when it didn't happen with you and you weren't fazed, I felt Finn was enough. And he is. But Bridie wants her own child.'

'As long as you remember Finn is like my own child.'

'I know that.'

'Is this what you really want, Dave?'

'It is. I've never felt like this about anyone before. And I don't mean that to sound harsh.'

'It does, but I'll live.'

'Sorry, how're you going?'

Why is it now, now that we're getting divorced that we're finally asking each other how we are and listening to the answer?

'I'm okay. Offer me a decent price for my share and we'll go from there. I'll have my things moved out. And I'd like to keep the car.'

Dave nods, he looks sad. Sad and relieved. I get off the call and wander to my bedroom, sit on the bed and cry. Magnus is by my side in an instant.

'No man, no house and no job, Magnus. Let's go read a fantasy.' Magnus wags his tail wisely, looks up adoringly and escorts me out.

Ricky and Hugo arrive full of art supplies and excitement, Fergus turns up with his whiteboard – he loves his portable whiteboard – and coloured pens to plot out sound and lighting cues.

'So professional!' Ricky whispers. 'He's really *that* guy.'

I nod and Fergus laps up the attention. I'm instructing Mum, Dad and Finn on shopping lists and places of interest. Finn is being a good sport about having a day with 'The Olds' who, I must say, are both springing about extolling the virtues of the campervan mattress. Them saying they've had a good night's sleep will never sound the same to me again. I've booked Finn into a day of flying foxes and rumbles tomorrow and Dad has been invited to join in as a male elder, so it's just the one day Finn has to hang with his grandparents, though he's in good spirits and I know they'll spoil him rotten as they drive around. I lend them my car and they head off as Darcy arrives at the gate.

'Sorry, had to get the kids to see their friends.' Her hair is pretty much standing on end again, I've never seen her look so luminous.

'And then I popped into Ace's. I can barely walk,' she says as she gets out of the car.

Fergus walks out of the garage and taps his watch. 'If you want to release one of these a day for the next week we need to get a move on.'

Darcy salutes him. 'Roger that!'

I head into 'hair and makeup', aka Ricky residing over my makeup case. I choose a different blazer for each clip, shake my hair out and head back in to the action.

Fergus is behind the camera, barking orders. Hugo and Darcy are on lights. Ricky performs last-minute checks as Fergus cues Hannah on the cello.

'Action!'

We tape five fantasies – *Ants, The Choir, Grand Designs, Highwayman* and *Huge and Swinging* – so they're ready to upload. Each one has its own colour and feel. Fergus cleverly manages to make sure I'm not backlit and even adjusts a few standing lamps to create different moods for each fantasy. He calls out for me to be bolder, to let go, to fly. Hannah makes adjustments as she plays our theme song and provides a few music cues through the fantasies.

Ricky fixes us lunch as Fergus reads us the riot act between clips. The man was born to produce. The others leave as he and

I go over the clips again and he tidies them up on his computer. We don't finish till nearly seven that night.

It reminds me of when Fergus and I first began working together in our twenties: getting out in the field, recording a story, working it through and editing it together before it went to air. Arguing over everything and loving every minute.

'You're not going to put Huge and Swinging out before something girly,' he declares. 'It has to keep building so each fantasy has you getting hotter and hotter till you're climbing the table to fuck each other's brains out.'

Of course this is the moment Mum enters with a tray of chicken sandwiches. 'Thought you could do with a snack,' she says quietly and backs out as fast as she can.

'Sorry, Mrs Law,' Fergus calls as he gets stuck into a sandwich, talking as he does, spilling pieces of chicken breast on his lap.

By eight o'clock we're ready to send the ants marching out into the stratosphere.

'Ready?' he asks.

Karen calls at that exact moment.

'The network are offering to drop the lawsuit and reinstate your super providing you make no public or cyber appearances of any kind for the next two years.'

I look at my frozen image on the screen. I think of the women who have shared their fantasies with me. And then I think of the house and the fiscal reality of losing all my super. What if this is their best offer?

'This may be their best offer,' Karen says.

'Give me five and I'll call you back.'

'You have two, I need to let them know.'

I hang up and tell Fergus what I've just been offered. He considers it.

'Well, I don't fucking know, what do you want to do?'

'I want to do this, but I'm scared. What if I end up with nothing?'

'Fuck that, look around you, you have family, you have mates. You have me and Hannah. I'm no friggin' Buddhist but I know doing something because you're scared ends you up in the shit.'

Magnus enters, tail wagging, ready for a walk. I close my eyes for a moment and make a decision.

I call Karen back.

'Tell them no thanks. I'm not interested in being silenced by them at any price.'

'Good choice,' she says. 'Things are just getting interesting.'

I hang up.

'Ready?' Fergus asks.

'I am.'

'Well you press the fucking button then, I'm not even meant to be here, this is your gig, Olivia Law at large.' He winks.

I press send and we high-five like teenagers.

30

watch TV with Mum, Dad and Finn, there's nearly a hundred thousand hits on the ant clip.

'It's because they've subscribed to you,' Finn explains.

Fergus calls me. He's on fire.

'You know what we need next? A fucking spinoff app, that's where the money is. Know anyone good with IT who won't fuck you over?'

'I do.'

Mum and Dad pass a tin of Roses chocolates around as we settle into watch *Die Hard*, Finn's choice – with quite a bit of encouragement from Dad. Again I'm struck by how happy I feel. No huge bells and whistles, just my family around me, Ugg boots on my feet, hazelnut whirl in my mouth and 100,000 hits on my YouTube clip!

A soft whirring sound pulls my attention away from Bruce Willis. I look to Finn who, unperturbed, shrugs. My eyes then travel to my parents, nestled in the expanse of the oversized leather sofa together, and I see it. Mum has one of Leo's vibrators placed on Dad's hip.

Dad smiles up at me, pleased with his world. 'Your mum found your friend's sports equipment in the linen cupboard. It's a miracle worker.'

'Dad's hip was giving him gip,' Mum adds, though avoids eye contact. She would have seen the packaging, she knows very well what the Ultra-massage Deluxe is more commonly used for. I draw my head back to the TV screen.

How funny that I've grown up considering my parents one way, basing a lot of my assumptions about them, Ava and myself on it, only to find nothing is as it seems and a shift in my 'history' necessitates a shift in my perception. Perhaps, like Ava, I'm more like my mum than I ever thought possible.

Mum discovers the speed dial on the vibrator and turns it up. I swallow hard and head to bed.

Leo is amused to say the least when I call him for the nightly round up of the day. I tell him about the network's offer I declined.

'They're going to have to do a lot better than that. It's over one million views and some pretty heated comments. Kingdom of Come wants to sponsor you.'

'You want to sponsor me?'

'Obviously *I* do, but it makes sense for my business, and there's a significant crossover in our markets.'

'I have a market?'

'Hell, yeah. Let's meet up when you're back in town, my lawyers are drawing up an offer. Think you'll like it. Run it past your dragon lady. Wait, why aren't you yawning?'

'Because I can't get the image of your vibrator on my father's hip out of my head.'

He laughs. 'Fair enough, would you like another image?'

'Don't go weird on me.'

He chuckles. 'Not one of those images, you take the lead there. But think of the woman who wrote that ant fantasy, she must be feeling pretty chuffed.'

'You think?'

'I do. And this is just the beginning, Olivia. What if *this* is the best time in your life? It never would have happened without Dave leaving.'

I tell Leo about the buyout from Dave.

'Tough, but sounds like you've made the right decision for you and Finn. You can always stay at my place; the garage door has been replaced. It's Margueritte proof.'

'Thanks, I'll have to start looking for an apartment of my own.'

'You want to stay in Sydney?'

'Where else would I go?'

'You can go anywhere. Do anything.'

I like that idea so much I yawn.

'And it's goodnight, Olivia,' he says softly as he hangs up the phone.

The next morning is a hub of activity at the house as Dad and Finn set off for their boys to men workshop with Dr Ace, and Mum, Darcy and I drive up the coast for Stella Supera's women in leadership luncheon on the Gold Coast.

The luncheon is held at the Versace Hotel. Mum's eyes bulge a little as she looks around at all the gilding.

'Oh my,' she says.

We're clearly not in Byron anymore. It's a bit of Beverly Hills on the Gold Coast – the huge tiled foyer, the endless pools with cabanas, the enjoyment of its own opulence.

Many ladies who lunch are assembled. As I enter, passing a woman in a Gucci ensemble with matching sunglasses and lapdog in a handbag, the feeling strikes me that this is exactly the sort of event Margueritte would attend.

I scan the room, no sign of her amidst the indoor palm trees and the three-tier china platters covered with crustless sand-wiches. Teacups are daintily held and the odd vodka tonic discreetly consumed.

What the hell am I doing here? I feel like an alien, even though just a few weeks ago I was as smooth as the calfskin leather gracing the backs of our padded seats.

'Olivia, baby.' Stella calls me over and embraces me whole-heartedly. Stella is a supreme being. A woman of integrity, style and huge reserves of gracious grit. If it wasn't for her, my name would still be on the banned list. What did she do to sway the board that I'm worthy of addressing them?

'Thank god we got you. The afternoon was going to be a long snore otherwise. And the ants, oh my god, the ants. Love, love, *love* them.'

She says this as she kisses and hugs Mum and Darcy.

'You've seen them too right, Mrs Law?' Stella asks sweetly.

'Oh um, no . . .' Mum stutters, her eyes beginning to blink.

Stella links her arm. 'Well you must, it's an eye-opener that's for sure. Your daughter is really shaking things up. Thank god. It's well over due. I mean I did my part in the '70's but somehow, between porn and this obsession with selfies, things have gotten out of hand. What Olivia is doing for women in the media, and women as a whole, is nothing shy of groundbreaking.'

'Oh,' Mum says thinly. 'That's nice.'

Stella is on a roll. Darcy nabs a passing finger sandwich. I continue to scour the room for mad women with lapdogs.

'It's not nice, and that's the point. It's raw, it's real, its –' Stella turns to me. 'Do you know which one I wrote?' She grins devilishly. 'Have a guess.'

I pause, mentally scanning through the long list of fantasies. 'Not the scuba diving one? I know you and Mr Supera –'

'No, no, no,' then she studies me closely and whispers in my ear, 'Four corners.'

My mouth drops open. 'Really?'

Stella winks then claps her hands. 'Okay, Olivia, I'm going to introduce you. It's just ten to fifteen minutes followed by questions, which I'm sure there will be plenty of.'

'I'm not overly prepared,' I confess. I scrawled some rough notes when I woke up this morning but that's it.

'Thank god for that. Speak from your heart, baby cakes. I'm so proud of you. You are too, aren't you, Mrs Law?'

Mum blushes and then, to my astonishment, says, 'I am, yes.' She raises her eyes shyly to meet mine. We exchange a smile and, for possibly the first time, I see a woman, Gillian, not Mum standing before me. I'm filled with admiration for her. Suddenly I couldn't give a hoot who else is in the room or whether they will applaud me or stone me to death. Mum and I are, for this fleeting moment, on the same page.

Mum, Darcy and I take our seats. There's a few murmurs and whispers, though they are possibly for Darcy's stunning kaftan, worn with her red locks wildly peeping through a turban of matching silk. Mum has her 'good' outfit on, she loves a pantsuit, this one is navy blue with gold buttons which she and Dad consider slightly bold but still smart. I've opted for a turtleneck houndstooth check Burberry woollen dress with high boots.

Stella takes the stage with her usual aplomb, she sports black leather pants, highlighting her fabulous shape, and a colourful kaftan top, compliments of Darcy's last season. She looks superb. Her presence quietens everyone and there's a hushed reverence.

Stella talks about the board and their work and today's topic, women, self-respect and the media. I look around the room. The women are aged mainly between their thirties and seventies.

Stella talks about change and paradigm shifts and the fact females over fifty-five are the most underutilised of talents and consumers. Not only do these women have unprecedented pulling power via their united economic strength, they make up an increasingly large portion of the media market. And yet they're the least catered to. Why is that?

I feel like calling the network and putting them on speaker-phone so they can hear this. It's exactly what Leo, Karen and even Fergus have been trying to tell me. I look around, lights are switched on in women's eyes all over the room.

And then Stella introduces me. There's applause, mainly led by Darcy. There's quite a few women staring into their teacups searching for their destinies and a way to avoid me. Here we go, I think, life is just a series of jumping off cliffs these days, and none of them have been lethal falls yet.

'Thanks so much for inviting me here today,' I start. 'As you're all aware self-respect, sexuality and the media are pretty hot topics in my life right now. Topics I wouldn't necessarily have bundled together a few weeks ago. But life has changed radically since then and . . . I'm glad it has.'

There are a few awkward shuffles.

'Not that experiencing the humiliation of having your job axed so publicly, and being ridiculed so heavily, has been a field day, it hasn't, but it's taught me a lot. One thing I've learnt is that we are connected by our fantasies far more than we'd ever care to acknowledge publicly. I thought it was just me, and that was the message my former employers wanted me to believe. But the women who were brave enough to share their own longings with me have shown me that's not the case. Women's fantasies do not all revolve around flowers on Valentine's Day and men who wash up. In fact, a great number of them hardly relate to men at all.'

A few women nudge each other. A few blush and one or two smile up at me.

'They do have these common threads. All the women who have shared their fantasies with me felt safe and confident enough in themselves to do so. They also felt free enough to let their imaginations roam. They all felt worthy of their own pleasure rather than shamed by it. And they all felt chosen and desired, whether it was by the object of their affections or themselves. They felt valued enough to express themselves.'

A few heads begin to nod. Hooray they're not throwing things!

'The silence we've been complicit in till now is over. There is value in expressing yourself, and if we stop accepting less the media will adjust. There is value in supporting each other as we do this. After all, the media is a machine of our own making and we have a choice in how we interact with it. So no more silence about what works or doesn't work for you, that goes for the boardroom and the bedroom. No more silence. Be brave enough to speak up. No more silence unless it's in a pillow-biting enjoyable kind of way.'

I take a pause and sip my water. Darcy and Mum nod at me.

'To conclude, I want to read you one woman's offering. It's my favourite of all the fantasies I've received and it's what's giving me the inspiration to continue. Sex, as we all know, is so much more than sex. Your sexual identity is key to how you connect with the world. You are not invisible. It took me losing just about everything I had to realise that. Sexual identity isn't about how much sex you do or don't have, or with whom. What I am talking about is your sexual identity, which is an expression of your own self-love. What I've learnt, the hard way, is the sexiest thing you can be is yourself.'

I read them *Le Monde*.

31

DISPATCH FROM THE INTERIOR

From: Kate Caffrey
To: Olivia Law
Subject: Le Monde
Date: 20 August at 11.06pm

When you left, there was nothing of me remaining. You had
battered my heart so heavily, punctured my soul so deeply,
I had no breath, no tears and no hope. All I had been before
you was demolished. I was an unmapped island in an
unending ocean of pain.

But slowly, over time, a long time, little pieces of me began
to float back, the island of me began to expand. Trees were
planted, they grew and bore fruit. I began seeing a reflection

when I looked in the mirror. I started tasting food again, felt myself smile.

And then I got bigger still and what was an island grew into an entire continent.

I keep a globe, one of those lamps that's a globe of the world, on my bedside table. I look at it at the beginning and end of each new day. I trace the countries and now, when I touch myself, that's what I see – all the islands and continents over the globe growing and merging, the way it was when the world first created itself. There is no edge to my terrain, no limit, no passport needed to the inner recesses of me. I am a reunited world, a globe of hope, that's what I feel when my hands reclaim myself and I fly through the boundaries of my own skin.

32

TO MY AMAZEMENT, MUM IS CRYING BY THE END OF MY PRESENTATION and I receive a standing ovation. Even the lapdog ladies connect with something in what I've said. Stella pretty much bowls me over in her warm embrace and holds my hand up like I've just won a championship wrestling match.

Women's iPhones come out and they tap frantically into the Twitterverse.

We listen to the other two speakers as Darcy finishes off two platters of sandwiches and mini quiches almost singlehandedly. My mother leans over to me.

'I've never seen Darcy eat so much, she must be working very hard.'

'Oh she is, Mum,' I reply as Darcy tops a scone with jam and cream.

The speeches conclude. I'm greeted by a few of the women who till now have been busy avoiding my gaze and deleting my phone number. I'm amazed by the warmth and generosity of the women around me. The big freeze has thawed. One woman, Jana Patton, who sent me the email axing me from the board, whispers to me that she and her husband have been watching the revenge fantasy on high rotation, that it sparked a fight followed by a furious round of lovemaking, breaking the drought in her own secret garden.

'Olivia,' Stella calls out, 'there's another five boards who want you to talk at their events. And when will the next story be released?'

'Tonight,' I reply as we all grab our coats and make our way to the exit.

'Oh goody.'

The network have already heard all about the event. There's some local media out the front. Stella hugs me close again and presents me with a huge bouquet of orchids.

'I thought they looked the most appropriate,' she whispers.

Darcy chortles. 'Right on, Mrs Supera.'

Stella ensures we will all be at the opening of Hugo and Ricky's stage one home and spa.

'I'm throwing them a huge party,' she bubbles.

'Wouldn't miss it for the world,' I assure her. 'And Stella, thank you. You've put me back on the map.'

Stella shakes her head. 'No, baby, you've done that by yourself, and you've taken us all to new terrain.'

I answer a few young journalists' questions out the front as we await the valet bringing the car. Mum falls asleep on the drive home, her head rolling around blissfully as we pass down the hills through to the river at Brunswick Heads.

By the time I drop Darcy off and we drive through the front gate I'm ready for a hot bath and an early night. I have a few hours of messages and emails to get through. It feels like the tide is turning, I can't wait to tell Leo.

All that changes when Finn runs up to meet the car, his face ashen.

'It's Magnus,' he stammers. 'He's collapsed.'

33

I JUMP OUT OF THE CAR AND FOLLOW FINN TO WHERE MAGNUS LIES at the base of the jasmine bushes.

'When?' I gasp.

'About a minute ago. He was fine when we got home, Ace gave Grandad some natives and we were planting them and I was throwing Magnus the ball.' Finn chokes on some tears. 'Is it my fault?'

'No, darling. Did you see anything around?' Finn shakes his head.

I lean over Magnus, his eyes are glazed, his breathing is shallow.

Dad and Finn help me scoop up his enormous frame and get him in the car. I call Atticus.

'Stay calm, I'll be waiting here,' he says.

A drive that should take twenty minutes takes ten. Dad says nothing but follows the sat nav directions to Atticus's as I sit in the back with Magnus on my lap.

'Come on, boy, please don't go' is all I can say, over and over. I call Leo who hears the tone in my voice when he answers.

'Magnus' is all I can get out before a rush of tears follows. I manage to tell him we're heading to the vet but it's not good. Leo is at Melbourne airport about to head to Sydney but he hangs up to book the next flight to Byron.

Atticus stands outside his house, waiting. He rushes to the car, studies Magnus and performs a quick check of his limbs.

I'm silently convinced Margueritte's hand is at play; she's poisoned him while we're out. But then Atticus says the words, 'Snake bite.'

He has located a puncture mark on Magnus's rear leg.

'But it's too cold for snakes isn't it?'

'It's sunny, and the beginning of spring is when they're at their most lethal. If it's a brown snake, and mostly likely it is, I don't like our chances.'

Magnus begins convulsing as we carry him into his practice and Atticus swiftly injects him with the antivenene.

Please don't go, Magnus, please don't go.

'He's not in any more pain,' Atticus says quietly.

'How long till we know if he'll pull through?' Dad asks.

'If he makes it through the next hour, he should be okay, then we have to watch him for the next day. It depends how long he's had the venom in his system. It looks like a severe bite. I'm sorry, Olivia.' Atticus is clearly preparing me for the worst.

Dad squeezes my shoulder. 'Better brace yourself, love.'

I stand over Magnus, tears pouring down my face as I talk to him and call his name and will him to live. I think of his constant company recently, his unadulterated adoration, his ability to pull us all together, his ability to heal. I watch his breath rise and fall, willing it to continue as the minutes pass. I scratch his ears the way he loves.

'Hold on, Magnus, you have to stay.' Another minute. No one speaks. It feels like an eternity.

Atticus checks his pulse again.

'It's holding,' he says carefully. 'Let's wait.'

I hold my breath and Magnus's breath deepens. It's almost like a sigh. I'm terrified it's his last gasp but then Atticus strokes him and says, 'That's it, Magnus. Good boy.'

A slight wag from his tail arouses a cheer from us all. Atticus administers a drip to keep him hydrated. Magnus stabilises.

'He's going to be okay?' I'm scared to ask.

'We'll need to keep him still and keep him here overnight, but yes.'

'Oh my god. Thank you, thank you.' I hug Atticus who kisses the top of my head.

'Nice to see you've eased off the drama then,' he jokes. I introduce him to Dad, who I can see is impressed with him.

'Can I stay? Not with you, with Magnus?' I request.

'I don't usually let people do that, but for you I'll make an exception.' He smiles.

I send Dad home with the good news and call Leo, who must have found a fast flight because his phone is switched off. I text him so he can see the news the minute his phone is back on. Poor Leo, what a terrible feeling he'll be sitting with on his flight.

Atticus brews me a strange Chinese tea concoction which I do my best to drink.

He's amazing with Magnus.

'He's fought really hard to overcome the venom,' he explains. 'Even with the antivenene, it's knocked him around.'

'But he's going to live,' I reaffirm.

'He has no plan to leave you,' Atticus says soothingly, which makes me bawl again.

'Hey.' He holds me in his muscular life-saving arms.

'I think you've needed a big release like this for a while.'

I cry more, thinking it isn't the only release I need and that I've cried more in the past fortnight than ever before in my life. I just nod. It seems simpler.

Atticus plays some Tibetan chants and cooks dinner. While we're eating vegetable soup I hear a car pull into the drive. Leo jumps out and we usher him through to his dog.

He, too, burrows his head into Magnus's ample fur and begins to sob.

Atticus leaves us to it.

'I'm so sorry,' I say as Leo throws one arm around me and pulls me closer while continuing to sob.

'Not your fault, kid. He's definitely going to be okay?'

'Atticus thinks so, I'm going to sit with him tonight. I thought I'd gone from being a dog-minder to a dog murderer.'

Leo laughs through tears then asks, 'What's that smell?'

'It's Atticus's Chinese herb tea for shock, have some.'

Leo takes a sip. 'Oh god that's vile.'

'I know.' We both giggle as Atticus returns with mats and rugs.

'I bet he'd rather be next to you two than up on the examination table,' he says.

We gently lower Magnus onto an old yoga mat with a blanket over it on the ground. Magnus's eyes are no longer glazed and he opens them to lick his lips and our hands.

Leo and I start crying again. Magnus throws us a 'what are you carrying on about' look and falls back to sleep.

Atticus brings in more blankets and a few pillows and leaves us to perform his nightly meditation and prayer rituals.

'He's horribly handsome,' Leo says when Atticus has gone.

'Yeah, I guess he is. For a monk.' I suppress a smile. Funny how a few days can change your perception. What is it Ace called it? Projection. It's a relief that Atticus, though undoubtedly a superior being, is more human to me again.

Leo and I spend the night fussing over Magnus and talking about everything and nothing. Eventually my yawns begin.

'Ah I've been missing those.' Leo teases.

'You mean you're over chatting to me?'

'It'll take me a lifetime for that to happen but your eyes are starting to close.'

'No, they aren't,' I argue though they do feel heavy.

'It's a good look on you, very sexy.'

'Ha. You'll keep.'

Our hands meet over Magnus, we both hold on as I fall asleep.

34

I AWAKE A FEW HOURS LATER. ATTICUS IS CHECKING MAGNUS, LEO IS out cold. Magnus's tail is back to a full-scale wag. It's as though nothing happened.

'He's good to go,' Atticus tells me as Leo stirs. Atticus looks to Leo and back to me and smiles. 'You're very good dog parents,' he says as he begins folding blankets.

We wave him goodbye as we head to our cars. Magnus hops into my passenger seat, king of the world once more. I realise my parents, Finn and I are all still at Leo's house and should probably make our leave.

'Don't be ridiculous,' Leo says when I suggest it.

'There's no way Magnus will want you out of his sight. The house has six bedrooms. I think we can manage. Besides, I know exactly what I want us all to do today. Your parents included.'

Storm clouds brew as we head back to Moksha. Finn is beside himself to see Magnus.

Mum stifles a tear and says, 'Glad you're back, dear boy.'

Dad nods stoically but I can see he's relieved. You'd think Magnus was our dog and we'd had him for years, though I'm learning dogs have an uncanny ability to fast-track their way into your hearts and remain there forever.

I introduce Leo to Finn, Mum and Dad.

Mum does her raised eyebrow thing and her voice goes up an octave, which is as close as I've ever seen her get to flirting. Dad commends Leo for his excellent sporting equipment. Leo thanks him graciously. Leo asks Finn to help him build a fire then presents us with his proposal as rain begins to bucket down. I'm wondering if it will involve Fleetwood Mac and vodka, neither of which my parents like. So it's to my great surprise, and my parents' delight, that he utters the words, 'Trivial Pursuit tournament.'

It's a full day affair, interrupted only by Fergus and Hannah, who join us for a round and hear the tale of Magnus's survival. Leo leads the way in the kitchen with a roast lamb. Mum and he compare recipes for mint sauce.

It's like a rainy day when you're allowed to stay home from school. We all keep watch on Magnus, who is back to manipulating us for scraps and requesting belly rubs when he's not sprawling in front of the fire till he gets too hot.

I look around the table as Mum proudly adds a green science and nature piece to her pie.

And once again I marvel at life.

Leo insists that I stay in the master suite while he takes a room next to Finn's. I'm in bed when my phone rings. It's Leo down the hall.

'Yes?' I say, answering.

'Figured it wouldn't be right without a goodnight call. Magnus is on the bed but it won't last, he's eyeing the door, my bet is you'll wake up with him beside you.'

'I'm so glad he's okay.'

'He's not about to leave you anytime soon.'

I laugh. 'That's what Atticus said.'

'Well the hot vet with the bitter tea knows his stuff. Are you interested in him?'

'No,' I say honestly.

'Thanks for a really great day,' he says after a beat.

'Thank you too, though I know why you like Trivial Pursuit.'

He laughs. 'Yeah, games you win are always more fun.'

The following morning I wake up and, just as Leo predicted, Magnus is at my side. We have our walk together around the estate. I have to remember this feeling, I think to myself. It's as close to peace as I've ever come.

Darcy sends a text. *Taking a break from sex fog, let's all do a walk and picnic at Minyon Falls. Blue skies. PS I actually climbed a tree to send you this, that's love!*

I text back an affirmative.

Fergus and I make plans to film the next batch of fantasies

tomorrow. He has questions, requests and lists to Africa for world domination, which I figure can wait one more day.

My YouTube clips have had nearly five million views. There's an email from a pharmaceutical company wanting to set up a meeting about potential sponsorship.

There are also emails asking me back on several boards, a few dinner party invitations back in Sydney from people who would have crossed the street to avoid me a week ago. Three more invitations to talk at events. And an email from the CEO at a competitive network.

I'm beyond stunned.

I call Karen, who of course is already at work, and tell her.

'You're going to have to make some big decisions in the next week,' she announces before checking in on Finn and rushing me off the phone to go into a meeting.

Leo, it seems, is not an early riser. We're all showered and ready to go hiking at Minyon when he emerges, but he's on board once we feed him coffee and toast. We leave Magnus inside for the day, not taking any chances with the slithery neighbours.

We meet Darcy, Ace, Rose and Dylan in the picnic area. Ace is in his element in these situations, delegating, instructing, checking backpacks. You'd think we were walking a lot further than the nine kilometres there and back.

In complete contrast with the previous day, the sky is baby blue without a cloud. The falls and surrounding forest make up part of the Nightcap National Park, one of those places that offers ancient calm and clarity. The air is beyond pure. The falls are in full force and are majestic.

Darcy grabs my hand as we walk. 'What up with you and the porn hunk?'

'No, it's not like that, we're really good friends,' I tell her. 'He'd make a good friend with benefits,' she muses.

'He has a chequered past and there's the crazy lady.' I begin rolling off a list, which doesn't include impotency.

'That's all past, he's into you. Bout time you had actual good sex instead of just talking about it.'

'Oh sex goddess of Mullumbimby and the greater world, that's just the problem.'

Darcy looks blank.

'He's had some medical issues,' I say *issues*, indicating my privates, hoping to god no one else hears.

'Permanent?'

'I don't know. Maybe.'

Darcy considers then squeezes my hand. 'Where there's a will . . . Baby, if anyone knows that it's you.'

'Ha. How's Dr Rumble-a-lot?'

'He's great with my kids, great with me, a certified sex god and isn't sticking it in anywhere else.'

'Darcy, that's amazing!'

'I never, ever thought it would happen again after Pete, that I could ever . . .'

I watch her trail off as Ace animatedly discusses fauna with Dad.

'I could marry him.' She sighs, squeezes my hand, kisses it and keeps on walking.

These are words I never, ever thought I'd hear Darcy utter ever again. Her devastation was so great after Pete. My heart sings thinking of it.

'Don't be a sook,' she calls back to me and we skip across some rocks over the rushing rapids.

The walk is perfect, not too long and not too hard but enough to make you feel connected to life and pleased with your efforts.

We sit at a picnic area, chomping on sandwiches. Leo and Finn skim stones. Mum looks up happily at the grand old trees. There's a few ants heading for the sandwich crumbs on her lap.

'Mum, you're going to get stung,' I say as I flick them off her.

Mum shrugs, unconcerned. Dad bites into his apple.

'Funny, your mum's never been worried by insects. Especially ants, they don't bother her at all,' he says as he chomps.

I nod, then I stop. Darcy and I stare at each other wide-eyed.

'Ant lady,' we whisper. Mum turns her head to us, smiles imperceptibly and nods.

I choke on my sandwich and fall off the rock I'm perched on. What I thought of my life has just turned upside down again.

All I can do is laugh.

35

BY THE TIME WE GET HOME I'M ITCHING ALL OVER. I HAVE A RASH AND I'm flushed. I check for leeches. Nothing. Of course I race to conclusions that are gory and lethal. I grab Leo, who is dicing onions, prepping a curry for dinner.

'Can you check my scalp? I think I might be dying. If I go unconscious just remember I'm allergic to penicillin.' I am totally strung out.

'Got it. You feeling upstaged by Magnus?'

'I'm serious, this could be it. Or menopause has hit in one afternoon.'

'Should I check your scalp first?' He kids.

I nod.

'The light is better in your bedroom. Follow me please.' He takes my hand and leads me to my room. He switches on all the lights and rummages in the top drawer, bringing out a small torch.

'Party trick.' He grins.

'That's not a vibrator.'

'No, it's a torch. Trust me, I was a doctor.'

I sit on the edge of the bed as Leo takes my head in his hands and inspects every hair on my scalp.

'No ticks here,' he announces.

'Then it's a virus,' I conclude miserably.

'Hold on, we need a full inspection. Strip,' he says. He does his best to keep a straight face.

I open my mouth to speak, nothing comes out. I perform a goldfish gulp and look at him dumbly.

'They can get in anywhere but they prefer warm hairy places,' he says in his best doctor manner.

I can think of a warm hairy place alright . . . 'It wouldn't, would it?' I whisper.

'Only one way to find out.'

He closes the door. I disrobe.

'I'm here in a purely professional capacity but if I weren't I would say, "Outstanding".'

I can't say that doesn't help ease my self-consciousness.

He holds the torch and scans my body lightly.

'Anything?'

'Nope.'

'Now what?'

'It's probably going to be best if you lay back and put your legs in the air.'

'You're kidding.'

Leo bats his lashes. 'I never kid my patients.'

He stands over me smiling fully now, holding the torch, inspecting. 'Superb.'

'Leo!'

'And there it is. Hold on.' He runs to the bathroom, grabs a needle and tweezers and returns.

'Here we go. I have to get the whole thing.'

'Oh god.'

'Hold still.'

'Olivia, Olivia, are you in there?' I hear my father approach the bedroom.

'I have a tick, Dad, Leo's getting it out,' I say, panicking.

'Hold still,' Leo calls, his head hovering dangerously close to me, so much so I'm fighting a rather huge urge to pull it closer.

'Need a hand?' Dad calls out. 'I'm quite good at –'

'Eureka!' Leo stands back up as the doorknob turns; I sit up and wrap the bedspread over me, avoiding the sequel to my hand mirror horror by a nanosecond.

'He got it!' I call as Leo holds it up proudly.

'Well done, where was it?' Dad asks.

'Head,' Leo and I say in unison.

'They can be tricky.' Dad comes closer to have a look.

Oh god, he's the ant inspector!

I rush them both out and head for a soapy bath to recover.

•

The following morning Fergus is reading the riot act for the day's filming as Darcy, Hugo and Ricky and I take notes. Magnus watches on closely.

'So do we have all the lights we need for Road Assistance, Dental Emergency, Four Corners, Orchid Show and Homecoming?'

His phone rings.

'Fuck it, hold on.' He walks out of the room.

'These just keep getting better!' Hugo says, looking over a fantasy. 'Just think, none of this would have happened if your love letter hadn't gone rogue.'

'True, perhaps I should be thanking the hacker,' I muse as Fergus re-enters.

'Then you'll be thanking the network,' Fergus announces.

'Sorry?'

'That was Harriet. One of the harassment claims was against one of the IT guys, he spilled the beans. The board were the ones who instigated it.'

'Why?' Darcy is incredulous. But to me it makes sense.

'I'm over forty-five and the ratings for my show were sliding. They needed a way to break my contract that made them look good.'

Fergus nods in confirmation.

'Well that certainly backfired.' Ricky's eyes widen.

'They would have been watching, waiting for some kind of stuff-up they could use against you. A video of you drunk and pining for Dave was like a treasure trove dropped into their laps.' Fergus continues, 'I feel like a goose.'

'What happens now?' I ask.

'You'd better call your lawyer. They'll be attempting to shut it down. The entire board may be sacked.'

'Promise?'

Fergus shrugs. 'Well I'm not fucking working with them if you're not there. Decide what you want and I'll back you. I'll come with you if you can pay me. You're getting more viewers on each of your clips than they have. You've got bargaining power, toots.'

'Promise?' I say again.

Fergus nods, he's emotional but keeping a lid on it.

'Five minutes then we start filming. Get a move on,' he barks.

I run outside to Leo and Finn, who are involved in a rumbling match, with Ace umpiring.

'Can't you guys just play frisbee?' I say then grab Leo and tell him the news.

'Quick, call Karen,' he says. 'Now you can play hardball.'

I do just that. The mirth in Karen's voice is palpable.

'No wonder they dropped the lawsuit.' She laughs. 'So what do you want?'

'An apology for starters.'

'That might be hard. What about your old job?'

'Not without an apology, equal pay and Fergus.'

I tell her about the other station's email. There's also been one from a friend of Leo's at a cable network. I pass on the details.

'Leave it with me,' she says. 'But you and Finn should get your arses back down here pronto.'

I head back into our 'studio', my head in a whirl, though one thing is clear – right now there's no place I'd rather be.

36

THE FOLLOWING DAY WE ALL HEAD OFF. MUM AND DAD IN THE campervan of rocking glory headed north. Finn and I on a flight. Leo decides he'll stay in Byron with Magnus for a few extra days. The thought of not having Magnus by my side saddens me. The thought of being separated from Leo provokes the same emotion.

Leo has offered me use of his Sydney house or the Byron one and I know I can go home to Mum and Dad if I need to, though I could only do that for a week at most. I'm going to have to decide where I want to live and find an apartment or something. But first I need a job.

Karen accompanies me to all my meetings. The network have agreed to reinstate me in my old job on my old wage, but they won't make a public apology or take ownership over their role in the debacle, and the board will remain as is.

'We'll pretend it never happened,' Len says carefully when he and the three lawyers meet us in Karen's office. He looks like he's been through the mill. Pretending it never happened would certainly allow him to stay in his position a bit longer, though according to Fergus the Death Star is hurtling towards his contract. 'She'll think about it,' Karen announces, 'provided she's paid equal to the other prime time newsreaders.' Len and the lawyers leave looking sombre.

I cannot for the life of me ever imagine walking into that place again. I couldn't be who I was before this all happened, even if I wanted to be. And the truth is, I don't want to be that woman anymore. I want to have more control over what I do and who I do it with, and over what I wear and how I look.

The other network offer me equal pay and a lot of support. I can either be on prime time and let go of my YouTube offerings or go late night and keep them, though there will be a series of conditions. I can't say the money and the security aren't very tempting but, in terms of my Goldilocks situation, it's still not the right chair.

I re-enter my house. It's like I never left because it's like I never lived there in the first place.

I grab some cases, pack my favourite clothes and cosmetics. My favourite photos. Finn is with Karen and Matteo having pizza. Dave is back in Hong Kong with Bridie. It's just me. I miss Magnus's constant nudge at my leg, his look of hope whenever I approach the fridge.

I wonder if Leo would consider a dog-share situation. Could Leo and I be housemates perhaps? But when he got the tick out I was just inches away from jumping him. Erection or not, he turns me on. But what will sex be like? And isn't that what got me into this situation with Dave in the first place? I think again of what Dave said at dinner that night. That I never talk. And what Leo said, that it wasn't about peeing in front of him, it's about intimacy.

I think of what Leo and I have shared in our short time of being friends. I think how fully myself I feel with him, how he makes me feel like I belong. Is that intimacy or lack of boundaries? I pack another case and ponder.

'So two down one to go?' Leo says about the meetings later on the phone. 'Can I ask you a question?'

I'm lying on the bed with cases all around.

'Shoot.'

'What do you want? What makes you happiest?'

'Making clips in your garage,' I say, laughing.

'Well, you have your answer. Whatever you agree to do, you need to keep that feeling.'

'How come you're so wise?'

'Not sure it's wisdom or just spending so much of my life stuffing up and wanting to stop stuffing up. Magnus misses you by the way. He's sulking.'

'The feeling's mutual. I miss being there.'

'I miss you. You've grown on me,' Leo says.

'What, like mould?' I tease.

'Exactly, a good one. You yawning yet?'

I stifle a yawn. 'No.'

'I could talk to you till sunrise if you like. Tell you about our new range of vibrators, I've already organised to have one sent to your dad.'

I laugh and yawn.

'Break legs tomorrow, Liv, and go stay at my house. The car's there too. I think we should swap. I like yours better than mine.'

'You want me to drive your Bentley, that's funny.'

We chat a bit more before I realise my eyes have closed and we're no longer on the line.

I fall asleep and dream I'm swimming in a waterhole. It's clear. I can see the glass bottom of a boat that I know I'll be boarding when I come up for air.

37

CAFFEINATED AND COLLECTED BY KAREN, DRESSED IN HER MOST superb Givenchy pinstripe woollen suit with a sexy black silk blouse and patent red stilettos, I sit in the car wearing my favourite red and black Chanel suit.

'The woman means business.' Karen looks me up and down.

Fergus meets us as we head into the pharmaceutical meeting. They want to sponsor us for huge pots of money in exchange for advertising female Viagra. I'm prepared for the meeting. Leo and I have talked at length. I know it's not what I want by the time we exit.

'Three down and still no cigar,' Karen says as we stop for lunch.

Darcy facetimes. 'I can't talk but I said yes to Bergdorf Goodman on the proviso they sponsor you. They will and so will their parent company. Come back and live up here and make your clips!'

I'm thrilled, mostly for Darcy, I know her range will explode and she'll keep a careful eye over it.

'Well, toots, is that what you want? We make your pics in Leo's shed . . . you know there's only so far we can go with that.'

'I know.'

Which is why, by the time I exit my meeting with the cable network I'm officially elated. Full control over content and presentation of a current affairs talk show and majority ownership and final say over Come As You Are, which will be distributed globally. Also majority ownership over the Come As You Are app.

'Bingo,' I say as we exit.

'With a cherry on fucking top.' Fergus has a satisfied grin, which makes me instantly suspicious.

'What have you done?'

'There's been a leak. Fuck knows how. The network have been outed for hacking you and setting you up. The board's being assembled now. They're all going to be fired.'

'How did the leak happen?'

Fergus and Karen exchange a look, shrug and keep walking.

I call Finn and Darcy, Mum and Dad, Hugo and Ricky. I pick up a few bags and get Karen to drive me to the airport.

There's two faces I need to see and one has fur.

38

I PRETTY MUCH LEAP OFF THE PLANE. LEO HAS MANAGED TO BRING Magnus into the terminal under the guise of being a 'therapy dog'.

I see them both and increase my pace. I don't care if it's unconventional, I don't care if it's unorthodox, I don't care if it only lasts a week. He's the person I want to share this moment, and myself, with.

Magnus beats Leo to the first embrace, jumping up and licking my face. Leo beams.

'We're both so happy for you,' he calls.

I take him in, think, *this is it, this is home*, and I grab him and kiss him for all I'm worth.

I pull back very quickly.

'What's that?' I say, pointing to his crotch.

'Well it's not a banana, kid.'

'But how? But you, but no . . . but how?' I marvel.

He laughs and kisses me again.

'It happened not long after I met you. Feel free to take the credit. I always thought it was purely physical. My therapist didn't. I think I was paying penance for my youth after the cancer, and I never wanted to go back to how I was. So I got good at punishing myself, and then got involved with Margueritte and got more fucked up. When you came, I felt something that I hadn't felt in a long time.'

'Clearly,' I say, my eyes wide.

'Not that.' He laughs. 'I haven't loved anyone other than my daughter and my dog for a long time, then came you and all those things I'd given up on. I want them with you.'

We head home and demolish each other in a way that will provide me with fantasy material for the rest of my life.

And the best thing?

It happens all over again the next morning. We barely leave the house for days. We talk and talk, we kiss for hours, we walk Magnus. Whatever else happens in my life I'll always be grateful that I have had this.

It took till I was forty-five, it took mass humiliation, slandering and a slobbering French mastiff hound. And it's been completely worth it.

39

DISPATCH FROM THE INTERIOR

From: Olivia Law

To: Leo Montgomery

Subject: Love

29 September at 10.55pm

It's the way you touch my hair.

Pat my tush.

Place your thumb lightly on the arch of my back.

Hold out the chair.

Grab me as I'm falling out of my heels.

Replace a fallen strap.

Laugh at my jokes.

Pick croissant crumbs from the side of my mouth.

It's the way your mouth moves when you speak my name.

Or say 'Jerusalem artichoke hearts'.

It's the way you always forget your keys and place your hand over mine to announce we're locked out.

And we wind up fucking in the backyard waiting for the locksmith to come.

You taunting me that he's pulling up and watching as I ride you.

Racing me to the finish line.

You drive me nuts.

And I couldn't be happier.

40

TWO MONTHS LATER, LEO AND I ARE WALKING UP THE STAIRS OF HUGO and Ricky's ultimate gay spa, part one. Finn, and of course Magnus, are by our side. The farmhouse now looks palatial.

Stella Supera calls out. 'Olivia, we all watched your show last night. Well done, and that train fantasy, hold me down and tie me up, John!'

John, Stella's husband, lifts his glass to toast me. He looks spent but happy.

Hugo and Ricky are on their most magnificent hosting form, both wearing white tuxes. Spring has taken hold and I'm wearing the Olivia kaftan.

Ace is manning the fire. I leave Leo with him and go in search of Darcy. I discover her in the bathroom.

'Sick as a dog. Fricking Indian at the movies.'

I look at her closely. I've seen that glow on her before.

'Darc, I don't think it's food poisoning.'

She stares at me and her face transforms. 'Noooo way.'

I nod. 'When was your last period?'

'No, I'm too old, my eggs have surely given up the ghost.'

'Ava calls it the closing down sale. You're definitely pregnant.' Darcy begins to cry and laugh at the same time. She races out to find Ace. I can just imagine him attempting to bring a talking stick into her labour.

And seven months later, he does, as unsuccessfully as I imagined. But the outcome is a very healthy, happy baby girl and they're both over the moon.

Leo and I base ourselves out of Byron, we justify that it's for the sake of Magnus. Finn is up every third weekend and school holidays.

Both Come as You Are and the current affairs show have a huge response and get commissioned for second seasons. But nothing compares to the success of the Come As You Are app that Daisy heads up. Through the hundreds of thousands of women's fantasies, I'm reminded daily that the sexiest thing you can ever be is yourself.

Sometimes, it's not till things are completely and utterly lost that you find the courage, most times by necessity, to find out who you really are. And if you learn to like that person, love them even, then anything is possible.

You probably won't look like you thought you would, do what you thought you would, and especially be where you thought you would be, but if you're open, I promise you, it'll be even better.

The upside of over is that it's just the beginning.

Acknowledgements

FIRSTLY, I'D LIKE TO ACKNOWLEDGE THE VERY TALENTED CLAUDIA Karvan who I came to with the original concept all those years ago. Thank you Claude for liking it enough to develop it with me, for the hours we spent giggling and imagining. And although its fate back then wasn't for it to be on screen, your input and confidence has been invaluable in the writing of this novel. Thank you.

I am blessed to be grateful to so many people, all of whom have made it possible for me to write this book and who have spurred me on in a myriad of ways.

My superb Publisher Vanessa Radnidge for continuing to rally me, cheer me, and hearten me. For backing my voice and believing in my stories . . . and me, thank you.

My lovely editor, Deonie Fiford for your knowledge, excellent insights and encouraging notes.

My fabulous publicist Jordan Weever-Keeny, Brigid Mullane and the entire Hachette team who have all provided such great encouragement and support and who work so hard for their authors.

My agent Dayne Kelly, thank you for making nothing impossible. Thank you also to the great team at RGM.

To my wonderful writing group Kelly Doust, Chris McCourt, Maggie Hamilton, Catherine Milne and Sarah Smith for your feedback, for urging me to go further and for sharing your own wonderful work.

Also a big thanks to: Jacqueline Hughes (Mum), Antonia Murphy, Emma Jobson, Joanna Briant, Maestro Heath Felton, Sarah Smith & Neal Kingston, Edwina Hayes, Jen Vinton, Ellenor Cox, Mel Rogan, Grania Holtsbaum & Monique Potter, Andrew Knight, Lauren Edwards, Stuart Page, Sarah Lambert, John Edwards, Rory Callaghan, Kerrie Mainwaring, Toni Malone, Paul Bennett, Jaison, Molly, Coco & Bodhi Morgan, Mark & Stacy Rivett, Caroline Teague, Marie Theodore-Daly, Dr Janice Herbert & Rod Adams, Tim Pietranski, Mark Keatinge, Katherine Hassler & Dr Darryl Hodgkinson, Ross & Danielle Priddle, Jonathan Wood, Dr Arne Rubinstein and of course Beau.